Better Left Unsaid

The Limitless Series, Book 2

Barbara Cutrera

Published by On My Way Up, LLC

ISBN: 978-1-944113-12-4

Second edition

For Angela, my easygoing, cheerful sister-in-law, who shows her love for her family and friends through her caring and dedication to them and to the world around her.

Chapter One

Cate felt the jolt of the impact and was momentarily stunned. Running late for work, she'd been hurrying down the sidewalk and simultaneously peering into her purse in an attempt to find her phone. The jarring collision she experienced when she ran into a stranger resulted in her landing on her butt next to her handbag, which had spilled some of its contents onto the pavement. Cate prayed that her iPhone wasn't broken and then looked up at the man who was asking her if she was all right. Probably in his early thirties, he was tall, handsome, and blind.

Oh, no, she thought. *This can't be happening. No.*

The stranger's dark glasses hadn't been knocked off during their collision, but he crouched down, reaching around in an effort to locate…what? Her? His white cane? She spotted it several feet to his right and scrambled to grab the cane before it rolled off the curb and into the street.

"Are you all right?" he asked, as he continued to feel for the cane. "Please, answer me!"

Cate frantically tried to think of a way to reassure him that she was fine. Her mind was blank. Snatching up the cane, Cate awkwardly held it out until the black grip touched the palm of the man's right hand. His fingers closed around it, and he swiftly put his free hand on top of hers. When she tried to pull away, he tightened his hold.

"Are you all right?" he asked again after thanking her for retrieving his cane. "Did you fall? You seem really small, and I'm a big guy. Please, tell me you didn't hit your head. If you did, then I'll call 911 right now."

Tears sprang to Cate's eyes as she struggled to decide what she should do. When the brown-haired stranger lifted his hand from hers and withdrew his phone from one pants pocket, she automatically shook her head. Of course, he couldn't see the gesture and raised the phone to one ear. She reached up with her right hand and squeezed his fingers, feeling the gold wedding band he wore as she did so.

"Look, don't play games with me," he said with irritation. "I'm only trying to make sure you're okay."

Tears of frustration escaped from the corners of her eyes, as she patted the man's hand. She laid a palm on his chest and hoped he'd understand that she wanted him to stay where he was. Then she hurriedly knelt, gathered the contents of her purse that had escaped, and then withdrew one of her cards from her jeans pocket. While she did this, the man put away his phone. Relieved, she touched the card to his empty palm. He seemed confused, and Cate felt guilty for not being able to explain further at that moment. As she patted his hand one last time, she noted that he wore a black Polo shirt with the words *Sight Unseen* embroidered on it.

I'll look up whatever Sight Unseen is when I take my break, she thought. *I'll make this right.*

Using the sleeves of her sweater to wipe away her tears, Cate rushed away, leaving the blind man standing on the sidewalk, calling out for her to come back. Despite the fact that she'd been running late and had lost time because of her unexpected encounter with the stranger, she arrived at work at 8:06. Employees were allowed a seven-minute grace period every day without being considered late. For Cate, who always seemed to be several minutes late for everything, the policy was a definite bonus.

She nodded in greeting to her coworkers as she made her way to her workstation. After hastening to log onto her computer, she pulled her phone from her purse and checked it. It seemed to function fine, and she breathed a sigh of relief. The device was fairly new and was a godsend for someone like her.

"Are you well, Cate?" her friend, Yana, asked from the workstation beside her. "You look as though you have been crying."

She nodded, deciding she would let her beautiful, statuesque Ukrainian-born friend sort out whether she was agreeing with the "okay" part or the "crying" part. When Yana suggested that she go to the restroom in order to collect herself, Cate figured she hadn't fooled the woman at all.

"Wash your face; then text me about what has made you cry," Yana suggested. "I will pull up your e-mails while you are away from your desk so that you can start working on them when you return."

Cate smiled gratefully and hurried to the restroom with her iPhone in her pocket. When she looked at herself in the mirror, she understood why it was evident she'd been crying. She had puffy eyelids and a slightly reddened nose. What little makeup she'd applied that morning was now decorating the cuffs of her purple sweater. The white areas surrounding her gray irises were slightly red, and strands of her black hair had come loose from her ponytail.

She tugged at the elastic band that held most of her hair away from her face, combed her fingers through the unruly mass, and then pulled it all back up once more. After that was done, she washed her face with soap from the dispenser on the wall, dried it with a paper towel, and studied herself in the full-length mounted wall mirror on the back of the door.

At five feet one inches tall, Cate was undoubtedly petite. She was also too thin. Despite her small frame and need to gain some weight, she had no trouble filling the C cups of her bra. Her butt had a nice little curve to it. Her black hair was slightly curly when she left it loose. Her gray eye color was rather odd, but she liked it. She thought that she looked reasonably attractive. She wished....

Stop wishing, she told herself. *No man is ever going to want you. It doesn't matter what you look like. How could you have a relationship with anyone?*

Cate texted Yana and then left the restroom, returning to her desk as her friend finished reading the message. She was relieved Yana's blonde hair was obscuring her face. She didn't want to see the pity in Yana's brown eyes. She hated pity.

"I am sorry that you had to go through that," Yana told her, as she put down her phone. "At least you gave him the card that states that you are mute. He will find a way to read it or have someone else read it to him. Then he will understand. It is not your fault you cannot speak."

Not my fault. How many times have I heard that?

3

She smiled, nodded to Yana, and then turned her attention to her work, which was to respond to emailed customer service questions relating to orders for Combine, a global online store. Because of the vast array of products, the inquiries were plentiful and varied. Since the staff in her branch of Combine only interacted with the public via computer, the one dress code requirement was that clothing had to be appropriate for someone who was out in public. Because the office was in Sarasota, Florida, most employees wore shorts and short-sleeved shirts to work for over half the year and then wore jeans and long-sleeved shirts or lightweight sweaters during the cooler months. Cate wore jeans and long-sleeved shirts or sweaters year-round.

At lunch, Cate ate in the office building's cafeteria with her coworkers and listened to them chatter on about how wonderful their partners were, how terrible their partners were, their children, their parents, their pets, and their plans for the upcoming weekend. As they prattled on about their lives, Cate was glad she'd been born mute. Had she been able to speak, she'd have nothing she'd want to contribute to such conversations. She could communicate with people through texts, emails, or by using pen and paper, but she chose not to unless she had something important she wanted to share or if she needed to answer a question.

The rest of the day passed swiftly, and it wasn't until Cate was on her way home that she remembered about Sight Unseen. Mentally slapping herself, she vowed to investigate once she arrived at her house. But that wouldn't be for another hour.

As she did every weeknight, Cate went to The Peking Palace for dinner. It had been four years since she'd started frequenting the place every Monday through Friday, and she loved it. A friendly Chinese family owned it, and only their teenaged daughter, who seated customers and took orders, spoke English. That was fine with Cate, since she didn't speak at all. The husband, wife, daughter, and three sons seemed perpetually happy and pleased to see her every time she entered. Cate knew it was strange, but eating dinner at The Peking Palace five nights a week made her feel as though she had a family. She even had her own personal table, a two-seater right off the kitchen. She figured no one else wanted to sit there, so that was probably why the family always saved the table for her. Yet, she imagined that perhaps they were saving it for her because she was somehow special to them.

As she did every weeknight, Cate sat at her table and ate, as she read using the Kindle app on her phone. After she paid her bill and left a generous tip, she smiled and nodded to the family as she left the restaurant. In return, they smiled, nodded, waved, and said things to her in Chinese.

It was a five-minute walk from The Peking Palace to her small home nestled in downtown Sarasota. In the midst of office buildings, shops, and restaurants was a row of old houses that had been beautifully restored on the outside. Their stucco exteriors were each painted a different bright color, and they shared lovely tiled roofs and beautiful architectural details of older Florida homes. One had to climb several steps to get to the gated archways that led onto the porches. The decorative iron bars with their spiked tops provided security by extending across the width of the huge arches on the porch sides, and the same bars edged the backyards. The landscaping of the small yards had been expertly executed. The developer who'd bought the run-down homes and flipped them had thought of everything that would make them attractive from the curb. The conditions on the inside were another matter entirely.

Shortly after the exterior work had been completed on the homes, the real estate market had crashed. The developer had needed to sell his investments as hastily as possible before he lost even more capital. So, the houses had sold for much less than they should have, considering their prime location. Cate, along with five other buyers, had been fortunate enough to get a home for an extremely reasonable price. Everyone on their block kept up their property and kept to themselves, and that had relieved Cate.

Her eight-hundred-thirty-five-square-foot, two-bedroom, one-bath house was painted flamingo pink and had black-and-white tiles on the floor of the large side porch. She climbed the steps to her gate, unlocked it with her key, and then closed it behind her. After unlocking the door to the house, she went in, depositing her purse on a worn, navy, overstuffed chair. There was no need to turn on the lights. Whether she was away or at home, the lights stayed on in every room twenty-four hours a day. Even the second bedroom, which was completely empty, had an overhead light blazing all the time.

The walls were in good shape, and the floors were level. However, the tan interior paint had faded a long time ago, and the carpet on the floors was threadbare beige shag. The water pressure in the kitchen faucet was always too low, and all of the light fixtures needed to be updated. Although the old refrigerator worked, the stovetop and oven didn't. There was no dishwasher. When Cate cooked at home, everything was prepared in her stainless steel microwave, which was the only kitchen appliance she'd bought, so far. Her mattress had been purchased new when she'd moved into the house as had the stackable washer-and-dryer combo in the closet next to the bathroom. The rest of the furnishings had been bought second-hand. This was partly because Cate had put all of her savings and most of her monthly income into buying and maintaining her home, but it was also because she loved the idea that the things she bought had some sort of history. She liked to imagine that everything in her house had a happy story that went along with it.

After changing into knit pajama bottoms and a long-sleeved pajama top, Cate used her phone to search the Web for Sight Unseen. She quickly learned that it was a local store that sold all sorts of items for those with low vision or no vision. Amazed by what sorts of products were available for the blind, she took her time exploring the website. Although the company did offer online sales, the physical location of Sight Unseen was not far from her home. She wondered how she'd missed it, although she had to admit it wasn't in an area of downtown she typically frequented. She had her routine and rarely strayed from it.

Tomorrow, I'll stray, she thought. *It'll be Saturday. There's no excuse for me not to go. It's the right thing to do.*

Cate sat on her couch and wrote out a note of apology to the blind man. Someone would have to read it to him, but it was the best she could do under the circumstances. She'd seen on the website for Sight Unseen that there were machines and software that allowed the blind to read print material, but she had no computer or printer at home. Her phone was the only way she could connect to the Internet outside of work. So, a handwritten note was all she had to offer.

Once the note was complete, she went to sit on the swing that hung on her gated porch. She enjoyed the silence of the evening and the cool March breezes. Finally, she went to bed. And, as she did every night, Cate had "the dream."

Cate had automatically and subconsciously detached herself from what she'd relived every night since the attack. It was almost as though she were watching a movie about someone else's real-life nightmare. One of her childhood therapists had told her it was a coping mechanism but assured her that wouldn't last forever. Cate was twenty-six, and it had lasted eighteen years. She prayed that it would last the rest of her life.

Chapter Two

The following morning, Cate dressed in a pink sweater and jeans and then set out for Sight Unseen. When she entered the store, she was impressed. The place had fabulous interior design that blended black, white, and stainless finishes. Large, colorful paintings adorned the walls. There were specific areas of the store designated for cooking articles, office items, adaptive computer software, guide dog items, children's toys, magnifiers, sunglasses, and much, much more. Intrigued by seeing the store in person, Cate began to wander and examine what was on display. She was looking at a magnification machine when a very pregnant woman in her late twenties who had deep green eyes and waist-length blonde hair approached her and asked if she needed help.

Cate withdrew one of her cards from the pocket of her jeans and held it out. She waited while the woman took it and read the pre-printed message: MY NAME IS CATE. I'M MUTE BUT NOT DEAF. THANK YOU FOR YOUR PATIENCE.

"Oh, my God! It's you! Logan was so worried!"

Frowning, Cate withdrew her phone and typed, **Logan?** Then, she held up the screen so the woman could read it.

"My husband. He told me all about what happened once I arrived at work yesterday. He scanned and read your card as soon as he got here, and that made him feel a little better. He was still concerned, though. He was thinking maybe you were actually hurt and couldn't tell him."

I'm fine, Cate texted. **I came to bring him a note, but it's handwritten. I'm sorry. I don't have a computer or printer at home.**

"That's no problem. Come with me. Logan's in his office. He'll want to talk to you himself."

Cate shook her head, but the woman insisted, adding "I'd really appreciate it. It would put his mind at ease."

Cate nodded and walked with the woman, who was wearing a Sight Unseen Polo shirt that was too big for her except around her midsection where it was stretched to its limits.

"I'm Beth Kirkland. It's nice to meet you, Cate. That's a lovely name. I've never seen it spelled that way. Is it Russian?"

Italian. It's short for Caterina.

"We actually thought about naming this baby Catherine Claudia until we found out we were having a boy this time."

This time?

"Mary Margaret is twenty-one months old. You'll get to meet her, too. We don't normally bring her in to the store, but we were short-staffed today and our babysitters were unavailable this morning. Usually, Logan and I take the weekends off, but sometimes working them is unavoidable. That's what happens when you own your own business."

Cate wondered how a blind person could safely parent a child but didn't text her thoughts to the woman who was carrying a blind man's second baby. Obviously, there was a lot she didn't know about blind people and how they functioned. She considered that fate had led her to bump into Logan Kirkland so that she could be enlightened.

Beth led her through a door at the back of the busy store. Cate followed the woman down a hallway and heard the beautiful sound of a baby's laughter. Then she heard Logan's voice, but he sounded different. Instead of worry and frustration, his tone was relaxed and…well, rather silly. When Beth and Cate entered what was obviously Logan's office, Cate saw why.

Logan was on his hands and knees, grinning from ear to ear. An adorable toddler who had brown ringlets framing her face and tiny bells attached to her shoes was running as fast as her little legs would allow while her father said, "Where's Mary Margaret? I'm going to find her! I'm going to give her a big hug when I do! Where could she be?"

The child giggled and ran, the silver bells allowing her father to hear her location in the room at all times. Logan crawled behind her. Cate got the impression that he was moving more slowly than he normally would in order to make playtime fun for his daughter. No matter where she went, he appeared to quickly discern her position. When the child stopped to look up at her mother and smile, Logan hurried forward, scooped her up, and proceeded to hug and kiss her. She squealed with delight, and Beth beamed at her husband and child. Cate smiled, but she was also struggling not to cry.

Why couldn't my own father have been as loving as Logan? I wish I could have a life and children with a man who would love me and our kids as much as Logan seems to love his.

"Logan, guess who's here?" Beth asked, as he got to his feet with Mary Margaret in his arms.

"Your mom?" he speculated, still smiling. "Or my dad?"

"Neither. It's the woman from yesterday morning. She's here and has a note for you. She's standing to my left."

Logan turned slightly to face Cate and said, "I'm so glad you tracked me down. I was kind of freaked when you didn't answer me."

"She says...texted...that she brought a note for you. She wanted to just give it to me and leave, but I asked her to come back here to meet you. I figured you'd feel better if she did."

"Definitely."

At that moment, Mary Margaret reached up and pulled her father's dark glasses off. He laughed and told her he wanted them back, but she didn't seem inclined to return them. Cate stared in fascination at the striking man's face. He was classically handsome and appeared strong and in control. His eyelids were closed, and she intuited that they never opened on their own.

"Sorry about that," he offered, as he wrestled the glasses away from his daughter while still holding her in one arm. "I hope that didn't creep you out. Most sighted people get unnerved by seeing someone who never opens his eyes."

Unable to reign in her curiosity, Cate texted, **Do all blind people's eyes stay closed 24/7?**

"No," Beth said, once she'd read the text aloud. "There are different types of vision loss and related physical manifestations. Some who are totally blind have eyelids that open and close, and they blink and all that. Each person is unique."

It didn't creep me out. It just made me curious.

"Curious is good," Logan offered, once Beth had read the text to him. "I'm curious right now. Beth, would you read me the note?"

10

Cate focused on Mary Margaret, who rested one rosy cheek on her father's shoulder. The child looked as though she were about to fall asleep at any moment. She appeared so contented that it made Cate want to cry again.

Beth read, "I apologize for barreling into you yesterday. I was late for work and not paying attention. I hope I didn't hurt you when we collided. I wish I could have explained at the time, but I've never interacted with a blind person before and didn't know what to do. Even people who are illiterate or can't speak English can understand I'm mute, because I can give them nonverbal cues as to why I'm not speaking to them. With you, I had no way to communicate. I hated to be rude or worry you, but I panicked. I'm sorry I stressed you out. Sincerely, Cate Nasello."

"It was totally understandable. Being visually impaired, I know about how challenging life can be when you're physically different from the majority. People are often afraid of what they don't know. We can only show them by example that we're not helpless, which I assume you're already doing. I've never interacted with a mute person. I'd like to know more so I can be better educated. Perhaps we could all have lunch sometime and –"

"Logan, I hate to interrupt, but I just had a contraction," Beth said with what sounded like nervous excitement in her voice. "If this baby comes as quickly as Mary Margaret did, you'll be delivering him here in the office if we don't leave for the hospital right away."

"We'll call a taxi and then your mom and my dad," Logan said evenly. "The staff will just have to manage without us today, unless they want to help deliver our baby."

"I hate to make you leave –" Beth began, but Cate raised a hand in order to stop her.

I should be going anyway. It was a pleasure to meet you. Congratulations on your new baby. Do you have a boy's name picked out?

"Luca."

Cate's stunned expression must have been evident, because Beth asked her if she was all right. She nodded, even though it was a lie. Then, she texted a goodbye and hurried out of the office, down the hallway, through the store, and out the front doors. Walking quickly, she headed for Whole Foods to do her weekly grocery shopping.

True, Whole Foods was slightly more expensive than several other grocery stores in Sarasota. However, Cate didn't have a car and didn't buy much in the way of groceries anyway. She never ate breakfast and enjoyed every weekday evening meal at The Peking Palace. So, that left lunches seven days a week and dinners on Saturday and Sunday. Having only a microwave to cook meals at home and a cafeteria at work that provided inexpensive lunches, she tended to buy a few frozen dinners for each weekend, some snacks, and a container of chocolate almond milk at the store. She considered herself fortunate when it came to her grocery bills. As for her meals at The Peking Palace, they were inexpensive enough since she typically ordered soup or a vegetable dish with rice or noodles. Once in a while, she'd splurge and get something on Fridays that would leave her with leftovers for part of the weekend.

Cate tried not to think about Luca while she shopped, paid for her groceries, walked home with her meager provisions, and put them away in her tiny kitchen. She managed not to really think about Luca until she sat on her faded, brown couch and wondered if Beth and Logan Kirkland were at the hospital and envisioned them holding their newborn son in their arms. Once that image entered her mind, she wept.

Had Cate's older brother, Luca, lived, he would now be thirty. She remembered him playing games with her when she'd been small. Other times, he'd held her in his arms and told her to rest her head on his shoulder. Even though he was only four years older than she, he'd been her protector. He would have done anything for her.

Just like Logan is with his little girl. Just like he'll be with his son. However he does it, he's obviously a great parent. Luca would have been a great parent if he'd been allowed to grow up, get married, and have kids. He'd have made a great man, period. I want him back!

But Luca wasn't coming back. No one was coming back. No one would protect Cate, except Cate. She was used to having no one.

Eventually, Cate went out into her little backyard and sat in the old metal lawn chair she'd found at the curb of one of her neighbor's houses. She'd scrubbed the chair clean, used a Brill-o pad to smooth the rusting finish, and then spray-painted it with green Rustoleum. It was a comfortable chair, and she liked to sit in it and watch birds drink and bathe in the concrete birdbath. She rarely saw anything except birds since there was no grass. As with the front landscaping, her property had rocks and drought-tolerant plants, but there was no grass or trees. She was okay with that, since it meant she didn't have to mow a lawn or do a lot to take care of the landscaping.

When a light rain started to fall, Cate went inside. Almost immediately, it began to storm. She sat in the worn, navy chair, tucked her feet beneath her, and pulled up the book she'd been reading the previous day on her phone. She became so engrossed that she didn't immediately realize that someone was ringing the buzzer on her house. Admittedly, no one ever rang the buzzer, and she'd almost forgotten what it sounded like.

Rising, she put the phone on the end table before going onto the side porch and staring through the front gate. The storm was raging, and a wet, ordinary-looking man stood on the top step holding something furry against his chest. He was soaked to the skin, and what looked like a little dog lay limply in his arms.

"Thank God!" the man exclaimed when he saw her. "My dog's hurt! Can I bring him on your porch and phone my wife? Please? I think he's dying!"

Cate moved closer in order to get a better look at the dog. Her keys were in the house, and she debated whether or not it was wise to get them in order to undo the lock for this stranger. Then, she spotted a cloth tag in the midst of the shaggy mass of fur he held and realized that the dog was actually a realistic-looking toy. She started to back away, but the man dropped the stuffed animal to the ground, grabbed her wrist, and yanked her forward. Her right temple, cheekbone, and shoulder slammed against two of the gate's iron bars, and she opened her mouth in a silent cry of fear and pain.

"Unlock the gate, Bitch!" he shouted. "Now!"

Her heart pounding, she shook her head and tried to break free. The man began to twist her wrist and repeated his order. The pain was intense, and Cate did the only thing she could. Awkwardly reaching through the bars with her free hand, she dug her nails into her attacker's forearm then dragged them downwards. He howled and released her right wrist as she drew blood. Stumbling back, she ran inside her house and slammed and locked the door.

Experiencing an adrenaline rush, Cate stood shaking and breathing hard in her living room. She paced the house, grateful for the tall gates on her porch and the high iron fence with its spiked bars that surrounded her yard. She was safe for the moment, but she knew what she had to do.

Cate lifted her iPhone and texted a message to 911. Finding it difficult to focus, she typed her name, her address, the fact that she was mute, and the information that someone had attacked her at her home.

Help is on the way. **Are you safe now?** **Are you hurt?** was the response.

I don't know.

Cate backed into a corner, slid into a sitting position, and huddled there with her knees drawn up. More texts came in, but she didn't respond. She was too busy staving off full-blown panic.

She jerked when someone pressed the buzzer on her house. Tucking her knees closer to her body, she listened as the buzzer was pressed three more times. She wondered if the man who'd tried to get her to let him in had returned.

Her iPhone rang, and she was so startled she almost dropped it. Glancing at the display, she saw the caller's ID and number and depressed the answer button. She thought of how odd it was to hold the phone to her ear, something most people took for granted.

"Cate, my name is Kirsten. I know you can't speak to me, but I also know you can hear me. The police and paramedics are outside your house right now, but they can't get in through the locked gate on your porch. If you're not seriously hurt, I want you to make a tapping sound three times so I can hear it. Then I want you to go outside and unlock the gate for them. I'll stay on the line until you've let them in. If you're badly injured or aren't sure, just stay still."

Cate rose and walked unsteadily to her kitchen. Withdrawing a spoon from a drawer, she held the phone near the counter and rapped the utensil against the surface three times. Then, she raised the phone back to her ear.

"I'm glad you're not badly hurt. Now, you need to let the emergency responders in. If you don't, then they'll have to call someone to force the lock on your gate."

14

Cate walked slowly toward the door that led to the porch. She picked up her keys and reminded herself that Kirsten was still on the line. She undid the lock on the door and opened it then heard men's voices and saw flashes of lights that indicated at least one police car and an ambulance were parked in front of the house. Her tennis shoes squeaked on the damp porch tiles, as she approached two policemen and two male paramedics. One of the policemen greeted her and asked if she would unlock the gate.

"We're here to help," he said reassuringly when she hesitated. "You're safe."

"Cate, you can let them in," Kirsten said. "They'll take care of you. Would you hand your phone to the officer who just spoke?"

She passed the phone through two of the iron bars then unlocked the gate as the man talked with Kirsten. Once she stepped back, the men slowly moved onto the porch. The policeman handed Cate her phone, which she brought back up to her ear.

"I'm going to end our call now," Kirsten told her. "You're in good hands. Take care."

Wishing she could verbally offer the woman her thanks, Cate listened as Kirsten hung up. The policemen urged her to move into the house with them and asked if she could explain what had happened. Her right wrist throbbing, she bit her lip and forced herself to text an explanation of her encounter with her attacker. She started to shake violently as she ended the text and handed one of the policemen her phone. He read the message aloud, and then the paramedics directed her to sit on the couch. She was relieved when the policeman passed her phone back to her. It was her lifeline.

"Cate, I'm Jake."

The paramedic sitting to her right was tall, broad-chested, and obviously liked to work out. He also had beautiful green eyes, sandy brown hair, and an engaging smile. Cate pictured him running marathons or playing volleyball on the beach with other handsome men in swim trunks and sexy women in short shorts and bikini tops. She liked the way his voice rumbled deep in his chest when he spoke.

"We're going to ask you a few questions," he went on. "Text us if we're doing something that doesn't work for you when it comes to us understanding what you need. Are we good?"

She nodded, enjoying the way he sounded when he asked. He was certainly easy on the eyes, but Cate sensed that there was much more to Jake than good looks and a nice smile. She wished she could smile back, but she was too frightened and traumatized. So, she sat and waited.

"My partner, Everton, is going to take your blood pressure, temperature, and check your vitals while we talk." Clearing his throat, he looked chagrined and said, "Well, you could text or write if you want. Or would you prefer to use gestures?"

Everton, who was a fit, handsome African-American man with box braids held away from his face with a cord at the back of his head and a scar that ran down across his left cheek, volunteered, "I'm fluent in American Sign Language."

Cate mouthed the words, "I don't know ASL."

"No sign language then," he said with a grin. "Why don't you text us about any injuries you might've sustained before I get started?"

Right wrist, shoulder, side of face.

Jake nodded and said, "We can see some bruising on your face. Everton's going to check your blood pressure and oxygen levels using your left arm and hand, while I look at your injured wrist and talk to you about your shoulder."

She shook her head, pulled her knees up to her chest, and wrapped her arms around them.

"Hey, guys," Jake said, darting a glance at the policemen. "You mind scoping things out with the other cops who were coming so that we can give Cate a little breathing room?"

Once they'd left the house, Everton asked, "You got someone you want us to call for you? Maybe it'd make you feel more comfortable?" When she shook her head, he said, "Okay, then. Let's start slow. Height?"

Raising her left hand, she held up first five fingers then one.

"Five feet one inches. Weight?"

She grimaced at the pain in her right wrist as she held up nine fingers then eight.

"Ninety-eight pounds," Jake noted. "You've got a small frame, but that's still a little underweight on the BMI chart. Do you have any health problems we should know about? No. All right. You're just a tiny little thing." When Cate couldn't help but smile, he said, "There you go. I knew you had one in there somewhere."

"Any drug allergies?" Everton prompted, as he gently drew her left arm toward him. "No? Good. Are you on any medications? No? Okay." Looking to Jake, he suggested, "Why don't you check out her pupils while I do the blood pressure and oxygen?"

Jake took a pen light and did just that. He then examined her temple and cheekbone before observing, "You can obviously use your right hand and wrist, but we can tell it hurts. You should probably have it and your shoulder x-rayed at Sarasota Memorial." When she shook her head, he cajoled, "At least let me look at your wrist before making any decisions. It's our job to make sure you're all right. Trust me."

Chapter Three

"Trust me," Jake repeated. "It'll be okay."

I haven't really trusted anyone in eighteen years, Cate thought. *I should try.*

She extended her right arm. Her heart was pounding almost as hard as it had right after her earlier attack. Jake supported her elbow and asked her to open her hand. She hadn't realized she'd had her fingers clenched into a fist. She relaxed them and held her breath as Jake caught a glimpse of the scar on her palm. He carefully pushed up her sleeve until it reached where his hand rested underneath her elbow. She inwardly cringed as he and Everton saw the six other visible pink lines.

"Defensive wounds," Jake said quietly.

"Old wounds," Everton noted. "You have some on this left arm, too?"

When she nodded, Jake speculated, "And on the front of your torso?"

She gave another nod, and his hold on her elbow tightened slightly.

"Anywhere else?" Everton prompted. "No? Okay."

"How long has it been since you were stabbed?" Jake asked calmly, but Cate heard the underlying anger in his voice.

She took the pointer finger of her left hand and "wrote" eighteen on her right arm.

"You were eighteen?"

She shook her head.

"You were stabbed eighteen years ago?" he asked in that same steady voice tinged with anger. "How old were you?"

She drew the number eight on her arm with the same finger.

Both men were silent for a while before Jake asked, "Is that why you won't go to the hospital to let them examine you? You don't want them to see your scars and have to explain?"

Cate jerked her chin toward her wrist, indicating that she wanted him to examine her so that they could be done. Everton cleared his throat, and the two paramedics focused on performing their exam. Jake made Cate lift and rotate her arm, which caused her great discomfort. She did it anyway. She had no intention of going to the hospital.

"Your wrist may be sprained," Jake said. "You need to let a doctor examine it and your shoulder."

Cate carefully disengaged her arm from Jake's hold and reached for her phone.

I'm not going to the hospital. I'll take some Advil and put some ice on my face, shoulder, and wrist.

Everton pointed out, "You need a splint in order to keep your wrist immobile when it's not being iced."

I can get one at Walgreens or CVS.

Before the two paramedics could voice any more concerns, a policeman re-entered the house and announced, "Well, we weren't able to locate the perpetrator, but we recovered the stuffed toy." Looking directly at Cate, he continued, "I want to commend you for being cautious and not opening the gate. This is a scam criminals had been using to rob, rape, kidnap, or murder people who are too trusting." Once he'd given Cate suggestions for staying safe, assured her there would be extra patrols in her area for at least the next week, and discussed places where she could receive counseling regarding the incident, he suggested, "Someone should escort you to and from work for the time being."

Cate was not going to ask her coworkers to take time out of their lives each day to chauffeur her around. She'd simply have to get some pepper spray and be conscious of anything out of the ordinary in her environment. At least that was what she told herself as the policemen and paramedics prepared to leave. Truthfully, she knew she was an easy target, not only because she was mute but also because she was so petite and slight.

After signing various papers for the police and the paramedics, she walked out onto the porch with them. As they bid her farewell, she closed and locked the iron gate behind them. Jake paused and looked back at her for what seemed like a long time before climbing into the driver's side of the ambulance. Watching everyone drive away, Cate felt as if she were a prisoner in her own home. Inside its iron bars and stucco walls was the only place where she could be truly protected.

Going back into the house, Cate locked her door, went to her bedroom, and collapsed on top of her mattress. It was 6:15. She didn't get ice to put on her temple, cheekbone, shoulder, or wrist. Instead, she draped her left arm over her eyes and tried to relax. The gate and doors were locked, and all of the lights remained on, as usual. She was safe. She slept and had the dream, but she remained detached as she always did.

She woke at 6:00 the following morning and rose stiffly. The injured areas of her body felt tight and hurt with every movement and touch. Somehow, she managed to remove her tennis shoes, socks, sweater, jeans, and panties using only her left arm. Unhooking her bra proved challenging, but she eventually succeeded. She went to her small bathroom and showered, which took longer than usual because of her current limitations. Once she'd toweled off, she painfully dressed in clean underwear and jeans. Hooking a bra proved impossible, and she gave up after several excruciating minutes of trying. Once she'd wormed her way into a green sweater, she put on socks then took an Advil before brushing her teeth. She left her black hair loose, since there was no way she could pull it back into a ponytail using only her left arm and hand.

Cate peered out of the kitchen window into her backyard. It appeared to be a sunny morning, and she longed to go outside in order to sit and watch the birds. Yet, she continued to be too afraid to leave the house.

I have to leave it tomorrow, she thought. *I have to go to work. How am I going to explain the bruising on my face? Will I even be able to type with my hurt wrist? What if I can't get my bra on? Yana will want to call out the Ukrainian Mob to search for the jerk who did this to me.* Pausing, she reflected, *Okay, that was a stupid thing to think. Yana's scared to death of the Ukrainian Mob. She'd never approach any of them for anything. I know the Ukrainians who live in North Port and aren't part of the Mob are terrified of them. Yana said her grandmother hides every time a stranger approaches the house. I can't live like that. I won't.*

"You should not have come to work!" Yana exclaimed when she saw Cate the following morning. "I wish you had let me come to your home yesterday after you texted me that brief explanation. I know you say you are better, but your face remains slightly bruised and your wrist slightly swollen. Does your shoulder still hurt?"

None of it hurts much anymore. It's just tender to the touch. Besides, I wanted to come to work so I could tell you everything in person. I know I could have texted, but that would have taken longer than emailing. There was a lot to explain, and my wrist hurt worse yesterday than it does today.

Cate typed an emailed version of Saturday's events and sent it to Yana. Once the woman had reviewed it, she said, "I am so thankful that you are all right, but you must be careful. You are vulnerable in many ways. You need someone to take care of you."

I've been taking care of myself since I was eight years old.

Startled, Yana echoed, "Eight?" Staring at the scar on Cate's right palm, she asked, "Is that when you were hurt by someone?"

Cate directed all of her attention at the screen on her phone and nodded.

"Eight," Yana repeated. "So young. There was no one else to take care of you? I cannot imagine it."

It's the truth.

"I know you would not lie to me. It is only hard for me to comprehend."

Our break time's over.

"You know I am here for you no matter what time it is."

Yes. Thank you. You're a great friend.

"As are you. I could not have made it through my divorce without your support. Having my husband leave me for another woman was devastating. You knew I still loved him. I grieved when he died the following year, despite the divorce. You were there for me through it all."

I'm a good listener.

Yana smiled then remarked, "It is more than that, and you know it. Now, let us get back to work. Routine will help you recover from your ordeal."

Will it? Cate wondered. *It hasn't seemed to help me recover from what happened eighteen years ago. All it's done is isolate me and make me miserable. Maybe if I didn't try so hard to stick to the same routine, I'd meet more men like Jake. There was something special about him. Living in my little bubble of a world isn't going to help me get to know any new people, much less a man like him.* Sighing, she wondered, *Why would Jake be interested in me anyway? I'm sure he has women falling at his feet every day. I need to forget about him and go back to my routine like Yana said. It will be for the best. Pretend like Jake doesn't exist, and get back to work.*

For the next six months, Cate did her best to forget about Jake. Gradually, her fear of being attacked by the man who'd hurt her faded until she was cautious but no more than she had been before the incident. She went to work, to The Peking Palace, and to the store. Life went on, but not a day passed that she didn't think of Jake at least once. She wished she could forget him. After all, she knew her longing for the man was ridiculous.

One October day, Cate left work at 5:15 and had just begun to walk in the direction of The Peking Palace when she heard a man call her name. She turned and saw Jake, standing about a dozen feet away from her dressed in a black t-shirt, blue jeans, and white athletic shoes. He was leaning against a red car that was obviously a classic.

Cate was stunned and excited but had no idea what to do with herself. She wished she'd chosen to wear something more stylish when she'd dressed that morning. She felt plain wearing a pink sweatshirt, jeans, and brown leather clogs.

"Hey, Cate," Jake said, flashing a grin that somehow combined total masculinity with boyish charm. "It's been awhile."

Cate nodded, moving closer and glancing admiringly at Jake's red car.

"It's a 1965 Ford Mustang GT," he said proudly. "It was my father's."

Cate wanted to communicate properly with Jake, but her phone had died right before she'd left work. She held out her hand and mouthed the word *phone* in hopes that he'd understand hers was temporarily out of commission. He handed her his. She texted, **Was?**

"What?"

You said the car was your father's. Did he give it to you? It's really awesome.

"Thanks. I agree. And no, he didn't give it to me. He was into cars and did the racing circuit. That's how we ended up in this area. Have you ever been to DeSoto Speedway?"

I don't drive. I never had anyone who'd teach me or a car to drive. The Speedway is past Bradenton. I'd have to take several buses and then a cab to get out that far. Isn't it in the country?

He nodded but asked, "You've never driven a car? You don't have a license?"

No. I can walk or take the bus anywhere I want to go.

"Not to the Speedway," he pointed out.

I've never wanted to go there.

Jake grinned, and Cate smiled.

"There it is again," he said. "You have a wonderful smile. You should let people see it more often."

I don't usually have a lot to smile about.

She regretted her words as soon as she'd typed them. She didn't want anyone's pity. Life had not been kind to her, but others should enjoy their own lives instead of focusing on her problems. She looked up at Jake, who was almost a foot taller than she was. He seemed so genuinely nice. She wanted to be able to smile for him, not drag him down.

"Did everything heal up okay after your attack?"

She nodded but typed, **My wrist still hurts sometimes, but it's not bad.**

"So, you never did go see a doctor about it?"

No.

"Mind if I take a look?"

Glancing up and down the busy street, she texted, **Not here.** When he frowned, she typed, **We're in a public area. I don't let other people see my scars. You could come to my house and take a look there unless you have plans. I don't know where you were headed and don't want to make you late.**

"I was running errands. I don't want to mess up your evening, but I am worried about your wrist and the fact that it still hurts off and on after all this time. If you're okay with it, then I'll drive you home and check it out. I'm not a doctor, but at least I have medical training."

Why not? she thought. *I need to take a chance for once in my life and just go with the flow. I can let the man look at my wrist. What's the harm?*

Jake drove her home. Once they'd passed through the gate onto the porch and Cate had unlocked the door to her house, she immediately gestured for him to enter. After she'd shut the door behind them, she turned toward him and extended her arm, proud of her decisiveness. When Jake pushed up the sleeve of her sweatshirt, he asked, "Did you ice your wrist like we told you to?"

I went straight to bed once everyone left. I slept all night. After I showered, I did take an Advil.

"Did you eat first?"

No.

"Why not?"

I never eat breakfast.

"But you didn't eat dinner that night."

And I haven't eaten anything yet today. I don't always feel like eating.

Jake guided her toward the couch and told her to sit then said, "I'm going to get you some water and something to eat. I won't be long."

Cate closed her eyes and listened as Jake went to her kitchen. He filled a glass with water from the faucet. The refrigerator and freezer doors were opened and closed. Cabinet doors were next. She heard him examining the stove. A minute of silence followed, and her stomach muscles twisted.

What is Jake thinking? Why doesn't he come back in here?

Returning to the living room, he sat beside her on the couch before beginning, "Your water pressure in the kitchen sink sucks. You have almost no food in the freezer or fridge. It doesn't look like your oven's worked in a while. You have a few snacks in the cabinets, but there's not a lot. What gives? What about food? I know you said you never eat breakfast. You're so damned tiny and…I don't know…delicate. Do you have an eating disorder? No. Great. You eat out a lot? Okay. It's only that it doesn't look like you're eating enough."

Cate plugged in her iPhone so that it could begin charging; then she extended her left hand in a wordless gesture for Jake to pass her his phone again. After he had, she raised the phone and began to type.

I've never eaten a lot. When I do eat, I eat as healthily as possible. I'm fine. I have my work and my home.

Scanning the room, Jake asked, "Have you had the furniture since you were a kid?"

No. I bought it once I was an adult. My house is structurally sound, but I don't have the money to fix up the inside or replace things that need to be replaced. My microwave, washer/dryer, and mattress are new. My sheets, comforter, pillows, towels, and clothes are always bought new. Everything else is second-hand. I like it that way. It makes me feel like those who owned the things before me are here with me all the time.

"Friendly ghosts," he muttered. "You need more than them."

You don't have to take care of me.

"I know. I want to."

You take care of people in your job all the time.

"Yeah, but I don't usually feel compelled to do it outside of work. Not like this."

Not Your dad? Your mom? A brother? A sister?

"Dad didn't need for anyone to take care of him. He died in a crash ten years ago. Ironically, he'd never had a really bad accident in all his years of racing. Mom couldn't handle life without Dad, so she remarried a few months after he died. She and her new husband moved to Indiana not long after they married. We don't talk much."

Siblings?

"My older sister is a truck driver. She's great, but she drives big rigs cross-country almost year-round. She comes to see me when she's in this area. She doesn't stay long, but we always have a great time when she's here."

What's her name?

"Hazel."

I like that name. It has character.

"Well, she is a real character," he said with a grin, and Cate couldn't help but grin back.

What was your father's name?

"Jake. I was named after him, but I'm not a Junior. I have a different middle name."

Do you have a last name? she teased.

"Genter."

Thank you, Jake Genter. I appreciate your willingness to help and take care of me, but you should probably go. I'm sure you have better things to do than sit around here and read my texts.

"I have lots of things to do, but I can't think of anything better. I haven't been able to stop thinking about you since we met six months ago. You don't know how many times I've wanted to come over here, but I didn't want you to think I was being inappropriate by pursuing you after I'd treated you for your injuries. I was so happy to see you walking down the street today. Even so, I was nervous about flagging you down because I didn't know if you'd want to see me again."

YOU were nervous about how I'd react? I haven't been able to stop thinking about you either but figured you wouldn't be interested in me. I've been trying unsuccessfully to forget you. You deserve more.

"What does that mean?"

Never mind.

"Come on, Cate. Tell me, or give me back my phone."

He seemed completely serious, and Cate tensed. Desperate to keep a conversation going for the first time since she'd been eight, she nonetheless texted, **No.**

"You're really small and light. I *could* just pick you up and take the phone. Hell, I could take you to the doctor or anywhere else for that matter."

It was the wrong thing for Jake to say. Actually, it was the worst thing he could have said. Cate sprang up from the couch and started to rush for her bedroom. She wanted to get in and lock the door as quickly as she could. She'd taken only three steps when Jake hooked her around the waist, effectively stopping her in her tracks. When she began to twist in his arms, he effortlessly turned her around to face him and demanded, "Stop! I was joking. I didn't mean it! I'd never force you to do anything against your will. Never! Jesus, Cate! Stop struggling! I'm sorry! Will you just trust that I won't hurt you?"

26

Chapter Four

Cate stilled, acutely aware that Jake was holding her snugly against him. Jake's phone remained in her left hand. Resting her forehead against his chest, she shut her eyes and tried to calm herself. Knowing what he was going to ask, she pulled back slightly, opened her eyes, and began to text.

One of my foster parents used to threaten me by saying he could just pick me up and carry me wherever he wanted because I was small and mute. I knew what he was threatening. Before Jake could apologize, she went on, **You didn't know. You couldn't have known.**

"I didn't know, but I feel bad that what I said reminded you of that asshole. It's obvious he scared the crap out of you." When she looked away from him and didn't text anything, he asked hesitantly, "Did he ever do more than threaten?"

Once.

"Was he the one who stabbed you?"

No. I was eight when I was stabbed.

"Cate, talk to me." Shaking his head, he continued, "You know what I mean. Please. I'm here. Let me be here for you."

I want to tell him, Cate realized, shocked by the revelation. *Not a day's gone by since we met that I haven't thought about Jake. I want this man, and I'm so, so lonely. Yana's my friend, but I can't even completely open up to her. But I want to with Jake. Surely, that's a sign I shouldn't ignore.*

Releasing a shuddering breath, she forged ahead and confided, **I was seventeen when the foster father drugged me and then –**

When she hesitated, Jake exclaimed, "He fucking *raped* you?!?"

Cate screwed up her face before texting, **Nice choice of words.**

"Sorry." Looking grim, he asked, "Is the piece of filth still alive?"

I don't know. I went to the police after I woke up the next morning and knew what he'd done. Thank God I don't remember the actual attack. I had to have an exam at the hospital. It was so embarrassing, but I made myself do it. I had to make sure he didn't do that to any other foster kids. The man and his wife went to jail for a while. I try not to think about them.

"How'd you do it?"

What?

"Survive all of that shit."

If I had given up, then they would have won.

"The man who raped you and his wife?"

Them. Those in society who think people like me who have physical challenges aren't as worthy of living as they are. My father.

"Your father? Did he treat you wrong because you couldn't speak?"

Cate chewed on her lower lip and considered whether or not she should answer. She'd already shared more with Jake than she had with anyone who wasn't a mental health professional. Because she'd been a minor who'd become a ward of the state after the stabbing, all of her records, including her therapy sessions, had been sealed and remained so. Child Protective Services people had relocated her from one part of Miami to another. This had allowed her to start over without having everyone around her know the specifics of her family tragedy.

"C'mon, Cate," Jake prodded, lifting her chin with two of his fingers. "You can tell me."

Cate looked into Jake's green eyes. With mild shock, she realized she wanted to tell him the whole truth, even though she feared it would push him away.

Protector, she thought. *He's a protector like my big brother was. Just like Logan Kirkland is. I've already told him about what that foster parent did, and he's still here with me. I should tell him about what my father did. I need to tell someone everything.*

After giving Jake a slight nod, Cate lowered her head and typed for a minute before showing him the screen. When Jake read the message, his mouth literally fell open.

"Your father was the one who stabbed you?" Jake asked in that deep, rumbling voice of his. "How many of you?"

Me, Mom, and Luca, my brother.

"Is your dad still alive? If he is, I'm going to find him and your foster father and beat them to a pulp. All of this is so fucking horrible."

After Dad stabbed us, he went into the garage and shot himself in the head. I remember hearing the shot. It was loud, even though I was lying on the floor of my bedroom on the other side of the house. Everyone died but me. I later learned I hadn't been expected to live.

"Do you know why he did it?"

I don't want to talk about this anymore right now. I've never told anyone except therapists since I was eight, and I stopped talking to them when I turned eighteen and the State quit paying for my treatment. Therapy is expensive.

"Not having therapy can be even more costly," he countered. "You're the most amazing woman I've ever met. Do you realize how brave you are? I can't believe what you've endured. It turns my stomach to think of what your father did, what your foster father did, and how alone you've been. No other man's said these same things to you?"

How would they know? Some men are interested in me, but when they find out I can't speak, they immediately back off. I've never been out on a date. Boys in high school always wanted to sleep with me. They figured I couldn't speak, so I wouldn't tell. So stupid. And they wondered why I didn't have sex with them. Ha!

Jake planted his hands on his hips and declared, "This is all so damned *wrong*!"

It is what it is.

"You don't expect anything more?"

Why should I?

"Because you should!" he growled. "Because no one should be treated like you've been treated or hurt like you were hurt!"

You're a paramedic. Don't tell me you're that naïve. I'm sure you've seen plenty of victims of domestic violence, neglect, rape, etcetera.

"I'm not naïve at all. I've seen a hell of a lot in the past few years. That doesn't make it right and shouldn't be accepted by anyone, least of all the victims. You should expect more from life!"

I did, and it got me nowhere. Since then, I expect nothing from life and get the pleasure of being surprised when something good happens.

"If that's the way you think, then you're in for a lot of pleasant surprises where I'm concerned."

Jake took the phone from Cate's hand and shoved it into one of the back pockets of his jeans. She was indignant – until Jake pulled her against him and slid one hand into her hair. He murmured her name, and she could tell that he was aroused and wondered why he didn't try to kiss her. Perhaps her limitations and past were causing him to hold back. Then again, she *was* vulnerable.

"I'm not out to use you," Jake volunteered as if reading her thoughts. "We're just getting to know each other. Also, you need to eat. Hell, *I'm* hungry, and I had breakfast and lunch today, which you didn't."

Cate went over to her phone, unplugged it, and texted, **I have frozen dinners, remember? We can eat then kiss.**

"Slow down!" he exclaimed, but he was laughing as he said it. "I want you, but not all the way right away. That would make me a totally selfish bastard. You deserve better than that." He gave her a lopsided grin and said, "As for the frozen dinners, they're not good for you. If your stove and oven worked and you had some real food in your fridge, then I'd cook for you. I'm no chef, but I'm good with chicken and fish."

Cate was suddenly hit by a wave of vertigo. She swayed. Jake was instantly there, effortlessly lifting her before carrying her to the couch. Once he'd put her down, he took her pulse.

"Don't try to get up," he ordered. "I'm going to get you something to snack on. Your blood sugar is probably low. Once I know things have leveled out, I'll go pick up some real food for us to eat. What do you like to eat besides frozen dinners?"

Anything vegetarian is fine.

"Christ, you're a vegetarian? I guess I won't be grilling you chicken anytime soon. Are you sure you're getting the right amount of nutrients? Maybe that's why you're so thin."

There are plenty of fat vegetarians in the world. Would you rather I be one of them?

"That wouldn't be healthy either."

Do you lecture everyone about being healthy?

"Only beautiful women I'm attracted to."

Cate blinked in surprise then texted, **You think I'm beautiful?**

"Of course. Even your name is beautiful. Your face and hair are gorgeous, and your eyes are so…unnaturally…so…."

Hold me again.

"You're killing me here. We've been over this. It's too soon. You need to eat."

After we eat.

"No."

I'm a grown woman.

"You told me you'd never been out on a date, so you've never been in a romantic relationship. We should try to take things slowly. We can build up to more if it works out. You need to be ready for me."

Ready for you? She asked, her body tingling from head to foot.

"We barely know each other. I like intense, but I don't want to overwhelm you.

Overwhelm me. I've never wanted any other man like I want you. I don't want to lose you now that I found you.

"No chance of that. I told you I haven't been able to stop thinking about you since we met in March. Dad told me once that I should always trust my instincts, and I have. He said I'd know when that special someone came along and not to let her slip through my fingers. You're pretty small, and I don't want to let you slip through mine."

Jake –

"When I was small, Dad was my hero. He taught me to pay attention to my intuition. I always have and always will. Everything seems to work out for the best when I do. So, I'm going to keep doing it. Sometimes, that means taking risks. That's what makes life exciting."

My life has never been exciting in any positive way. I want to change that. I want to explore it with you.

"Good, because if you really want to explore what's between us, you'll be getting a dose of excitement. I love it. Why do you think I became a paramedic? Some of my work is definitely routine, but a lot of it is filled with adrenaline. What kind of shape are people in when I get to them? If they're fighting to survive, can I save them or keep them alive until an M.D. can?" Stroking her hair, he asked, "What do you do for a living?"

Resolve emailed customer service issues for Combine.

"The on-line store?"

Yes. It's not exciting in the least. But it can be challenging, depending on the problems in question. I don't have to be able to speak in order to do it, so it's perfect. I get paid well enough. It's not what I wanted to do, but it works for me and Combine.

"What did you want to do?"

Be a rap singer.

Now it was Jake's turn to look surprised. When Cate giggled soundlessly, he grinned and asked, "Okay, Miss Smarty Pants. Really. What did you want to do before you took the job at Combine?"

I majored in journalism in college. I wanted to write news stories for a magazine, a paper, or a television station.

"What stopped you?"

Discrimination. After I graduated, I applied for those types of jobs. I was turned down each time, even though I'd worked on the staff of the college paper and done an internship at a TV station. I had an overall GPA of 3.5. It didn't matter. I couldn't speak, and they couldn't understand how a mute person could investigate and write news stories. I applied for and got the position at Combine to pay the bills but kept applying for the jobs I really wanted. After a couple years, I quit applying. The constant rejection was too deflating.

"Do you write for yourself?"

I've gotten away from it. I used to keep journals where I put down my thoughts, poems, or stories. I stopped when I quit applying for jobs in my field. Instead of making me happy, my writing was making me sad. It reminded me of what I couldn't have.

"You never know what the future has in store for you," Jake pointed out, as he got to his feet. "Right now, your future includes a snack then some take-out. After that, we'll see."

Jake went to the kitchen and returned with a bag of organic yucca chips. Cate sat up, ate several, and then drank some of the water he'd gotten for her. He agreed to try a chip and was amazed to discover that he liked it. When Cate stopped eating, he finished off the small bag then declared he was going to get them some "real" food for lunch. She gave him her extra set of house and gate keys and promised she'd stay on the couch while he was gone. She broke her promise the moment she heard his car back out of the driveway.

Cate picked up what little clutter there was in the living room and then went to her bedroom, straightening the comforter with its black-and-white swirling patterns. Next, she artfully arranged the decorative pillows she had piled near the head of the bed. Once that was done, she went to the bathroom and brushed her tangled black hair.

Why am I doing this? she wondered. *Jake is a nice guy, but I shouldn't get my hopes up. He's hot, and probably every woman around wants him. How can I compete?* Staring at her reflection for a long time, she thought, *He said I'm beautiful and amazing. Unless he's a really good liar, why would he say that? If he wanted to use me, he certainly could have and then left. I gave him the opportunity. Would he really do everything he did today and act the way he did if all he wanted to do was to have sex with me? And why does he want that? I don't even know what it's like. It sounds like he's had a lot of experience. He could have anyone but says he wants me.* Sighing, she told herself, *If he's lying, then I never have to trust another man again.*

She returned to the living room a minute before Jake reentered the house, carrying bags of food from The Peking Palace. When she laughed noiselessly, he asked, "What? Did I do something stupid?"

Not at all. It's only that I eat there for dinner Monday through Friday. I love that place and the family who owns it. I even have my own table near the kitchen. I can't speak, and they can't speak English. So, we smile, nod, and wave a lot. It's nice. Plus, the food is fabulous.

"I'm glad I trusted my intuition then. I'd never been there, but something told me it was the right place to stop. Jesus. This just keeps getting better and better." When she raised an eyebrow at him, he said, "I believe everything happens for a reason, not that we always know what the reason is. Sometimes we never know, but there's always a reason. Everything's connected, good and bad."

I've always felt that way. If I hadn't, then I would've killed myself a long time ago. There has to be more to life than simple randomness. For instance, I didn't want to be attacked last March, but my 911 text brought you to me.

Jake shook his head with what appeared to be wonder and muttered, "I freakin' love this."

This?

"What we're doing here."

But we're not doing anything.

"We're doing *everything*. God, I'd like to drop these bags and just take you to bed right now."

Then do it.

"No. I love sex, and I've had no problems doing one-night stands with other women. But I want more than that with you." Shaking his head but smiling, he said, "Damn, I sound like some guy in a chick flick. I'm not going to screw up what might be the best thing that ever happened to either of us by giving in too quickly."

Are you for real? Maybe I hit my head a little too hard on one of those bars six months ago and am in a coma dreaming all of this.

"You're welcome to pinch me if you want to make sure I'm not a figment of your imagination."

You're such a tease! she typed, grinning as she did so.

Jake deposited the bags of food on the coffee table, took Cate in his arms and said earnestly, "I love that smile. I'm seeing it more and more as we spend time together. If being a tease gets you to smile more often, then I'll make sure to flirt as frequently as possible. Hell, I'd stand on my head if it'd get another smile out of you."

You can stand on your head?

"No, but I'd try if it'd make you happy. I get the impression you don't really remember what it's like to be happy on a regular basis. You want a handstand? I can do one of those if there's a clear wall nearby."

Another time. I know you're hungry. Let's eat.

"Where are we supposed to sit? I didn't see a kitchen table."

I don't have one. I didn't need a table just for me, especially when I mostly eat frozen dinners and leftovers. I usually sit on the couch.

"That might be tough with all the food I brought. How about if we use the coffee table and sit on the floor?"

For the next thirty minutes, they concentrated on eating. When they finished, Jake insisted on throwing out empty containers and putting the leftovers in the refrigerator while Cate sat on the couch. She was tired, full, and happy.

"Take off your sweatshirt," Jake directed, once they were both seated on the couch again.

What? I thought you told me we weren't having sex right away.

"We're not. I want to examine your shoulder. If your wrist is still hurting off and on, then I'm wondering how your shoulder's really doing."

I'm not ready for you to see the scars on my chest and stomach.

"So, how'd you think we were going to have sex if you won't take your top off?"

I don't know. I guess I wasn't thinking.

"When you're ready for me to see your scars, then you'll be ready to make love with me."

He didn't say "sex." He said "make love." Maybe it was a slip of the tongue, but I don't think so. Jake Genter doesn't strike me as a man who says anything he doesn't mean. Will I ever be ready for him? God, I hope so.

Chapter Five

"This man did all of that for you and then told you he would drive you to work each day so that you would be safe?" Yana asked Cate the following morning after she read Cate's emailed explanation of the previous night's events. "Why did you not let him bring you?"

He's a paramedic. He can't keep regular hours and babysit me all the time. He has his own life. He wasn't happy when I told him that, though.

"No, I would think not. And he is hot?"

Very.

"I am so happy for you, my friend. I hope he is for real."

Me, too. Rubbing at her eyes, she added, **I'm SO tired. Jake and I stayed up talking until 3:00 a.m. Then, I couldn't fall asleep because I was so wound up. I can barely keep my eyes open. I hope it's not a slow day.**

Fortunately, Cate's workday was fast-paced and productive, if exhausting. When she left at 5:10, she considered not going to The Peking Palace. After all, she had leftovers from the restaurant in her refrigerator. However, she didn't want to miss her nightly visit to the family.

She was reading at her table while eating stir-fry tofu and vegetables with rice when Jake Genter planted his backside onto the seat of the chair across from hers. He wore a red shirt and a disapproving expression. With a deep sigh, Cate bookmarked her place then texted, **What's wrong?**

"Do you realize what an easy mark you are? You're tiny, mute, and a total creature of habit. Hell, I'm surprised no one grabbed you before last March."

Well, no one did.

"And no one will, not as long as I'm around to do my damnedest to stop you from putting yourself in harm's way."

The one time I was attacked by a stranger I was behind a locked gate on my own front porch!

"You've been lucky. Luck doesn't always cut it."

What do you propose? You're never going to let me out of your sight?

"If I had my way, then yes. Realistically, that won't work. Additionally, I think you'd get pretty pissed off at me if I tried that."

You've got that right.

One of the owners' sons appeared with a plate of chicken lo mien and deposited it in front of Jake, who thanked him and then told Cate, "I ordered when I walked in."

I didn't hear you.

"Obviously. You were so freakin' engrossed in your book that you weren't paying attention to anything but reading. You tend to zone in on what you're doing and block everything else out. That also makes you an easy target."

I am who I am. I don't want to be anyone else.

"I'm not trying to take away your independence. I only want to make you more aware and keep you safe. I don't want anything to happen to you."

The way Jake said the last sentence gave Cate pause. She pointed the tines of her fork at his plate and gestured for him to eat before returning her attention to her own food. Once again, they ate without attempting to converse, which would have been challenging for Cate, who'd have to alternate between eating and texting. When they were done, she insisted on paying for their dinner as a "thank-you" to Jake for the previous day's meal.

"This time," Jake told her. "Never again. I'm old-fashioned in that I think a man should pay for dinner, a movie, or whatever when he's out with a woman. Dad told me a gentleman should treat a lady right in every way, and he always knew what he was talking about when it came to that sort of thing."

No wonder your mother couldn't live alone after he died.

Jerking his chin up in what she assumed was agreement, Jake said, "You look beat. Let's go."

Where's your car?

"In your driveway. I knew where you'd be and that I'd be walking you home, so I drove there and left it."

Just then, Cate wished he'd driven it to The Peking Palace. She was beyond tired and would have welcomed the ride. She didn't share this with Jake, as the two of them stood and prepared to leave the restaurant. She smiled and waved at the family, and they smiled, waved, and said things to her in Chinese as they always did. Jake wished them a good night, and they bid him farewell in the same manner.

"They're really sweet people," he observed, as he and Cate walked back to her house. "How long have you been going there for dinner five nights a week? Four. Four months? No? Four years? Impressive."

Not knowing what he meant by this and too exhausted to think about it much, Cate texted, **When do you have to go to work? I don't want you to change your schedule because of me.**

"I tend to work four days on, four days off, three days on, and then three days off. That does vary depending on the need and availability of the crew, but my schedule's pretty stable. Burnout can be high for paramedics, and they want to give us as much work/life balance as possible in order to cut down on turnover rates. I worked day before yesterday, but now I have several days off. We pull twelve-hour shifts as a rule, but that can go longer if it's a busy day or night at 911. It's never been a problem for me since I like the excitement. I've been doing it for six years and have no desire to stop."

How old are you?

"Twenty-eight."

Did you always want to be a paramedic?

"No. I didn't know what I wanted to be until Dad died in the crash when I was seventeen. That was the deciding factor, and I've never regretted my career choice."

Did Hazel always want to be a truck driver?

"Hey, you remembered my sister's name!"

Of course. Well?

"Yeah, she always dreamed of driving a big rig and being on the road. She's known as Her Royal Highness Hazel on the highways. She loves her life, and I'm happy for her. She's fun, brazen, and loves me to death. What more could I ask for?"

Luca, my brother, could be a lot of fun, too.

"How old was he when he died?"

Twelve. He was the one who taught me how to speak.

"Speak?"

He gave me confidence to communicate even though I was born with no voice box. My parents got me in some therapy thing when I was a baby and continued it as I grew. I could make my mouth move the right way so that people could read my lips. I have great conversations with deaf people who read lips and can speak, since they can read my lips and I can hear their speech. If they're deaf and mute, then I'm out of luck, although they can understand me. Anyway, Luca used to practice with me all the time. I'd move my mouth to emulate the ways speaking people moved theirs. It was tricky, but I learned it well enough. I silently talk to myself at home off and on so that I don't lose the skill.

"I wondered how you knew the correct way to form words if you'd never uttered any. You must have had awesome teachers."

I did. I was fortunate. My parents had money, so I got help early on.

"What did they do?"

Trying to act nonchalant, Cate texted, **My mother didn't work outside the home. My father was the head of a drug cartel. Luca and I didn't know it. I found out after Dad…after they all died. Luca and I just thought he was a very successful businessman. Dad provided for us well. We lived in a fancy house. Our parents drove expensive cars and went to all sorts of social events. We had designer clothes, and Luca and I went to a private school. We took big vacations. Luca and I had no idea all the money was coming from drug trafficking. We were thankful for what we had, but things were never good at home. We would rather have been poor and had a nice family life.**

They had reached the steps of Cate's house by the time she finished the text. Jake said nothing as he read it while she unlocked and opened the gate. Once they were in the house, he exploded, "Your father was a fucking drug lord?!?" When Cate shrank back from him, he gritted his teeth, clenched his fists, and forced himself to calm down before saying, "I'm not upset with you. I'm unbelievably pissed that you had a father who made his money off other people's misery, obviously didn't treat you and your brother right, and then stabbed all of you before blowing his brains out! Shit! Where was this?"

Miami.

"Christ. The crap you had to go through…." Gingerly putting his arms around her, he asked, "Did his business lead to him stabbing his wife and kids then killing himself?"

Supposedly the Feds were finally able to get enough dirt on him to bring his operation down. He found out and decided they weren't going to best him. At least that's what they pieced together from conversations he'd had with other associates who were arrested later.

"He was going to kill his family and himself in order to keep the authorities from winning?" When she nodded, he let out a low whistle then asked, "Didn't you have other family who could've taken you in after the attack?"

Cate nodded.

"Yes? You had relatives, and they let you become a ward of the state instead of taking you in?"

The authorities found out my father's family was all tied into the drug operation. Most of them were arrested, too. As for my mother's family, they were ashamed that she'd knowingly stayed with a drug kingpin and didn't want to have me around as a reminder of what he'd done for a living and of what he'd done to Mom, Luca, and me. They didn't want to have to explain to others. I think they couldn't handle looking at me because they felt guilty. What could they say to make it okay for me? Nothing. So, they let the State of Florida handle things.

"Have they ever tried to contact you, Baby?"

After everything I've told him, Jake's not running away. He's really listening to me and just called me Baby, although I don't even think he realized he said it. This is good. Really good. So, why am I feeling so scared?

"Cate, I want you to do something for me." When she nodded cautiously, Jake said, "I want you to tell me how many times you were stabbed."

I won't tell you. When he appeared ready to argue the point, she texted, **I won't tell you; I'll show you. After everything I've shared, you're still here. I feel like I can show you and you**

won't disappear on me. Tell me I'm right, and I'll take off my sweater.

"You couldn't be more right."

Experiencing a mixture of elation, daring, relief, and joy, Cate felt as though she'd been freed from an emotional prison. And, like a prisoner who'd been locked away for almost two decades, she wanted to be totally free to live life to the fullest without reservations or censure.

She slipped her iPhone into one of the pockets of her jeans and stepped back. Going slowly, she carefully pulled off her sweater and tossed it onto the couch. Nervous, Cate extended her arms so that he could see every scar.

I can do this and stay calm. It's going to be okay. Then, unexpectedly, *I'm glad I wore the lacy, pink bra today and not a plain, white one.*

Jake allowed his eyes to roam over her bare flesh. She watched as he took in the pink lines he'd already seen on her right hand and arm. Next, his gaze went to her left arm, which had five scars on it. Finally, he let his eyes move to her chest and the four marks there. He ended by noting the three scars on her upper belly.

"Eighteen," he said before surprising Cate by wiping at his eyes. "Eighteen stab wounds inflicted eighteen years ago. Good Lord. Were your mother and brother stabbed as many times?"

She shook her head, as a tear escaped from her left eye and trickled down her cheek. Withdrawing her phone, she typed, **Dad got Mom in her sleep. She never made a sound, and it only took one…one time. When he stabbed Luca, Luca woke up and yelled for him to stop. I could hear Luca yelling for me to lock my door. I was running toward it to do what he said when Dad came in and started stabbing me. Unlike Mom and Luca, I wasn't asleep when he started to attack. I put up my arms and stumbled back. I stopped him from seriously wounding me for a few seconds, but then he got me in the chest. I fell to the floor, and he stabbed me a few more times in order to finish the job. The odd thing was that I didn't hurt. I guess I was in shock. Dad wasn't a really loving father, but you never expect your parents to stab you. I was so stunned that I didn't feel anything, except how hard it was to breathe. That was when I heard the shot. I prayed Mom and Luca were okay. Help arrived; then I** lost consciousness. **When I woke in the hospital, several nice people came in to tell me everyone else was dead but me. I kept insisting they'd made a mistake. I couldn't accept that Mom and Luca had died. I still have trouble accepting it.**

"What you just did…what you told me…showed me…." He bent to lightly kiss her before saying, "I don't think I've ever gotten a more meaningful gift in my whole life."

It's a gift I've never given anyone. Please, remember that.

"You better believe I'll never forget it."

Jake kissed her again, but this time he cupped her face in his hands. The kiss was filled with the passion she'd longed for the previous day. Stuffing her phone back into one pocket, Cate wrapped her arms around him and kissed back. Not having any experience made her feel awkward, but Jake didn't seem to mind. He skimmed his fingers along Cate's bare back, making her shiver with pleasure.

Suddenly, he stepped away from her and announced, "You'd better put your sweater back on or else I won't be able to stop myself from making love to you."

If I'm going to put anything on, it'll be pajamas. I'm so tired.

"Go change then. I'd like to hold you while you fall asleep."

I'd like that.

"You mind if I spend the night? I don't mean for sex. I can move to the couch once you're asleep. I just want to be close to you. I'll sleep in my clothes."

I'd like that, but what if this thing between us doesn't work out?

"If we don't take a chance, then we'll never know. I feel like I need you more than I've ever needed any woman. I'm so drawn to you, Cate. Let me see if I can love and protect you."

All she could do was nod as she thought, *Love and protect. Jake Genter wants to love and protect me, and I want him to do exactly that. I wonder if he'll let me do the same for him.*

Chapter Six

Feeling simultaneously elated and drained by all that had happened between her and Jake over the past couple of days, Cate finished undressing in her bathroom and then put on pink knit pajamas. After brushing her teeth, she opened the door and froze. The lights in the living room and kitchen had been turned off.

"Do you need anything before we lie down?" Jake called out from her bedroom. "Oh. Sorry. I kind of forgot you can't answer. Hang on. I'm coming."

Immobilized by fear, Cate stood panic-stricken in the bathroom doorway. Jake padded barefoot toward her. His smile became a worried frown as he approached.

"Tell me what's wrong," he urged. "When she pointed to the two dark rooms, he appeared perplexed and assured her, "Everything's all right. I was the one who turned off the lights." When she shook her head and bit her lip, Jake asked, "What's the problem, Cate. Explain it to me."

I never turn off the lights. They have to stay on all the time. "Why?"

Bad things happen when a house is dark. People get hurt. They might get stabbed or raped.

Awareness flooded Jake's eyes. Without a word, he went to the kitchen and flipped on the light before walking to the living room and doing the same. Then, he came back to Cate and asked, "Better? Good. When was the last time you turned off a light?"

Eight years ago before I got my first apartment. Ever since I've been on my own, I've kept every light on all the time. It makes me less afraid.

"You sleep with all the lights on?"

Yes.

"What if there's a power outage?"

It's only happened three times. Each time, I brought flashlights and lots of batteries into the bathroom and locked the door then slept on the floor. Even then, I kept waking up off and on.

"Do you think you could turn some lights off if I'm here with you? I don't know if I can sleep with all of them blazing."

Her heart racing and her hands trembling, she typed, **I don't know. Just the thought of it makes me totally anxious.**

As he led her to her bedroom, Jake suggested, "How about if we leave on the lights in the living room, kitchen, hall, extra bedroom, and the bathroom but turn off the overhead light in your bedroom and just leave on that little lamp in there? Could you handle that?"

I don't think so. Maybe you should just go. You shouldn't have to deal with this. You should be with some nice woman who's had a normal life and can give you what you need.

Once Jake finished reading the text, he put his hands on his hips and insisted angrily, "You have no right to tell me what I need. I've been with plenty of women who've had so-called *normal* lives. I never felt anything like love when I was with them. It's different when I'm around you. But if you really want me to leave, then tell me."

I don't.

"Good, because I don't plan on going anywhere."

Even if you have to learn to sleep with the lights on? she texted with a nervous smile.

"Even if I have to do that. Hopefully, you'll eventually feel more comfortable about turning them off."

We could try what you said and just leave the lamp on in the bedroom.

"Are you sure?"

No, but I'd like to try.

Leaving on the bedside lamp, Jake switched off the overhead light. When Cate tensed, he motioned for her to move toward him then suggested she get under the covers while he stretched out on top. She shook her head then typed that she wanted him to lie beside her and hold her against him so that she wouldn't be so afraid.

"If I get under the covers and hold you, then we're going to end up making love."

I'm fine with that.

"Cate, you don't know what you're getting into. If we have sex this soon –"

I can't tell you what you should do, but you can tell me what I should do? I'm twenty-six! I want you! I want to start living and feeling, not only putting one foot in front of the other and expecting nothing! I want to know what it's like to love, to be comfortable with a partner, and to have an orgasm! Every night I dream about what happened when I was eight, but I feel nothing. I don't want to feel anything when I have the dream, but I should feel something, no matter how awful it is! It's abnormal not to feel! I understand that now! You've shown me that, and I love you for it.

Jake wrapped his thick arms around Cate's small waist, pulled her against him, and slanted his mouth across hers. She clutched at the fabric of his shirt and held on as all that he was swept over her. Within seconds, she was lying on her back on her pink sheets, while Jake pulled away and then hastily removed his jeans and shirt. She scrutinized his handsome face, athletic build, and defined muscles. Jake pushed down his boxers, and Cate became both wet and scared.

How will that fit in me? she wondered. *I'm tiny, and he's…well…big. At least he looks big. Maybe all men are about that size. How would I know?*

Jake climbed onto the mattress, hooked his fingers around the waistband of Cate's pajama bottoms, and tugged downwards. Once they were off, he helped her to remove her shirt. When the shirt had been tossed to the floor, he laid her back, covered her mouth with his again, and slipped one middle finger between her legs. Had she been able to make any noise, Cate would have cried out with surprise and pleasure. She would have continued to cry out, because Jake didn't stop. She wanted more.

And more was what she got. Jake took her hands and brought them to his erection while he played with and sucked on her nipples.

"Feel me, Baby," he directed. "God, yeah. Like that."

As Jake grazed his teeth along Cate's neck, she urged him to enter her. In response, he inserted a second finger into her channel.

"You're so goddamned wet," he moaned, his eyes hooded and his breaths shallow and rapid. "I've got to be in you right now! Spread your legs, Baby."

She immediately obeyed. Jake sat back on his heels then leaned forward in order to gather Cate into his arms. He pulled her up against his chest and then eased into her in one, fluid movement.

Oh, God! she thought, even as she ground her hips downwards. *God, he's big, but it feels so amazing.*

"Oh, Baby. Can you take more?"

More? There's more?

Cate nodded, and Jake began to thrust in and out, harder and deeper. Her lips formed a silent *Oh!* as one of Jake's arms tightened around her waist while his free hand rested on the back of her head. She felt herself begin to pulse wildly around his cock. Gripping his shoulders, she watched his face as he claimed her. As she clenched around him when her climax hit, she sensed she was laying claim to him, too. He surged deeper before stilling and crying out, succumbing to his own release, and Cate came again. Jake cradled her against his chest and said nothing while she shuddered in his arms.

"Fuck me," Jake said, as he eased out of Cate. Lying back and pulling her against him, he repeated, "Fuck me."

Although exhausted, somewhat sore, and completely sated, Cate managed to reach for her iPhone and typed, **I thought I did.**

"You did, Baby. I always like intense, but I've never had intense like that. I…I *felt* that." When she raised her eyebrows, he clarified, "I felt it in my heart. It might have been explosive, but I sure as hell was making love to you. 'Fuck me' is an expression that means –"

I get it now. That was fabulous.

"Yeah, it was." Sighing, he added, "It was also the most reckless thing I've ever done."

Reckless?

"We should have used a condom. When's the last time you had your period?"

Her eyes widening, Cate typed, **Almost two weeks ago.**

"Jesus Christ!"

Cate counted to ten then texted, **It was one time.**

"We're both adults. You know for some people it only takes one time."

Oh, my God. What would I do if I got pregnant? What would Jake do? Oh, my God.

"Don't panic, Cate. I don't regret what we did, although I do regret not stopping to think about protection. I was so caught up in you that it totally slipped my mind."

What are we going to do if I get pregnant?

"I'd hope we'd figure out things together. I told you before that I think everything happens for a reason. I've slept with lots of women over the years and never forgot to use protection until tonight. That can't be chance."

Maybe. Maybe not. Aren't you scared?

"Oddly enough, no. Hell, I find it kind of exciting. Talk about the thrill of the unknown."

But I'm so screwed up, and I'm mute, too.

"You have plenty of reasons to be screwed up, and I've got my own crap to deal with. I'll introduce you to that soon. As for you being mute, so what? Everyone has challenges."

You don't.

"Oh, I have plenty of challenges."

Such as?

"For starters, I'm dyslexic. Are you going to tell me you don't want me because I have a learning disability?"

You have a reading disorder?

"Yeah. My parents got me help through the school system once they figured out what was wrong. I function fine, although every once in a while I mess up and do something like read *Brian* instead of *brain* if I'm really tired." Jake kissed the top of her head and said, "You've already shared a lot with me about your past. We can embark on a crash course in Jake 101 tomorrow."

But I'm really scared about everything at this moment.

"I get that. What can I do to make it better?"

Hold me and start the lesson in Jake 101 tonight.

Tucking her against his side, Jake began, "Whatever you need, Baby. Let's see. I guess I'll start with my folks. Both of my parents were mechanics. That's how they met. They got married when he was twenty-one and she was eighteen. Hazel was born two years later. She was seven when I came along. Believe it or not, I was born in the backseat of the family car in the middle of a snowstorm in Indiana. Dad delivered me with Hazel in attendance. She later described my birth as gross *and* awesome. That's Hazel for you.

"As Dad became more and more well-known in the racing circuits, we made the rounds. We settled in Bradenton when I was four. Cars were a huge part of our family life, and I sort of grew up at DeSoto Speedway. I had a good time as a kid, although school was a struggle until I really learned how to retrain my brain when it came to the dyslexia. Still, life was generally good. That all changed when Dad died in the crash."

What happened?

"There was a freak accident during a race. His car burst into flames. Everybody was devastated, and I don't mean just the family. Everyone loved Dad. He was such a nice, giving person. When I was little, I wanted to grow up to be like him."

But you didn't want to race?

"I did race, but I quit after Dad died."

What about being a mechanic?

"I'm actually a damned good mechanic, but that wasn't what I wanted to do for a living. I didn't know what I wanted. However, after the crash, I knew I was meant to be a paramedic, to help people in that way."

Did you feel like you could have saved your father if you'd been a paramedic at the crash scene?

Jake was silent for a long time before confiding, "There was no way anyone could have saved him. No one could get close enough, although people tried. Afterwards, all we heard was how Dad was such a great man who didn't deserve to die like that. Everyone said he should have lived to be old and to see his grandchildren and great-grandchildren."

You're making me think about maybe being pregnant.

"Until you get your period in two weeks – or don't – that's pretty much all we're going to think about. Even so, I'm already hard. All I want to do is make love to you again right this minute. It's crazy, but it's true."

Very crazy, but true for me, too.

"Foolish."

Totally.

"But we're going to do it again."

Yes.

"You know we shouldn't."

I know.

"I thought you were scared."

I am. I still want you to make love to me.

"And damn the consequences?"

No. Welcome the consequences.

"God, Cate. Are you one hundred percent down with this? I don't have any condoms with me, but I could go buy some." When she shook her head and reached for his cock, he said, "Then it's official. I freakin' love you."

Her heart swelled with love for Jake, the paramedic she'd met six months earlier, the man she barely knew. What they were doing was completely irresponsible, and Cate felt alive with the anticipation of it. She hadn't felt anticipation in eighteen years and didn't hesitate to roll onto her back once more and part her knees for Jake.

"Wider, Baby," he rumbled. "Jesus, you're so beautiful. I usually like to take my time, but it's not going to happen tonight. You make me want to come just looking at you. Christ!"

Jake thrust hard and deep, and Cate quickly climaxed hard and fast. Jake pushed her knees further apart and kept going. She felt another climax begin to build, as he lowered his body on top of hers without altering his rhythm. He fisted one hand in her black hair and buried his face against her neck before surprising her by saying, "I knew it was you, Baby. The moment I saw you, I knew you were the one."

She arched her back and let out a silent cry of ecstasy. Jake grunted; then he growled as he came. As they both stilled, Cate wondered whether or not she'd lost her mind and decided she didn't care. She was *feeling* again for the first time in almost two decades. Nothing mattered except her love and lust for Jake and the overpowering urge she was experiencing to truly live again.

Chapter Seven

The first thing twenty-six-year-old Cate saw when she woke from the dream was Jake's handsome face. He was sleeping soundly beside her. She felt no different waking from the nightmare than she had since she'd been eight. Part of her was relieved, but another part of her was disappointed.

Perhaps I'll never be able to feel anything about what actually happened, she speculated. *Maybe my mind can't cope and won't ever allow me to really remember what it felt like to experience everything. Would that be so bad? What if I remember and have a nervous breakdown? I probably should have had one eighteen years ago.*

Sighing, Cate rolled over to look at her clock. Disbelieving, she stared at the display. It was 10:04 a.m. She glanced around for her phone but didn't see it. Then, she spotted one corner of it. The thing was underneath Jake's pillow. Trying not to wake him, she eased her right hand underneath. She was dismayed when her movements woke Jake, who opened his eyes and smiled lazily at her.

"Good morning, Sunshine," he said then stretched. "You okay, Baby?"

She grinned and texted, **More than okay. I love it when you call me Baby. What I don't love is that I'm already two hours late for work. I'm a few minutes late every morning but never more than that. I have to shower, get ready, and walk to the office.**

"Play hooky for the day. Spend time with me. I can take you to visit my apartment and to check out other places I go."

I shouldn't.

"Do you miss work often?"

Hardly ever.

"So, miss it today. Let's have a great day together. We should probably get to know one another better, all things considered."

You mean in case I'm pregnant?

"I mean because I have no intention of having a future without you in it. Are you with me on that?"

She pretended to think about his question for a full minute.

"Cate, you're torturing me!" he laughed. "Are we in this together or not?"

"Together," she mouthed.

"Thank God for that. You scared me, Baby." Lightly touching her temple and cheekbone, he observed, "You're so unbelievably beautiful."

Thank you. I think you're pretty gorgeous yourself.

Jake chuckled, shook his head, and opened his mouth, probably to refute her observation. After holding up one finger in order to tell him to wait, Cate texted her supervisor. Feeling guilty for lying, she apologized for not texting sooner but typed that she wasn't feeling well, had overslept, and wouldn't be in to the office that day. She then texted Yana, letting her know about her absence and vowing to text more shortly. The supervisor, who knew that she didn't often miss work, texted back that he understood and hoped she'd quickly feel better. Yana texted back that she knew something was going on and asked if Cate was all right.

I actually texted in sick, but I'm more than all right. But I might already be pregnant.

Yana's reply took so long in coming that Cate wondered if her message had gone through. However, she finally got a text back asking, **What do you mean?**

Remember Jake, the paramedic I told you about? We ran into each other again last night. We were going to take things slowly. It didn't work out that way.

Yana responded, **This is very serious. Is this man pressuring you?**

No. And I feel safe with him. I feel love for him.

To this, Yana replied, **That is why this is serious. I told you that you are vulnerable. You have been so alone for so many years. He could be using you. You said you may already be pregnant. Do you realize what that will mean? What if he leaves? How can you be sure he is not a serial killer?**

51

Cate laughed noiselessly then typed, **I can't be sure of anything except that this feels right and good. I have to try to trust someone and to love someone or else I'll continue to exist alone and depressed. Please be okay with this. You're my best friend. I want you to be comfortable with my decision to be with Jake.**

Yana typed, **I will not be okay with this until I meet the man and see for myself that he seems to only have good intentions toward you.**

Cate handed the phone to Jake so that he could read the chain of texts. Once he'd reached the last one, he suggested, "Would she meet us at The Peking Palace for dinner tonight? I don't want your best friend to think I'm some sort of bad guy out to hurt you."

After texting Jake's suggestion to Yana along with the information that he was the one who'd suggested meeting that night, Cate leaned forward and lightly kissed him. As she was quickly discovering, Jake rarely did anything lightly. He pushed his tongue into her mouth and kissed her passionately, so passionately that she barely noticed when her phone vibrated with Yana's reply.

See you at 5:30. Be careful, my friend.

Cate smiled as she read the text. She didn't want to be careful. She wanted Jake and everything uncertain that came with him. She was tired of living in such a limited world, even though it was the life she'd created for herself due to circumstances beyond her control.

She and Jake rose, and Cate plugged in her phone to charge while they showered and dressed. Jake put on the clothes he'd worn the previous day, while she dressed in jeans and a maroon sweatshirt. He retreated to the kitchen to find something to eat, while she applied some makeup, pulled her hair into a ponytail, and brushed her teeth. After polishing off a protein bar, Jake rinsed with mouthwash and told Cate they were going for a drive. She slipped on her shoes, grabbed her purse and phone, and then followed him to the red 1965 Mustang GT.

When Jake lowered the top, Cate texted, **I've never ridden in a convertible. Won't we get cold?**

"It's October. It's, like, seventy-five degrees. You're wearing a sweatshirt and jeans. I think you'll be fine."

Where are we going first?

"Around the area to places I go, and then we'll go to the condo building where I lease an apartment. I want you to see where I live, work, and play."

Cate loved riding in the Mustang with the top down. It was wonderful to experience the sun on her face, to see the unobstructed view of clear blue skies, and to feel the wind all around. They drove past Jake's work, restaurants where he liked to eat, bars where he liked to drink, and his childhood home, which was a modest white bungalow twenty minutes away in Bradenton. They ate lunch at The Salty Dog on Siesta Key then walked hand-in-hand along the beach before returning to Jake's car and heading back to Sarasota in order to go to his apartment.

The building was in the heart of downtown. It appeared to be older but had been restored. As they walked toward the front doors, Cate froze. Logan Kirkland was walking toward them with his white cane, carrying Mary Margaret in a toddler carrier backpack. Cate frantically tapped on Jake's arm and pointed to Logan then texted, **Stop him, please!**

"Hey, Buddy!" Jake called out. "Hang on a second!"

Logan turned toward them and asked, "Yes? What can I do for you?"

"I'm not sure. My name's Jake. My girlfriend asked me to stop you. If you'll hang on a second, she'll explain after she texts what she wants me to read." As Cate typed, he glanced at the screen and continued, "She says to tell you her name is Cate and that you'll understand. She wants to know how your wife and new baby are doing."

"Nice to meet you, Jake. Hi, Cate! Beth and Deacon are great."

Deacon? I thought you were going to name him Luca.

"We decided we liked the sound of Deacon Kirkland better," he told her once Jake had read her text to him. "Deacon's already trying to crawl. Beth and I took the day off to spend some uninterrupted quality time with the kids. I just took Mary Margaret to the park for a little while to give her some one-on-one time. She seems to be accepting her little brother, but we each want to show her individual attention so she doesn't resent his appearance."

"Cate texted that that's a great idea," Jake told him. "And congratulations from me on your recent addition to your family."

"Thanks. Why don't you come up and see Beth and Deacon?"

We don't want to intrude, Cate typed. **I'm sure Beth is tired.**

Once Jake read this aloud, Logan laughed and said, "With two kids under two-and-a-half, we're both pretty tired all the time. We're loving it, though. Beth's also still the same wonderful, hyperactive woman that she's always been. She'd be thrilled to see you and show off our son." Hesitating, he said, "If you're heading home or something, then we can do it another time."

"Actually, this is my home," Jake said. "Cate has a house not too far from here, but I've lived in this building for almost a year. I'm surprised we haven't met before today."

"Me, too." As the two men shook hands, Logan said, "Cate and I met last March. She was at our store the Saturday morning Beth went into labor with our son."

As Mary Margaret shook the small stuffed bear in her hand, it made a jangling noise. Logan laughed and told them this was their cue to go inside. When Jake asked why, Logan said that his two-year-old daughter was potty training and waved the bear around when she needed to go. The toddler shook the bear again and said, "Now!"

"I guess we'd better hurry," Logan chuckled. "Come on."

Beth, Logan, and their children lived in a three-bedroom, two bathroom, fourth-floor condo. The place was decorated in an eclectic fashion that was attractive and inviting. Beth obviously liked vibrant colors, but Cate immediately noted a variety of textures on the furnishings. She suspected the couple had combined their wants and needs in order to make their apartment a true home for both the blind and the sighted.

"Beth bought this condo before we met," Logan told them once he directed them to have a seat on the couch. "When we became a couple, I moved in here, and she moved into Sight Unseen. Make yourselves at home. Mary Margaret and I will be right back."

"What's Sight Unseen?" asked Jake. After Cate had texted an explanation, he remarked, "Very cool. I'd like to check it out in person with you."

"Cate, hey!" Beth Kirkland exclaimed, as she entered the living room wearing jeans and a blue knit top.

Beth was holding her six-month-old son in her arms. The baby's hair was brown like his sister's, but it didn't appear to be curly like hers. Cate didn't know much about babies, but she thought he looked big for his age. Of course, his father was tall, so perhaps he merely took after him.

"It's so great to see you!" Beth cried, leaning forward to give Cate a brief hug. "Logan said you ran into each other downstairs. At least you didn't run into each other like you did in March. Did Logan tell you he figured out how you can actually talk to him? It'll be fantastic for both of you!"

Chapter Eight

Cate was too stunned to move. Her mind was racing. Had some new technology been invented that would allow her to speak? Was there an operation she didn't know about? If there was something that would enable her to talk like a normal woman, would she try it?

Of course, I would, she thought. *To be able to tell Jake I love him and to chat with Yana and —*

"You okay, Baby?" Jake asked gently. When she nodded, he observed, "You look a little pale."

I was wondering how I can talk to Logan.

"Through Siri," Beth said, shifting her waist-length blonde hair out of her way as she repositioned the baby in her arms. "Logan was saying that if you texted him, he could use voice command to tell Siri to read your texts. That way, you could talk to him without speaking yourself."

It was an excellent idea, and Cate wondered why she hadn't thought of it right away. She texted this, held it up for Beth to read, and smiled, but she was actually struggling not to cry. For a few seconds, she'd felt hope that she could somehow be granted the ability to speak. The realization that there was nothing new available hit hard.

Logan returned to the room with Mary Margaret. Cate noted that he didn't use his cane in the condo and moved around as easily as if he were sighted. She assumed this was because he was totally familiar with every inch of the Kirkland family's place. She suspected that he took off his dark glasses when he was at home alone with his wife and children.

Mary Margaret looked very pleased with herself, and Cate figured the toddler had peed or pooped in the potty. Logan confirmed this, and all the adults clapped, except Beth since she was holding Deacon. She told her daughter how proud she was of her and asked for a kiss. The little girl tugged on her father's jeans and said, "Up!" He lifted her so that she could bend forward and kiss her mother.

If I'm pregnant, then how will I communicate with my baby until it learns to read? Will it bond with me if it can't hear my voice? What if it doesn't love me?

"Cate, would you like to hold Deacon while I take a quick potty break myself?" asked Beth. "Or maybe your boyfriend would like to hold him?"

I'm so sorry. Where are my manners? Jake Genter, this is Beth Kirkland.

"Great to meet you," Jake said genially. "I'd love to hold him, but Cate can go first."

I've never held a baby in my life. Have you, Jake?

"Yeah. Being a paramedic, I've actually delivered a few babies over the years." He flashed Cate a grin and muttered, "Hazel was right. It's gross but awesome."

Before Cate could object, Beth rose and deposited Deacon in her arms. Cate was afraid but excited and looked to Jake for guidance. He assured her she was doing a fine job and reached out to gently draw one large finger along the boy's cheek. Deacon grabbed his finger.

"He's a big boy," Jake remarked. "How much did he weigh at birth?"

"Almost ten pounds," Logan volunteered. "Mary Margaret was a little over five pounds when she was born. Beth said delivering a five-pound baby was painful enough, but having one twice that size was pretty tough. At least they both came really quickly, but I think we're done. We're happy with our daughter and son."

Cate stared down at the baby in her arms. If she was pregnant and had a ten-pound baby, then she'd need a C-section. She doubted there was any way her tiny frame could allow for the birth of such a large baby. Deacon shifted in her lap and looked as though he wanted to root around for a breast on which to nurse. She wanted to tell him she was sorry she couldn't oblige, but she obviously wasn't able to convey this to Deacon, not that he would have understood. It made her sad.

"What's wrong, Baby?" Jake asked, as he tucked some of her black hair that had come out of the ponytail behind one ear. "Are you okay?"

Unable to use her phone to text with the infant in her arms, she shook her head, knowing Logan couldn't see the gesture. Jake frowned then kissed her before asking if he could hold Deacon. He expertly lifted the baby from her lap and joked that the boy was heavy.

"Sorry," Jake told the boy when Deacon stared at Jake's chest as though he were searching for a breast. "No way are you getting any milk out of me."

Beth returned to the living room, and Jake passed Deacon back to his mother, who asked Logan for a blanket so that she could cover herself while nursing the baby. Cate retrieved her phone and texted that she hated to leave but that she and Jake had to be going. After she'd programmed Logan and Beth's phone numbers into her Contacts List, she and Jake made their apologies and left, promising to get together with the couple and their children soon.

"What was all that about?" Jake asked while they rode the elevator up to his floor. "You looked scared and upset not long after we got there and while you were holding the baby."

When Beth said Logan knew how I could talk to him, I thought maybe there'd been some new discovery about a procedure or a machine that would make it easier. I was hopeful, but then I got dejected. It's a great idea about using Siri to help me "speak" but not the same as actually talking. I want to talk to you. And what if I am pregnant and can't talk to my child? I couldn't even talk to you while I was holding the baby because my hands weren't free to text. What if my baby wouldn't bond with me? What if it was embarrassed by me as it got older? I never thought about these things before since I never thought any man would want me or want to have kids with me.

"I want you and want kids with you. If you're not pregnant now, you will be someday. We'll make it work. We'll find a way, just like Beth and Logan. Do you think Mary Margaret and Deacon are going to be embarrassed by Logan? I mean, every kid gets embarrassed by his or her parents sometimes, but I doubt if they'll be uncomfortable with their father's blindness. I get the impression that they're not being raised to think of it as an issue. We could ask the couple for tips."

It still wouldn't help me to speak to my child or to you. When I was little, I used to wonder what I'd sound like if I could talk. I stopped wondering when I was eight and realized I was going to live but was going to always do it in silence. I figured that what I had to say was better left unsaid.

He pulled her against him, tilted her head up, and traced the curve of her jaw with one thumb before saying, "It'll be okay, Baby. Modern medicine is allowing for the development of all sorts of things. You're twenty-six. Who knows what they'll come up with in your lifetime?"

She nodded but remained unconvinced. When the elevator doors opened, Jake took her hand and led her down the hallway to his two-bedroom, one bath apartment that was decorated in the "bachelor" style. The furniture was comfortable, modern, and sparse. There were some dirty dishes in the sink, and his bed was unmade.

"I'm not a slob, but I never saw the need to keep everything spic and span when it was only me here."

What about women you've dated or just had sex with?

"I went to their places. Only my male friends like Everton come to my apartment. We're family. Everton and I have been partners for the past two years. We're a great team. That's why they keep us together. We have a phenomenal track record. He's also my best friend."

How did he get the scar on his face?

"Everton lived the stereotypical story of a young black kid with no dad around and a drug-head mom. He found family by becoming part of a gang. He got out when he was fourteen and someone knifed and killed his best friend. That was the night he got the scar. He was done and went to the cops for help. He was lucky and got it." Glancing at his watch, Jake said, "It's almost 5:00. We should head for The Peking Palace. I don't want to be late and make a bad impression on your friend. After all, she's already wondering if I'm a serial killer."

Jake?

"Yeah, Baby?"

After dinner, will you drive me out of the city in the convertible? I want to feel what it's like to ride outside in the dark and see the stars from the car.

"You know I will. Will you do something for me?"

Anything I can.

"Will you let me teach you to drive soon? Everyone should know how to drive."

I'd really enjoy that.

"Good. Will you do something else for me?"

What?

"Think about letting Everton teach us both sign language. I want to be able to talk with you face-to-face without having to wait to read your texts. Plus, even babies can learn how to sign things. If we do have kids together, then that could be a big help."

But if I sign, then people will think I'm deaf, too. It will be confusing to those I meet who don't know me. I don't want to unintentionally mislead anyone.

"Everton's not deaf and didn't learn how to sign in order to mislead anyone."

That's true. Why DID he learn sign language?

"Because his baby girl is deaf, and he wanted to communicate with her."

Everton's got a baby girl?

"Well, she's not a baby girl anymore. She's sixteen."

Sixteen? How old is Everton?

"Thirty-four. He and Ava's mom were eighteen when Ava was born. A year later Ava's mom died of an aneurysm. So, there was Everton – nineteen, a widower, in college, and with a one-year-old daughter. Ava was officially diagnosed as being deaf a month after her mother died. Somehow, Everton managed to take care of Ava, learn American Sign Language and about the deaf community, work, and finish school. His only support was Ava's grandmother, who always treated Everton like he was her son and not her son-in-law. She learned ASL and had Everton and Ava move in with her so she could help out. She's a fabulous woman called M'Dear."

M'Dear?

"Yeah. No idea where she got that nickname, but it fits her perfectly. She's a great lady. You'll have to meet her and Ava soon.

Everton and Ava are blessed to have her. There's so much love in that family."

A family filled with love, Cate reflected. *What I always wanted but never had.*

Unable to stop herself, she burst into tears. Jake came over to where she stood, putting his big arms around her before kissing the top of her head and saying, "Your best friend's going to think I made you cry before dinner. What can I do to make you happy?"

She decided this was a rhetorical question since he didn't release her in order to let her text a response. She hugged him as tightly as she could and mouthed the words, *I love you,* even though he couldn't see her face.

"I love you, too," he murmured.

Startled, she pulled back and mouthed, "How?"

"People don't always have to use speech to express themselves. I knew what you were saying. I didn't have to hear it to know. Actions speak louder than words sometimes."

As they left the apartment, Cate decided she'd let actions speak louder than words later that night when she and Jake were in the car. She knew what she was going to do, what she had to do in order to prove to Jake that she really did want him. No matter how strong he seemed, she sensed that he feared rejection. Despite the fact that she didn't understand why he found her so appealing, she wanted to provide him with reassurance that *she* wasn't going to leave *him.* She knew exactly how she'd do it.

Yana was waiting for them when they arrived at The Peking Palace. As Cate and Jake greeted the Asian family and joined her statuesque friend, Cate thought of how odd it was not to sit at the little table near the kitchen. Once the threesome was seated, she texted, **Yana Tarasenko, this is Jake Genter.**

Cate watched her best friend and her boyfriend exchange pleasantries. Jake appeared totally relaxed, but Yana was noticeably wary. Once they'd ordered their food, Yana asked Jake why he'd taken Cate to bed so quickly after telling her that they should take things slowly.

Grinning, Jake said, "You don't pull any punches, do you? I'm glad. I'm a pretty straightforward person and would rather be upfront about everything. I did want to take things slowly with Cate, even though I *knew* from the moment I saw her that she was the one for me. For six months, I had tried to ignore what I'd felt during our first meeting. But we had a random encounter a couple days ago. The second day – yesterday – one thing led to another, and it just…happened."

"Why did you not use condoms?"

Yana! Jake's already told you enough. I think this is all too invasive.

"I disagree. Do you protest because he is hiding something?"

"I'm not hiding anything," Jake replied calmly. "To answer your question, I didn't have any with me because I had no plans to sleep with Cate that quickly. But once we got started, we were so into what we were doing that the thought of condoms didn't come into my mind. That's the first time that's ever happened in my entire life. I figured it was confirmation that Cate was the woman I was meant to be with."

"And if she is pregnant?"

"Then we were meant to make a baby together."

"Such self-assurance!"

"Guilty as charged."

"Will you marry her if she is pregnant?"

"I want to marry her before we find out."

This was news to Cate, and it was both exhilarating and frightening. Yet, she didn't share her surprise with Yana. Instead, she kept quiet, which wasn't hard for her to do.

"Marry her! You have only known her on a personal level for a few days!"

"Love is love."

"But that is crazy!"

"Love makes people do crazy things. My father told me when I was young that when I found the love of my life I shouldn't hesitate. I took his words to heart. I'm not hesitating. We only live once, and I make the most of every day. If Cate won't marry me, I'll settle for living with her for the rest of our lives. I'd much rather make it official."

Yana turned to Cate and said, "This is insane, my friend! You know nothing about this man!"

From the moment we met, Jake's shown me respect, kindness, concern, patience, and understanding. I've felt his sincerity from the beginning and his love. He hasn't pushed me,

hasn't tried to force me to do anything I wasn't comfortable with, and has made me feel alive for the first time in eighteen years. The thought that we might have already made a baby together is kind of terrifying for several reasons, but I want it to be true at the same time. I want to live, Yana.

"I know you do, but your desire to live a normal life is making you reckless."

Maybe so, but being reckless is better than simply existing.

"But what if you go insane like your father? What if you stab your children like he did?"

Cate instantly felt as though she was going to pass out. She stared open-mouthed at her friend and wondered how Yana had known the truth and how long she'd known. Did her other coworkers know the truth as well? She suspected if they hadn't known before, then they would after that night.

Shaking with rage, Cate lifted her phone and texted, **My father did go insane. He was a bad person who was unbalanced. I'm a good person who would never do anything to harm anyone. The fact that you could even suggest that tells me you're not the woman I thought I knew at all. The fact that you know what happened to me and my family shows me you've gone behind my back and are NOT my friend. How dare you deceive me? How dare you play with my emotions? I trusted you, Yana! You're no better than those Ukrainian Mob goons you fear.** Turning to Jake, she texted, **I need to go. Now. Please, take me away from her. Take me home.**

Jake, who was radiating fury toward Yana, said, "Anything you want, Baby. I'm sorry your so-called friend here turned out to be the enemy."

"I am not the enemy!" Yana declared. "I am only looking out for Cate!"

"If you truly believe that, then *you're* the one who's insane," Jake shot back.

"I will report you!" Yana shouted. "I will call your company and tell them you went back to see Cate after you treated her as a paramedic!"

"Too late," Jake said with a satisfied smile. "I told you I'm a straightforward guy. The first day I met up with Cate on the street, I talked to my partner about it and also called our bosses. They know me and know what a stickler for honesty I am. They said it had been six months since I'd treated Cate, so there was no problem. Call them all you want."

"I will tell everyone at work about what happened to you, Cate!" Yana cried. "They will all know the truth!"

Tell them. Let them know what a traitor you are. I'll be talking to our supervisor tomorrow about all of this anyway.

"You little witch!" Yana screeched. "I hate you!"

Jake apologized to the restaurant's owners and tried to give them fifty dollars, even though they hadn't gotten their meal, yet. The parents refused his money and went over to Yana and pointed at the door while saying things to her in Chinese that sounded extremely uncomplimentary. It was during this exchange that Jake hustled Cate out and to his car. Within a few minutes, they were at her home, and she was pacing and furiously texting Jake.

I can't believe her! I trusted her! I thought she was my friend! How could she do that? Why would she do that? How am I supposed to trust anyone when things like this happen? How can I trust you? How can I trust myself? How can I go back to work? Everyone already thinks I'm weird because I can't speak. Now, they'll be looking at me with even more pity, because they'll know that my drug lord father took a knife out of the kitchen drawer and then killed us! He killed us, Jake! All of us! The Cate I was died with my brother and mother! She died when her father kept stabbing her and then blew out his brains afterwards! She's been dead for years, and I'm what got left behind! I'm nothing but a walking ghost! I should have died with the rest of my family! I shouldn't have survived! Why did I survive?

Chapter Nine

"Don't, Baby," Jake said quietly. "You survived because you were meant to survive. I don't pretend to know why, but maybe it was so you could help me."

Help you? You don't need any help. I'm the one who's all messed up.

"I need more help than you know. I've been…struggling ever since my father died."

Struggling? You mean depressed?

"Yeah. I never was like that before the crash. It totally sucks, which I know you get."

I'm sure plenty of other women were there to comfort you before you met me.

"All other women wanted was for me to show them a good time and to listen to their problems. Not one wanted to understand me. You took what I gave, but you also gave me what I needed. You wanted to know about the real me."

So, my protector needs protecting, Cate thought. *He may not have had my struggles, but he's obviously had his own. He's human, not some superhero. I can't expect him to be in charge all the time. That would be so selfish of me. It sounds like he needs me as much as I need him.*

Cate put down her phone and slipped her arms around Jake's waist. As he lowered his mouth to hers, she moved her hands down and gave the cheeks of his backside a squeeze. He deepened the kiss, as she brought her palms to his front and ran them up his flat belly and the contours of his pecs. He stopped kissing her and rested his forehead against hers, as she reached for her phone.

Being with you feels so right, but I don't know what to do about anything else anymore. I don't think I can go back to work at Combine, not after what Yana said tonight and what

she'll do tomorrow. I don't really want to be there anyway. I want to write, but that seems to be a dead-end dream for me. Plus, I need my income in order to live. If I quit Combine, then what would I do?

"Marry this impulsive, dyslexic paramedic named Jake and let him take care of you?" he suggested, and she heard the barest trace of anxiety in his voice and knew it stemmed from fear that she'd reject him.

Yes. A thousand times yes, even though it's crazy for both of us.

"People run off to Vegas and get married on the spur of the moment all the time. Crazy is in the eye of the beholder," Jake said with a wide grin. "Okay, so here's what we'll do. You quit your job. I'll move in here with you. What's your house note and homeowner's insurance cost?" After she'd told him, he went on, "That's less than what I pay for my apartment rent. You have no car, and I have no car note because I have my Dad's Mustang. I only have to pay insurance on it. We'll have to pay for food and utilities, plus cable and Internet."

I don't have cable or Internet here. I don't own a television or home computer. I didn't have the extra money.

"You do now. I've got to have cable and Internet service, Baby. You really do, too. I own a computer and my kick-ass flat-screen TV. We'll have Frontier come run the wiring and hook it all up."

I won't have health insurance if I quit my job. Especially if I am pregnant, I need that.

"I'll add you to my plan at work. Hell, I might be going from an individual plan to a family plan overnight if we find out we've already made a baby together. If there is a kid coming nine months from now and you want to be a stay-at-home mom, then I'm down with that. We need to review finances more thoroughly, but I'm thinking we can make it on my salary alone. If not, then you'll have to go back to work. Either way, you write. You can make your dream of reaching people through your writing happen, Cate. You can make anything happen. You just have to believe it."

I can't make myself speak.

"Smart ass. No, you can't, not in the traditional sense. Find a different way to speak. Also, learn sign language with me. Build a life with me. We'll enjoy the good stuff and deal with the bad. We'll live, love, and make love every chance we get."

I feel a little better about things, but could we go for that drive out to the country another night?

"Whatever you want."

Make love to me again.

"I'll make love to you whenever you want and wherever you want. I just need to make one call before we do anything else." Jake withdrew his phone from one pocket and gave the voice command, "Call Hazel." He waited for a few moments before saying, "Hey, Sis! I'm going to put you on speaker. There's someone I want you to meet." Once he'd punched the button, he said, "You're on, Hazel."

"Hey, little brother! Are you with your girlfriend?"

"She's not my girlfriend anymore."

"But you told me yesterday you were in love with the most beautiful woman in the world. You said you didn't think you could make it until the next day before seeing her again."

Cate's heart soared as she heard Hazel Genter's words. She wondered what else Jake's older sister might share during their call.

"I did say those things. A lot's happened since then."

"Such as?"

"A lot, as in we totally connected, had unprotected sex, and decided to get married as soon as we can, preferably before we find out if Cate's pregnant or not."

"Pregnant? Jesus, Jake! Are you kidding me? You always use condoms."

"It didn't even occur to me once we got started. It didn't occur to Cate either, but she'd never really been with a man before." Looking chagrined, Jake whispered, "Sorry, Baby. That just slipped out."

It's okay. It's the truth.

"Christ, Jake! I know you're an impulsive guy who likes intense, but this is nuts! Talk about impetuous! You *must* be in love. You've never done anything this harebrained in your life!"

"Thanks for the vote of confidence, Hazel," he said wryly.

"I have complete confidence in you, which is why I know this must be the woman you're destined to marry! I'll be in the Sarasota area a week from this Thursday and have a few days to hang out before I go back on the road. You think you two can hold off on getting married until then? You always said when you tied the knot, it would be forever, and I don't want to miss my obviously crazy little brother's wedding. Did you call Mom, yet?"

"No. I don't want her here, Hazel. She didn't talk to us before she married that guy, so why should I tell her about my marriage to Cate?"

"Because she's our mother, and she should know that her son is getting married and might be a father in the next nine months."

"You can tell her if you want. I'm not calling. I'll send her some pictures, just like she did with us."

"Is Cate hearing all this?"

"Yeah. I have no secrets from her."

"Good, but I don't want her to think we're terrible kids to our mother."

I don't think that, Cate texted. **It just sounds complicated. Tell her that and also that I want her to be here when we get married.**

"Cate texted she wants us to wait until you're here and that she doesn't think we're bad children."

"Thanks," Hazel said. "Jake told me you were beautiful, really tiny, totally sweet, and that you couldn't talk. If he gives you my number, will you text with me tomorrow? If you're going to be my sister-in-law, then I want to get to know you better right away."

Of course. That would be awesome. We could talk without actually talking. Jake says you're an amazing big sister.

When Jake relayed this information, Hazel laughed and remarked, "He's an amazing little brother. He can be a handful, though. He's a totally good guy who's done way too much for women who didn't appreciate him. I'm glad to hear you're different. I use voice commands to text while I'm on the roads, so we should be able to really get to know one another."

I'd love that.

"Tomorrow then," Hazel said once Jake had read the text. "This is so freakin' wonderful, Jake! Do I need to buy a fancy dress for the wedding?"

Jake looked to Cate, who shook her head and texted, **The beach?**

"No fancy dress. Cate wants to get married on the beach."

"Hallelujah! I *hate* fancy clothes! I could probably manage a sundress if jeans are too casual."

Cate shrugged, and Jake said, "I want to see you in a dress. I don't think you've worn one since your own wedding."

"I'll see what they have at the next truck stop."

Jake chuckled and said, "I can't wait to see what you come up with. Love you, Hazel."

"Love you, Jake. Love to you in advance, Cate!"

She sounds fabulous, Cate texted once Jake had hung up.

"She is. I hope you love her. Since she's on the highways all the time, you two can talk through text whenever you want."

"Her husband doesn't mind that she drives a truck year-round?"

"Her husband was also a trucker. They were married for three years and then they divorced. She says she's happy being single. I know she can take care of herself, but I worry about her being alone in her eighteen-wheeler hooking up with whatever guy strikes her fancy. I can't do anything about it. Hazel is…well, Hazel."

Are you sure you don't want your mother –

"I'm sure," Jake cut her off. "She made her choice. I'm making mine."

As they moved toward the master bedroom, Cate made up her mind to "talk" to Hazel about Jake's past and present. Her man did, indeed, have his own issues, although they weren't quite as dramatic as hers. Still, it sounded as though he was burdened by the tragedy of his father's untimely death and what he perceived as a betrayal by his mother.

Is that why I sense he's afraid of rejection by me? He's slept with lots of women but appears to have never connected with any of them. I have to find out more.

The following morning, Cate woke at 5:00, showered, dressed, and then sat on her couch in order to draft her letter of resignation. Jake came out of her bedroom wearing the same clothes he'd had on for two days. He told her he was going back to his place in order to eat, shower, shave, and put on clean clothing, but he promised to be back by 7:30 in order to drive her to Combine. As much as she wanted to prove to herself that she could face Yana and her other coworkers alone, Cate wanted Jake there. She needed his support – and possibly his protection.

They entered the offices of Combine at 8:00 a.m. Cate almost laughed. It was the first time she'd been punctual for anything in eighteen years. The slight smile that had been playing on her lips disappeared when she saw Yana, who stood glaring at her. Several other coworkers threw Cate and Jake furtive glances and looked embarrassed.

They know, thought Cate. *They know what my father did and what Jake and I are doing.* After mulling this knowledge over in her head for a minute, she wondered, *What difference does it make? I didn't ask for my father to be a drug kingpin. I didn't ask for him to stab us all then kill himself. I didn't ask to be born mute. And what Jake and I are doing is our business, not theirs. It's time for me to stop hiding and start making myself heard.*

As Yana moved toward her, she handed Jake the envelope that held her resignation letter, crossed her arms in front of her, grabbed at the hem of her gray crocheted sweater, and lifted it over her head. The pale yellow tank top she wore underneath adequately covered her breasts and the scars on her belly, but the scars on her arms and chest were clearly visible. Everyone in the room stilled, stared, and gasped. Cate studied the faces of her coworkers, who looked at her either with pity, horror, or both. Cate didn't care. She wanted them to see. She knew now what she was going to do with her life and her desire to write, and she experienced blessed relief at the realization.

No more hiding. No more sweaters unless I'm really cold. It's time to live again.

Chapter Ten

Hi, Hazel. It's Cate.

Good morning, Cate! How are things today?

Very strange but in a good way. Jake is talking to the guys who are running fiber-optic cabling to my house. He's moving in with me and says he can't live without cable and Internet. I don't know how he got them to come out the same day he called.

That's Jake. When he wants something, he usually figures out how to get it.

Did you find your dress last night at the truck stop? ☺

No, but I did find a hula guy for my dashboard.

Hula guy? I've never seen one of those. I've only seen hula girls.

Me, too. That's why I snagged the hula guy. He's really hot and is great company, although I'd much rather talk to you than him.

I want to learn all about you and tell you all about me, but could we talk about Jake this first time? Things are moving fast, but it feels right with him. There's just so much I don't know. I think I should know.

Definitely. If you're going to be his woman and have his babies, then you need to know everything. He'll give it all to you, but it may take time. Some of it, he doesn't even realize. He is a guy, and men can be dense. Of course, women can be pretty dumb sometimes, too.

Will you tell me what you think I should know? I'm not even sure where to start.

I'll do my best. What I leave out, I'll tell you as I remember or if you ask. How's that?

Good. Thanks, Hazel.

I'm happy to do it. I only want the best for my kid brother. Let's see. Dad's name was Jake, and Mom's Irene. Our lives revolved around our family and cars. Dad was loved by everyone. He gave his all to everyone. Mom was a good wife and mother. I was seven when Jake was born in the backseat of the car. I'm sure he's told you the story.

Gross but awesome.

☺ Yeah. He was always such a wonderful son, brother, and friend. His hero was Dad and rightly so. Dad was the best. Jake couldn't have had a better role model. When Jake was having so much trouble learning because of his dyslexia, it was Dad who insisted on helping him with the exercises that would teach him to retrain his brain. Mom and I helped Jake with schoolwork until he caught on, but Dad was his main instructor. Jake was motivated because of how Dad went about teaching him, but he also wanted to please Dad. It pushed him to do his best. Always. He was almost eighteen when Dad died.

What happened? Jake said there was a crash, and no one could save your father. He said it made him want to be a paramedic. I get the feeling there's more to the story than that. What am I missing?

Jake's sister took several minutes to reply. Cate wondered whether or not it was because the woman was uncertain how to answer or because she was dealing with some sort of traffic issue. Eventually, Hazel began to text again.

Sorry, Cate. I had to think about how I wanted to explain. Jake would probably rather wait to tell you more about the accident himself, but you should know right away.

Know what?

Jake feels responsible for Dad's death.

What? Why?

Dad wasn't feeling well that night. He told Jake, and Jake told him he shouldn't race. Dad didn't want to let the sponsors or supporters down. Jake told me later that he thought that Dad might be having a stroke or something, but Jake was only seventeen. Dad was in his forties and a seasoned racer. He was also Jake's hero. How do you argue with your hero who's older, wiser, and also your father? Jake gave in, even though he felt like something wasn't right. During one of the laps, Dad lost control of his car. He hit a couple of other cars, flipped, and crashed into a wall. His car burst into flames, and he was trapped. After another long pause, Hazel resumed by texting, **We could hear him screaming as he burned to death. People rushed out with fire extinguishers, but it looked like the car was going to explode. No one could get close enough to do much of anything. Like I said, the whole thing was wrong. Cars don't usually explode like on TV, but the threat was real that night. Jake tried to get to Dad, but some other guys pulled him back. He was yelling for Dad, even though we all knew it was too late. It was a mercy when Dad stopped screaming. Everyone was stunned and crying.**

And Jake blamed himself for not insisting that his father pull out of the race that night.

Yeah. He fell into a deep depression, especially after Mom lost it and married that guy and moved. I did what I could for

him, but it was rough. He finally came to the conclusion that the best way for him to help other people not lose loved ones was to become a paramedic. That way, he could treat them and hopefully save them so their families wouldn't have to suffer like ours had. Whether they were victims of car accidents, violence, illness, or whatever, he wanted to stop the hurt for the patients and the people who cared about them. It was a noble goal, and it brought him through his depression, although he never was the same happy-go-lucky kid he'd been. I'm proud of the new Jake, but I'll always miss the old one. Maybe you can bring him back. He's fallen for you hard. He's never fallen for any woman. He's been desperately lonely, even though he's dated a lot and hangs with his buddies. It's not the same as having a partner to hold you when you need it most.

What about you? You don't have a partner.

My husband turned out to be an idiot. I'm fine with being independent and single. I like driving on the open road and doing my own thing. But if you guys are going to start having kids, I might change my route so I can be around Sarasota more often. I want to be a part of my nieces' and nephews' lives.

I may not even be pregnant.

If you're not, then I get the idea you will be soon. Jake's an intense guy. You'll probably be popping out babies every year.

Cate giggled soundlessly and texted, **Most likely I'm too small to pop out anything. If we do have babies, then I suspect I have C-sections in my future. I'm kind of trying not to think about it at the moment since the events of the past few days are making my head spin. To think that just last week I was extremely into routine and almost totally isolated.**

Jake will definitely change that.

He already has. I'm loving it. I really like you, Hazel. Thanks for being so open with me.

I'm a pretty open kind of gal. I can't wait until next week.

Me neither.

I'm coming up to a traffic jam. I think I'm going to have to go for now. Let's do this again soon. Text anytime.

You, too. Bye, Hazel.

Bye, Cate.

Cate put down the phone as Jake came in from outside and said, "They're wrapping things up. You'll have to sign since you're the sole homeowner. I guess we have a lot of things to work on."

Getting a marriage license would be first on my list. Then, I'm going to get my own computer. I know what I want to do, Jake. I figured it out.

A light knock came from the door that led onto the porch, and Jake said, "Once they're gone, I have to know. You look really excited."

Cate signed the papers, but Jake insisted on paying the bill. Once the technicians had left, Cate texted, **Cate Speaks.**

"What does that mean?"

I'm going to start my own blog and call it "Cate Speaks." I probably won't make any money doing it, but I want to have my say. I want people to know what it's like to be mute, to go through what I did with my family, and to try to come to terms with it all. I want them to know that no matter what they're facing, they're not alone. You showed me miracles can really happen. Maybe if I grow and change, others will be inspired to do the same. I may still have to get another job.

"I told you I don't mind being the only one working outside the home."

If I start "popping out babies" like your sister hopes, then I may have to work outside the home so that we can afford a bigger place.

Jake laughed and said, "One thing at a time. First, we get married. Then, we find out if you're even pregnant. After that, we start renovating this place."

Renovating?

"Baby, the outside's in great shape, but the inside's in a pretty sorry state. Paint will be easy, but we've got to redo floors, get a workable kitchen, and get rid of some of your things and some of mine. It won't all fit in here."

We can get rid of any of my furniture, except the new mattress and stackable washer and dryer. Oh, and I want to keep my new microwave. The rest of it can go.

"No more friendly ghosts?"

I'd rather share my house with friendly, living people.

Jake smiled down at her then reached out to stroke one cheek. He ran his thumb along her lips then bent to kiss her before saying, "I love you, Cate. Promise me you'll never leave me."

As long as you love, respect, and take care of me, then I promise I'll do the same for you. God, this is scaring me out of my wits, Jake! It's so impulsive! I haven't done anything impulsive in my life.

"And I've always been impulsive."

You're not going to be impulsive and decide you're tired of me one day and leave, are you?

"No way. I'm loyal to those I love, Baby. I can't deal with people who don't stand by their families."

Like your mother?

Jake rested his chin on top of her head and said softly, "Yeah, like my mother. She couldn't live her life without Dad, but she made the choice to live it without me and Hazel. Just because we were adults didn't mean we didn't need Mom anymore, especially after we lost Dad like that."

Where is she?

"Indiana. She moved back up there after she remarried. She sends cards for our birthdays, and she calls now and again. I don't answer my phone when I see her number."

Maybe she's embarrassed by how she handled things.

"She should be. I'd never abandon my kids, no matter how devastated I was if I lost you. They'd need me even more. I don't get it. I guess I never will."

Jake?

"Yeah?"

Call her. You can tell her you don't want her to come to our wedding, but she's your mother. She may not have done the right thing, but that doesn't mean you have to retaliate by acting the same way.

"I can't, Cate. Hazel will call her. She doesn't talk to Mom much, but she'll call her for this. Don't ask me again, Baby. I just can't do it."

I understand. Will you do something else for me, though?

"If I can."

Don't rule out talking to your mother for the rest of your life. You don't have to plan on doing it, but don't make up your mind to never let it happen. Please. I never have the chance to see my mother or brother again. Mom could have done a lot of things differently, but I'd give anything to have her and Luca alive today. Even if my relationship with her wasn't good, at least I'd know she was out there and loved me. She should have left Dad a long time before his attack on us and his suicide. She didn't protect her children or herself. Maybe she didn't know how, but I know she cared. If Dad hadn't killed her, she'd still have the opportunity to change. I'd hope for that, even if I resented her for what she didn't do.

"For you," Jake muttered. "I won't rule it out because of you."

Thank you. After kissing him, she texted, **I love you, too.**

Chapter Eleven

"Jake! Oh, my God! This is freakin' awesome!"

Cate grinned as she watched her future husband and future sister-in-law embrace on the steps of her house. Hazel had arrived moments earlier in a rental car, and Jake had rushed out as if he were eight instead of twenty-eight. Even in the dwindling light of day, Cate could see the love and happiness reflected in their faces and actions as they greeted one another. A pang of sadness pierced her heart as she thought of Luca, imagining that she and her brother would greet each other in the same fashion had he been alive and come to visit.

Whereas Jake was tall, muscular, brown-haired, and had chiseled features that gave him stunningly good looks, Hazel was not much taller than Cate, was not classically beautiful, had extremely large breasts, and needed to lose about seventy-five pounds. Although the siblings both had deep green eyes, Hazel's hair was dyed red. She wore bright, red lipstick. Cate thought she was beautiful because she could *feel* the beauty emanating from the woman.

"Sweet Jesus!" Hazel cried, as she broke away from her brother and turned to look at Cate, who was standing in the doorway that led out onto the porch. "Cate, you are absolutely gorgeous! Look at those gray eyes and that awesome black hair! Oh, my God! You really *are* tiny, aren't you? If you are pregnant, I sure don't know where that baby's going to fit! Jeez! Can I give you a hug?"

Cate nodded, and Hazel practically smothered her with the hug before saying, "I so can't wait for tomorrow night, but I haven't found a dress, yet."

Withdrawing her phone, Cate texted, **That's okay. I haven't found mine either.**

"What? But it's *your* wedding!"

I know. I've been so busy that I haven't had time to look for a dress. Jake's been working his regular job, but we've also been working together and separately on the house. I painted all the rooms with one-coat paint, and Jake and some of his friends from work ripped up the carpet in the hallway, living room, and two bedrooms. They found wood floors in perfect condition underneath. So, they cleaned and sealed them. Now, we have great, new old floors.

"What about the furniture?"

We got rid of mine, brought in some of Jake's, and bought a new oven and fridge. We've got two small desks set up in the living room for our computers. Thank God, it's a small house. Otherwise, there's no way we could have done it all in a week, regardless of how much help we had! When I wasn't working on painting walls, I did some intensive research and set up a blog site. I'll post my first "Cate Speaks" blog after the wedding. Everton's taught us a few words of sign language. I haven't had time to breathe, much less get a dress for tomorrow.

"We'll fix that in the morning and go shopping. Jake, what's your schedule?"

"Everton and I changed things around because of the wedding. We should be working this weekend, but we got friends to take our shifts. We're both off until Monday."

"What are you two wearing to the wedding?"

"White Oxford shirts and khaki pants."

"Who's marrying you?"

"A woman who specializes in beach weddings. We found her online, met with her last night, and reviewed what we wanted. It'll be short but sweet."

"What about pictures?"

The woman performing the ceremony has package deals and can provide a photographer. We got to see pictures from other weddings and were happy with them.

"What time's the wedding?" Hazel asked.

We'll be there at 6:30, have the ceremony before sunset, and then kiss while the sun's going down behind us. As long as there are no evening showers, it should be perfect.

"It will be," Hazel said with certainty. "Jake, I'm going to take Cate shopping tomorrow. We'll meet you at the beach right before 6:30."

"Hazel, it's not your wedding. You can't run the show."

"Somebody has to! This is your only wedding, remember? I'm not going to let the two of you make it just another wedding. It's got to be magical, even if it's simple. Trust me."

Jake said his sister's name in a warning tone, which she ignored. She asked Cate if she trusted her. Cate shrugged and smiled.

"This is your wedding, but neither of you knows what in the heck you're doing. At least you got the woman marrying you and the photographer lined up, but there has to be more. What about a cake? What about a reception?"

For the four of us?

"Why not? Jake, you and Everton can handle that, and let me add some special touches to the ceremony. I promise it'll be wonderful."

"I know you're really good at this kind of thing, Hazel. But it's up to Cate. She's the bride."

I'll trust you.

"Hallelujah! You won't regret it. I swear."

I'm sure I won't. I'm glad for the help. Thank you again for being my Maid of Honor.

"I'm thrilled beyond belief! Can I see the inside of the house now? I'm really curious after all you said you've done in a week."

"Sure. Like Cate said, we wouldn't have been able to accomplish it all if it hadn't been a tiny house to begin with. We'll show you to your room. It's pretty sparse, but it's a decent guest room right now. We put my old bed and a nightstand in there, but we don't want to add anything else. If Cate is pregnant, then that'll be the nursery."

When Hazel entered the living room, it was evident that she was impressed. Cate smiled slightly, but Jake had a wide grin on his face. With the new gray paint highlighted by the white baseboards and crown molding, the gleaming wood floors, and the addition of his black leather couch and chair, expresso TV stand, and flat-screen TV, it looked trendy yet inviting. The two small black desks and desk chairs were tucked in opposite corners of the room behind the couch. They had yet to hang pictures. Cate wanted to frame photos of their wedding and hang them, leaving space for pictures of their baby – if it existed.

They led Hazel to the extra bedroom. It was painted a cheerful yellow and, as Jake had described, held only a queen-sized bed and a nightstand. Jake put his sister's suitcase near the closet and motioned for her to follow them, continuing the tour.

The master bedroom remained unchanged, except for the green paint and shiny wood floors. The kitchen, with its new stainless refrigerator and oven, now had deep red walls. The hallway was painted gray like the living room.

"I don't know what it looked like before, but this is great."

"The outside looked great, but the inside looked like crap," Jake informed her. "Cate wanted to fix it up but couldn't on her own. The only things we still have to do are to have someone regulate the water pressure in the kitchen and to change out all the light fixtures."

Would you like to see the backyard before it's too dark? I like to hang out there and watch the birds.

"It's so cute," Hazel remarked once they'd gone outside. "But there's only one chair. I saw a swing on the side porch, but where's Jake supposed to sit out here? I also didn't notice a kitchen table or end tables in the living room. You've got to have those."

"Thank you, Your Royal Highness," Jake teased. "We've done a hell of a lot in one week. Yes, we still need to buy a little table that will fit in the kitchen. We don't think there's space in the living room for end tables. Take a deep breath and chill."

As they returned to the house, Hazel said, "I talked to Mom."

Jake stopped where he stood and asked tightly, "And?"

"And she sounded upset but said she understood why you didn't want her here. She asked me to send pictures. She wants to know if she's going to be a grandmother."

"Why? So she can *not* be a part of her grandchildren's lives like she's not a part of ours?"

Jake, please. It's the night before our wedding. Try not to let this cloud what's supposed to be a happy occasion. You can be angry with her after this weekend.

He nodded but remained tense. The three of them sat in the living room and talked for several hours. By the time they went to bed, Cate's fingers and her right wrist were aching from all the texting she'd done, but it had been a wonderful evening. Hazel was, indeed, an amazing woman and had entertaining stories to tell of life on the roads as a female big rig driver.

As she'd done every night for the past week, Cate got ready for bed and then went into the bedroom before Jake shut off all of the overhead lights in the house. There were nightlights in the living room, kitchen, hallway, and guest room, but the small lamp on Cate's bedside table and the bathroom light remained on at all times. So far, this new routine had worked for Cate, and it had been explained to Hazel, who now knew the story of Cate's stabbing but not the rape. Hazel promised to remember not to turn off the bathroom light if she rose to answer nature's call during the night.

"Do you like her?" Jake asked, as he tucked Cate against him in the bed.

"I love her," Cate mouthed then snuggled closer and drifted off to sleep.

Cate woke the following morning and sighed deeply. She'd had the dream *again* and still felt nothing upon waking. She wondered if her response to the nightmare would ever change and speculated that perhaps it wasn't meant to.

As she stared at Jake's strong chest and watched it rise and fall ever-so-slightly with his breathing, she thought of the days ahead. She was preparing to marry a man she'd met briefly six months earlier and had only truly known for less than two weeks. If she wasn't pregnant, then she should start her period on Monday. If she was....

Do I want to be pregnant so soon? I have no doubts that I want to be married to Jake, and he definitely wants to be married to me. But maybe we should have more time to get to know each other before having a child. Especially with my limitations, we'll have more challenges than the average couple. Beth and Logan Kirkland are making their situation work. Maybe we should approach them like Jake suggested. They could tell us what to expect when it comes to raising kids who have a...disabled parent.

Cate hated the word *disabled* and tried not to use it, but sometimes it seemed to be the only word that fit her situation. She was literally not able to speak, which made her disabled. Semantics didn't lie.

Push all this worrying aside until Monday. My cycle's as regular as clockwork. If I don't get my period by Tuesday, I can take a pregnancy test and find out one way or another. If it's positive, then Jake and I can figure out what to do in the next nine months and afterwards.

"What are you thinking, Baby?" Jake mumbled, as he opened his eyes and turned his head toward her. "I know we only learned a few signs and probably suck at sign language right now, but can you sign anything to me that might tell me what's going on in that mind of yours?"

She immediately signed, "Love you."

Jake grinned broadly and signed, "Love you."

Then, she signed, "Baby."

He cocked his head and asked, "Good or bad thoughts about a baby?"

When she shrugged, he said, "If you don't get your period next week, then you go to your doctor and get a blood test so we know for sure." Are you still scared because it's so sudden or because you're mute?"

Yes to both. I'm sure about you and me, but I'm not at all sure about us being parents so quickly when we still have to get to know each other.

"We're going to make it work, Cate," Jake insisted. "I love you more than anything. Whatever happens in our future, we'll face it together."

I like the way that sounds. Let's put that in our wedding vows for tonight.

"I'll email the woman performing the ceremony and tell her to add it. You and Hazel have some shopping to do. Have fun, Baby. I'll be waiting for you at the beach. Don't stand me up, okay?"

She heard a trace of fear in his voice and scooted over until her head rested atop where his heart beat. Wrapping her thin arms around his waist, she squeezed him as tightly as she could. His fingers were suddenly in her hair, and she felt his hardness brush against her side. Lifting her head, she smiled at him while reaching down to caress the tip of what they both wanted to be inside of her.

"Jesus, Baby," he groaned. "You don't know how much I want to make love to you right this moment."

Cate forced herself to stop, retrieve her phone, and type, **Do it. I want you to take me a different way in honor of our special day.**

"Fuck me, Baby. I'm glad I closed the door to our room last night and that Hazel's a pretty sound sleeper."

Cate was soon kneeling on the mattress with Jake behind her, gliding in and out with practiced ease. When she bent her arms and lowered her top to the pillow, Jake made the rumbling noise in his chest that she so adored. She gasped as he drew his tongue along the back of her neck while exploring her body with his hands.

"Move your knees further apart," he directed, his breathing becoming more erratic as she did so. "Perfect, Baby. So perfect."

The words *filled to capacity* floated through Cate's mind as Jake thrust more urgently. Her black hair spilled over her neck and shoulders. Jake groaned, threaded the fingers of his right hand into the mass of loose curls, and tugged gently. Cate arched her back and came.

"More, Baby?" Jake rasped once she'd stopped shuddering.

She didn't hesitate to nod, and he wrapped his hands around the fronts of her thighs and drew her up until her knees no longer rested on the bed. She gripped the sheets with pleasure at this unexpected change in position, as Jake began a pattern of swiveling his hips and then plunging into her before almost withdrawing and repeating the movements. Her center was throbbing, and she ached for release. When Jake pulled her legs wider as he plunged down again, the climax slammed into Cate so hard she thought it might kill her. From behind her, she heard Jake suppress a growl as best he could, probably in an attempt not to wake his sleeping sister while he came.

Afterwards, Jake eased out of Cate and gently lowered her onto the mattress. Between the intensity of her orgasm and their unusual position, her muscles quivered and her limbs seemed weighted down. Too tired to move, she smiled drowsily at Jake. As she drifted back to sleep, she heard him say, "You have no idea what a blessing you are. I love you, Baby."

Chapter Twelve

Cate woke alone. Totally comfortable where she was, she hated to get up but knew she had to. Rolling out of bed, she dressed in pajamas and a robe, got a fresh pair of jeans, underwear, and a red, long-sleeved sweater, and went to the bathroom. She was about to close the door in order to shower and dress when she heard Jake and Hazel talking in the kitchen. Jake was crying.

Stunned, Cate pushed the door until it was almost shut and strained to hear the exchange between the brother and sister. A part of her said she shouldn't eavesdrop, but another part told her it was in her best interest – and Jake's – for her to listen. She wondered if he was crying because of something she'd inadvertently done or failed to do.

"That was over ten years ago," Hazel said soothingly. "You were seventeen. You told Dad he shouldn't race. He was the adult. He shouldn't have raced, but it was his choice, and the accident happened because he was so focused on not letting other people down that it blinded him to the risks."

"You don't understand, and I can't explain it!" Jake insisted.

"When will you let go of this guilt? You hide your depression really well from everyone else, but you can't hide it from me. I've literally known you since you were born. Hell, Cate's known you for two weeks, and she knows something's not right when it comes to you and Dad's death. Have you talked to her about it? Have you cried in front of her?"

"No."

"You have to tell her about your depression and what's at the root of it. She's told you about all of her crap. You need to reciprocate. She'll be your wife, and she'll be the mother of your children. She's barely bigger than a minute herself, so being pregnant might not be so easy for her. She knows that and still wants you and your babies, little brother. You told me she's the best thing that's ever happened to you. Prove it, and talk to her."

"Not on our wedding day." Sounding more in control, he said, "She's had a lot of adjustments to make in the past couple weeks. I'll talk to her once things are more settled."

"Are you taking any antidepressants?"

"No. I manage fine without them."

"I can tell."

"A man can't freakin' cry on his wedding day, but a woman can? You don't think Cate hasn't cried in my arms because she wishes her brother and mother could be here for all that?"

"That's the difference. She's cried in your arms. You're crying in mine, which is fine. But you need to cry in *hers*. She's your partner. Let her in all the way."

"Soon." Clearing his throat, Jake said in his normal voice, "Thanks, Sis."

"I seem to recall bawling on your shoulder a time or two myself. Reciprocity, remember?"

Cate quietly closed the bathroom door and showered. She wondered how long it would take for Jake to shed tears in her presence. When she emerged, ready to go, Hazel was seated on the couch, drinking coffee. Jake was gone.

"Did you hear him crying this morning?" Hazel asked soberly. When Cate nodded, she said, "He wants to be strong for you and doesn't understand how he can let you see that part of himself that's still hurting so much. It worries me."

Pulling her iPhone from her pocket, Cate texted, **I get that he feels responsible. I have survivor guilt myself, although that's a little different. Rationally, I know it's not my fault that I survived and the rest of my family died. However, at some level, I feel like I betrayed Mom and Luca by living. It makes no sense, but it's a real feeling.**

"Yeah. Jake knows what I reminded him of is true, but he continues to blame himself. I wish he would take some medications or talk to a therapist or something. It would probably help. It's been ten freakin' years!"

Do you think he'll ever reconcile with your mother? I asked him not to rule out the possibility, but I don't know if he agreed just to placate me.

"I don't know. Mom changed after Dad's death, but then we all changed. I would tell you to reach out to her, but Jake would feel totally betrayed by you if you did. He can deal with me having sporadic conversations with her, so I'll keep updating her and see what happens. Maybe when you have kids, he'll try to at least talk to her. Anything would be an improvement." Standing, Hazel announced, "It's your wedding day. Let's get moving. We have dresses to find and fun things to do."

They arrived at the Mall at University Town Center thirty minutes later. Despite Cate's protests, Hazel insisted that they start at one of the large department stores at one end. She cited the availability of nice dresses for special events and told Cate to splurge on a dress that made her feel like a queen.

"You're getting married tonight. Indulge."

But I'm too tiny for any of these dresses, and they'll be too expensive.

"Not if we go to the juniors' department and see what they have. It's your wedding dress! If you find the right one, then it's worth every penny. You're supposed to trust me, remember?"

The dresses in the juniors' section of the first department store were not appropriate at all. Everything in Cate's size was too flashy, too short, or "too skanky," as Hazel put it. So, they moved on to another large department store after having lunch at the Cheesecake Factory.

At first, Cate was dismayed by the selection in the juniors' department. The dresses seemed similar in style to those of the other store. She wondered if the parents of teenaged girls really approved of their daughters' wearing of such clothing. However, as she wound her way through the racks, she began to see dresses that were more classic in their design. When she rounded one rack, she spotted a dress that she knew would be perfect – and expensive.

The garment consisted of a white sheath gown with a white, crocheted, long-sleeved shell that went over it. It would be fitting for a beach wedding and would artfully conceal the scars on Cate's arms and torso. Although she wasn't embarrassed by them anymore, she had no desire to see them highlighted in anything sleeveless or strapless.

Maybe they won't have my size, she thought. *If they do, maybe it won't look right. If they do and it does, then I have to get it.*

Hazel's right. This is my one and only wedding, and I'm already not doing what most women do when they get married. I have no family or friends to celebrate with me. There won't be a lot of fanfare. So, why not get a dress I love?

"You found it," Hazel said from beside her. "God, I hope they have your size. I think it would be perfect for you. Take a look, and I'll keep my fingers and toes crossed."

They had her size.

Cate went to the dressing room while Hazel waited right outside. As she slipped the gown over her head then reached back to zip it up, Cate prayed it would fit just right. It did. She stared at herself in the mirror and smiled. Then she opened the door of the fitting room.

"Oh, my freakin' God!" Hazel exclaimed. "It's, like, meant for you! Oh, Cate! Please, tell me you'll get it no matter what it costs. Hell, I'll buy it for you if you won't spend the money. You have to get married in that dress! Promise me."

I promise.

Hazel let out a whoop of delight that made several nearby customers look disapprovingly in their direction. Cate didn't care. She was ecstatic. Now, all she needed was a pair of shoes to go with the dress.

Forty-five minutes later, Cate decided on a pair of dainty, white sandals. She paid for them and the dress without hesitation or concern and followed Hazel to the women's department. Hazel found a comfortable but not-too-casual long-sleeved green dress and black sandals they both agreed would be just right for her. Once she'd paid for her items, she asked Cate what jewelry she was going to wear and whether or not she and Jake's wedding rings matched. That was when Cate almost had a panic attack.

I didn't get Jake a ring! Oh, my God! How stupid of me! How could I forget about getting his wedding ring? I don't even know his ring size!

"Deep breaths, Sister. I know his ring size, and we'll get a nice gold band at one of the jewelry stores in the mall. It won't be hard. Now, what about your jewelry?"

I don't wear any. My wedding ring will be the only jewelry I've worn since before...since I was eight.

"Well, that makes things easy. You're so beautiful you can get away without wearing jewelry. You don't even really need any makeup, although I know you wear a little. It's obvious you like to do your nails and toenails, though. Let's get a mani-pedi and then go to the salon here so that they can do your hair real nice for tonight."

After we find Jake's wedding band.

They found the simple ring at a nearby fine jewelry store. Cate hated the idea of getting Jake a plain gold band but was totally against buying him anything ornate. Her father had worn flashy rings, and the mere sight of them sickened her. However, she wished she could personalize the ring in some way and texted an inquiry to the man behind the counter.

"We do laser inscriptions on the insides or outsides of wedding bands and other jewelry. You could put the date, a meaningful word or phrase, or your names. Actually, you can put anything you want as long as it's not too many characters."

After considering her options for a few minutes, Cate typed what she wanted inscribed and where. The man went to the back of the showroom and gave the ring to another man who was obviously the store's jeweler. They talked, and the jeweler set to work. Soon, the clerk returned to where Cate and Hazel waited at the counter. The words *Forever, Baby* were clearly inscribed on the outside of the band. Cate smiled, pleased with what she'd done.

"He'll love it," Hazel told her. "He's so scared he's going to lose you."

I know. That's why I selected those words.

Hazel hugged her and said, "I love you, Cate. Jake's a lucky man, and he sure as hell knows it."

And I know I'm a very lucky woman. That doesn't mean I'm not still terrified about how quickly all this is happening.

"That's totally understandable. It will be okay."

When they left the mall at 4:30, Cate's black hair hung in loose curls, and her fingernails and toenails were an iridescent light pink. Hazel's red hair had been arranged in an up-do, and her nails were a dark shade of red. They loaded their purchases into Hazel's rental car and headed for the house, which Hazel told Cate had already been vacated by Jake.

"I texted him while you were in the dressing room and told him to vamoose by 4:00. He's getting ready at Everton's. We should have plenty of time to change and put on makeup before heading out."

I'm always late for everything. We'll never make it.

"Of course, we will!"

They arrived at the beach on Siesta Key a few minutes after 6:30. Cate shivered in the cool October air as she walked beside Hazel, who was carrying Jake's ring. They scanned the area looking for Jake, Everton, the female Justice of the Peace who was conducting the ceremony, and the photographer but saw none of them, yet.

"We could sit while we wait," Hazel proposed.

I'm too nervous. I'd rather –

"Jesus, Baby! You scared me."

Cate pivoted. Jake, who'd come up behind her, now put his arms around her shoulders and smiled. He murmured that she looked stunning before gently kissing her, but she caught the glimpse of fear in his eyes.

He wondered if I was going to stand him up, she thought. *How could he think I'd ever do that to him?*

You know I'm always late for everything. What made you imagine our wedding would be any different?

The tension in him eased, and she smiled and lightly kissed him on the jaw. Lowering his head, Jake nuzzled her neck before whispering, "You look so beautiful. I wonder if my hard-on will show in our wedding photos."

She laughed soundlessly, and Hazel cried, "Okay, you two! If you want a sunset wedding, then stop horsing around. There'll be time for that later."

After Cate and Hazel had hugged Everton in greeting, both of them were introduced to the female Justice of the Peace, a young, blonde woman who wore a navy blue pantsuit and flats, and the older, male photographer, who was dressed in a navy shirt, jeans, and loafers. Within minutes, Jake and Cate stood on the sand only a dozen feet from the water, and the photographer snapped some shots of the two of them before asking Everton to stand beside Jake and instructing Hazel to take her place beside Cate. He took several more pictures then moved aside as the Justice of the Peace stepped forward and prepared to begin. A small crowd of beachgoers gathered once they realized a wedding was about to take place, but Cate and Jake had suspected this would happen and didn't mind.

"Hey!"

Everyone turned to look at the brunette woman jogging across the sand toward them, a bald man carrying video equipment trotting in her wake. When they came up to the wedding party, the smartly dressed brunette said, "I'm Dana Montgomery from Gulf News 7, and this is my videographer, Tim. We're filming a story about things that draw tourists to the area. We noticed you had a photographer but no videographer and wanted to know if you'd like for us to film your wedding. Beach weddings are always popular for locals and out-of-towners. A few seconds of footage would be a cool addition to our piece. It's going to be an awesome sunset in about thirty-five minutes, and you should catch it on video as well as in photos."

Cate looked to Jake, who shrugged and said, "It's up to you, Baby. My intuition tells me it'll be worth it."

She beamed and nodded. The videographer and the photographer had a hasty conversation regarding lighting, got into position, and waited. The Justice of the Peace stood several feet in front of the couple and began to speak.

"We're here today to celebrate the marriage of Jake Anthony Genter and Caterina Maria Nasello. Jake and Cate have written their own wedding vows. Jake?"

He took Cate's hands, looked into her eyes, and said, "Everything happens for a reason. You're my reason for being. I knew it the moment I met you. I want to share everything with you, Baby. You have all of me forever. Whatever happens in our future, we'll face it together. I'll love you for the rest of my life and beyond."

Cate blinked back tears at Jake's heartfelt words but smiled up at him and squeezed his hands before turning slightly toward Hazel and nodding. She looked back to Jake, as Hazel withdrew a piece of paper from one concealed pocket of her dress and unfolded it before beginning to read the vows Cate had written.

"I've never been able to talk, but you know that doesn't mean I can't *speak*. In such a short time, you've helped me to move on from simply persevering through my life's tragedies to actually living. Whatever happens in our future, we'll face it together. My heart will always belong to you and only you."

Jake's green eyes were alight with love, desire, and happiness. Cate was certain that her gray eyes must be projecting the same emotions, as the Justice of the Peace said, "And now the rings."

Jake accepted Cate's ring from Everton, while Cate held out her hand to Hazel for Jake's wedding band. Earlier, the couple had agreed to exchange rings wordlessly. After all, Cate couldn't talk, and the act was self-explanatory and affecting enough without commentary.

When Cate saw her wedding ring, she blinked in surprise. The emerald-cut diamond was pink. She hadn't known pink diamonds existed. The gemstone was surrounded by tiny white diamonds and had a simple gold setting. She loved it but was slightly confused and would ask Jake about his selection later.

Instead of slipping Jake's band onto his finger without pause, Cate held it out to him. His brows drew together, but he accepted the ring and noticed the inscription. After he'd read it aloud, he shut his eyes as if trying to hold in a swell of deep emotion. Then, he opened his eyes, handed the ring back to Cate, and watched as she slipped it onto his finger.

"No matter what happens in your futures, you'll face life together," declared the Justice of the Peace. "Love conquers all."

They were pronounced husband and wife, and everyone in the crowd clapped and cheered. Jake and Cate kissed, and Jake literally swept Cate off her feet without breaking their contact. When he returned her feet to the ground, they broke apart and then kissed again. By the time she realized what was happening, the sun had set behind them.

The light from the videographer's camera illuminated their little group, and Cate offered the crowd a sign she knew, the one for "Thank you." Everton translated this to those present, who gave the couple their congratulations and good wishes. As the strangers began to wander away, Dana Montgomery approached. She then proceeded to stun the entire wedding party into silence.

Chapter Thirteen

"What do you think?" the newscaster asked once she'd finished pitching her proposal to the bride and groom. "The ceremony was totally amazing and unique, and I think we could make the video reflect how magical tonight was for you. Well?"

"*I* think it would be freakin' awesome!" Hazel volunteered. "What a wedding present!"

Cate held out one hand to her sister-in-law, accepted her iPhone, and then texted, **You don't need permission from your station?**

"I'll get it," the woman assured her. "This is fantastic, and they'll love it. If they don't, then you'll still have the video. If you don't like it once it's done, then you just keep it. No one else ever has to see it except you, if you'd prefer. Please. Let us do this for you."

"They could come to the reception with us, the Justice of the Peace, and the photographer and get more footage," Everton suggested. "That way, the final product could include video, photos, and narration or whatever of the whole evening."

I'd love it!

"Hey, I thought *I* was the impulsive one," Jake chuckled.

I've become pretty impulsive myself since we met that second time.

"That you have, Baby," he murmured then kissed her. "Let's go!"

Cate, Jake, Hazel, Everton, the Justice of the Peace, the photographer, the newscaster, and the videographer went to their respective vehicles and drove to The Peking Palace. Jake drove slowly, and he and Cate got to the restaurant after the others had parked and were obviously already inside. One front window had a sign in it that read, *CLOSED FOR PRIVATE EVENT*. When Cate raised an eyebrow, Jake explained that he'd paid the owners to reserve the entire restaurant just for them and their guests. Tears pricked the backs of her eyelids.

The Chinese family who owned the restaurant was waiting inside. The men wore suits, and the mother and daughter wore traditional silk Chinese dresses. The father and sons bowed to Cate and Jake and spoke in their native tongue, while the daughter translated.

"Our family is honored to be present for this celebration and to have been chosen to prepare your wedding dinner. We have treasured you for four years and are thankful you have found love with a man who appears honorable and strong. We hope you bring your many sons and daughters here so that we can continue to be family and see yours grow."

Cate was deeply touched and wiped at her eyes while thinking, *It may already be growing. We'll know on Monday.*

A wide array of dishes had been prepared in honor of the occasion, and Cate knew she'd be sending food home with everyone present and would still have plenty left to refrigerate and freeze at the house. After everybody had eaten, Jake nodded to the owner, who disappeared with his sons into the kitchen. They returned with a two-tiered white wedding cake that had been decorated with what appeared to be tiny pink diamonds.

"The 'diamonds' are actually edible decoration," Jake explained. "I wanted them on the cake since I gave you a pink diamond wedding ring."

Why pink? I love it, but why that color for the main stone and the cake decorations?

"Because it's different and beautiful, like you. It's also your favorite color. You wear it at least three times a week and have little girly things all around the house that are pink. Hell, the house is even pink. Look at your nails today. They're painted light pink. It's totally feminine, totally sweet, and totally you." After brushing his lips across her temple, he murmured, "And I do love you more than anything, Baby."

And I love you more than anything, Jake. Thank you for putting so much thought into my ring and the cake. It makes everything even more meaningful.

They cut the cake, which turned out to be the best Cate had ever tasted. It had the perfect hint of almond extract in it, and this was balanced by the buttercream frosting and pink sugar jewels. Everyone had a second piece as they relaxed and talked. It was an unusual reception, to say the least, as Cate communicated through her texts and the Chinese family talked through translation, thanks to their English-speaking daughter. Despite the challenges, everyone had a wonderful time. Cate was enjoying herself so much that she didn't notice that the videographer was filming everything.

The reception wound down shortly before midnight. The Justice of the Peace left first, followed shortly by the photographer, newscaster, and videographer. Everton was the next to depart. Hazel walked outside with him as Cate and Jake thanked the Chinese family for everything they'd done for them.

"I'm going to crash in the extra bedroom at Everton's," Hazel told the couple when they stepped outside. "He already took my bag with him when he and Jake were at the house earlier."

You don't have to do that, Cate insisted.

"I want to. It's your wedding night. It should be just the two of you in your house. Everton said his mother-in-law and daughter won't mind if I sleep over."

"It's all good," Everton assured them. "Hazel's welcome at our house. Why don't you two come over for lunch tomorrow? That way, Cate can meet M'Dear and Ava."

I'd love to meet your mother-in-law and daughter, but I don't want to impose.

"There's no such thing as imposing where M'Dear's concerned. Think you'll be up by noon?"

"Maybe," Jake said with a smirk, which attracted a playful swat on the arm from Cate. When Jake parked the Mustang in the driveway five minutes later, he and Cate stared at the iron gate on the porch. A large, white-and-pink bow had been affixed to one of the bars near the lock. Cate looked quizzically at Jake, who admitted he hadn't been responsible.

"Hazel," he said after looking at the bow once more. "Remember how she said she wanted our wedding to be awesome? What do you want to bet she got Everton involved and gave him the extra set of keys? He and I weren't together all day. She must have gotten them to him. I bet M'Dear and Ava came over while we were getting married and having the reception and took care of whatever Hazel had in mind. You want to go see?"

Cate was already out of the car. She hurried up the steps, unlocked the gate, and went to the door. She opened it, stepped into the living room, stopped, and gaped. Jake came up behind her, laid his hands on her shoulders, and whistled.

"Christ, I love my big sister."

Strips of outdoor lights that resembled dragonflies were plugged into every outlet and artfully strung around the room. The couple soon discovered the entire house was populated with dragonflies. Cate loved the glow and beauty of the lights and wondered if they could leave them up all of the time.

"Jesus," Jake muttered, when they reached the master bedroom and viewed M'Dear and Ava's handiwork.

The dragonflies were also present in that room, but they'd been joined by bouquets of pink-and-white roses in vases that had been placed on the nightstands and dresser. A large, white basket rested in the center of the bed. Upon inspection, they discovered it held an interesting combination of pink articles meant for a baby – a blanket, onesies, booties, dresses, toys, towels, and miniscule hair bows.

I think Hazel wants to be an aunt in the worst way, Cate texted. **It's all so adorable!**

Grinning, Jake said, "If you are pregnant, then I sure hope it's a girl." Hefting the basket off the bed and bringing it to a corner, he said, "Are you nervous about Monday?" When she nodded, he admitted, "Me, too. Either way, it'll be good. Any predictions?"

I think you got me pregnant that first time we were together. You…freed me. What happened between us was too powerful not to link us in a concrete way.

"And if you're wrong? Are we going to start using protection until we get to know each other better, or are we going to keep making love and trying to make babies?"

No protection. I want as many babies as we can have.

Cate did, but that wasn't the only reason she typed the words. She knew that Jake, who had an irrational fear about her abandoning him, would interpret her declaration as a promise to be with him always, which was the truth. She simply hoped he believed her and prayed that her tiny body would be up to the challenge of having normal pregnancies.

"You're serious?" he asked intently.

Completely.

"How many kids do you want?"

Let's see. I'm twenty-six, and you're twenty-eight. If I'm pregnant now, then this baby will be born when I'm twenty-seven. If I have one every year or two until I'm thirty-nine, then that puts us with up to a dozen kids or so. Looking around the small bedroom, she added, **I think we'll need a bigger house.**

"Fuck me, Baby. You'd be willing to have a dozen kids with me? Are you joking?"

No joke, as long as my body can handle it and I can learn how to communicate with our babies. I want advice from Logan and Beth Kirkland. We'll see how things go with the first baby. I want as many children as we can have, but I may not be able to do it for more than one reason. I'm still scared of the unknown, although your crash course in living has made me less afraid.

As he pulled her small body against his large one, Jake said, "I'm glad to hear it. How about if we start your driving lessons Monday night after I get off work? We never did take that drive out to the country, and I can teach you the basics where no one else is around. I'd say we could do it tomorrow, but I want to spend as much time with Hazel as possible until I have to go to work Monday morning. She'll have to get back on the road Monday anyway."

Cate agreed and then kissed Jake. What she didn't tell him was that she planned to withhold the results of the pregnancy test from him until they were out in the country. He and Everton would have to work a twelve-hour shift, and he wouldn't get home until it was time for dinner. He'd be dying for her to tell him all, but she'd make him wait and then surprise him with the results and more once they were in a remote part of the county.

She'd expected Jake to initiate sex the moment they were both naked, but he didn't. Instead, he hooked one arm around her waist and gently drew her down onto the mattress until her back rested against his front. He spooned her tiny body with his and protectively draped his arms around her.

"I'll always take care of you, Baby," he murmured. "I swear I'll never let anything happen to you."

Cate wanted to tell him there were certain things he couldn't control, but she didn't have her phone. Even if she had, she didn't feel as if it was the right time to remind him of reality. He needed to feel as though he could protect her from any potential dangers in the world.

I've lived through enough in my life, she thought, as she fell asleep. *Certainly nothing else horrific can happen to me now....*

The sound of her brother Luca's screams were what woke her. Her heart pounding, Cate scrambled out of bed, almost tripping on the hem of her long, pink nightgown. As she rushed for the door, she heard Luca's cries of pain and his pleas for their father to stop.

Stop what? she wondered. *He's hurting Luca? How? Why?*

"Cate, lock your door!" Luca yelled then let out a blood-curdling scream.

Panicked, she hastened to close the door and depress the lock on the side of the handle. Her shaking finger was about to push the button when her father forced open the door, causing her to stagger back. It was dark in her room, but the light in the hallway was on. She could see the silhouette of her father and heard his labored breathing as he held the large knife in his left hand. She could also see the blood on the blade, which he lifted as he approached her.

"Daddy, no!" she mouthed, as he brought the knife down. Her palm burning as he sliced it open, she cried noiselessly, "Please! No!"

She automatically raised her arms in order to shield her face and chest. Her father kept stabbing, and she kept pleading soundlessly for him to stop. Every piercing of her skin brought with it terrible pain and a growing sense of betrayal and confusion. She didn't understand at all and wondered if her mother and Luca were still alive. When the blade of the knife found its way past her arms and sank into her chest, Cate gasped at the resultant agony and tumbled to the ground. She lay in shock as her father continued to stab her. She could see the crazed look on his face, thanks to the light spilling in from the hallway. Unable to look at him any longer knowing that he was killing her, Cate shut her eyes and waited for the final strike. Suddenly, there were no more strikes.

Opening her eyes, Cate realized she was alone in her room. She turned her head and saw that her carpet was stained with blood. It was difficult for her to breathe, and it felt as if she was being stabbed all over again each time she inhaled and exhaled. She wanted to get up and go to Luca to check on him, but she couldn't move. As she debated on how she could manage to rise, she heard a loud *bang!* and wondered what it was. It hurt her ears.

Cate had no idea how long she stayed on the floor. There was an eerie silence in the house, and it only served to heighten her fear. At that moment, she wished more than anything that she could speak. Even if no one heard her, she thought it would make her feel better if she could cry out for someone to help her, her brother, and their mother.

Eventually, there were sirens. Faint voices of men and women could be heard from outside the house. Then the voices were inside. Red and blue flashing lights were visible through the sheer curtains on the windows. She listened as the men and women yelled orders to one another or let out exclamations of horror and dismay. Someone said it was too late for the white, adult female in the master bedroom. More voices, closer this time, said they'd found a juvenile white male who was also already dead. Tears spilled down her cheeks, and she prayed God would take her soon to join her mother and brother. The light to Cate's room was switched on, and a man and woman in uniform stared down at her for a few seconds as she squinted up at them. Then they sprang into action and declared that they'd discovered a juvenile white female who'd also been stabbed but was still alive. As they knelt on the floor beside her, she knew they were kneeling in her blood and wondered what it felt like to rest their knees on the wet carpet. They asked her for her name, but she was too weak to even attempt to mouth the word *mute* to them. The last thing she heard was a man telling someone there was a white, adult male dead in the garage due to what appeared to be a self-inflicted GSW. Cate wondered what a GSW was, as she waited for angels to carry her away.

Chapter Fourteen

"Baby! *Baby!* Wake up! Shit! Cate! Baby, open your eyes!"

Cate's eyes snapped open, but she had no idea where she was. Disoriented, she found herself panting as though she'd run a marathon. It hurt every time she inhaled and exhaled, but she couldn't stop breathing hard. In fact, she was breathing so hard that she thought she might hyperventilate.

"Baby, look at me!" Jake demanded. Taking her face in his hands, he ordered, "Focus on me!"

She automatically did as he asked, although it didn't seem to help. She was still so confused, terrified, and in pain.

"That's it, Baby," Jake said more calmly. "Just keep looking at me. I'm not going anywhere. I'm keeping you safe."

The dream, Cate thought. *I was eight again and…and I felt it all.*

Tears coursed down her cheeks. There was so much pain in her body, mind, and heart that she didn't know what to do with it all. She hadn't felt it in eighteen years, and she thought she might shatter at any moment.

"I'm here, Cate," Jake said soothingly. "You're okay."

In a daze, Cate shook her head and mouthed, "Daddy killed them."

"Yeah, he did," Jake said grimly.

"Daddy hurt me," she mouthed. "It hurt so bad."

"I know," he murmured, his own eyes shining with tears.

Cate attempted to push away from Jake, and he reluctantly released her. She frantically scanned the room for her phone. Spotting it on one of the nightstands, she snatched it up and started typing.

He was our father! How could he do that? How could he do that to his wife and children? If you could have seen the look on

his face as he stabbed me again and again and again! It hurt so much! Every time the knife sank into my flesh, there was so much pain! I begged him to stop, but he kept stabbing! He was my father! I loved him! Why didn't he love us? How could he kill us?

"Baby, he didn't kill you that –"

Shut up! I want to speak! I want to talk and have my say and have people hear me! I want –

Her phone battery died. Cate stared at the device for a few seconds and then hurled it across the room. She longed for a voice so that she could scream with frustration, anguish, and rage. Her tiny body shook as she tried to quell the torrent of emotions that was threatening to consume her after eighteen years of lying dormant.

She'd missed her mother and brother and had periodically cried for them. She'd struggled not to wallow in self-pity. She'd fought to do well in school and gain some sense of security in the midst of an unhappy childhood that had literally turned into Hell on Earth. She'd resented her mother's family for leaving her to suffer and recover alone and then to be placed in the foster care system. She'd loathed the man who'd drugged and raped her, robbing her of yet another thing that should have been a normal first for any girl or woman. Throughout it all, she'd hated her father for what he'd done and hated herself for surviving.

Jake reached for her, but she stumbled out of bed. Unsure as to where she should go or what she should do, Cate lurched across the room toward the bedroom door. In her distress, she didn't notice the basket in front of her and tripped. Flinging out her arms, she landed on her hands and knees. Breathing heavily and still crying, she stared at one small, pink baby bootie that had ended up on the floor in front of her. Collapsing to the ground, Cate sobbed.

Jake suddenly lifted and carried her back to bed. As he placed her on the mattress, climbed in beside her, and covered them both with the comforter, she tried not to focus on how awful she felt. She'd known it was unnatural to feel nothing about the nightmare and remembered longing to feel something, even though the thought had frightened her.

I got my wish, she thought dully. *I feel it all. What a freak I am. I should have died with my family. Why didn't I?*

"Stay with me, Baby," cajoled Jake. "I'm here for you. I need you to be here for me, too. Don't leave me."

Leave him? I can't even get up on my own right now. How could I leave him?

"Don't do this," he continued. "I can freakin' see you withdrawing into yourself. It's going to be okay. You can get help. You're a survivor. You'll survive this."

What if I don't want to? She thought. *I'm so tired. My own father gave me life, and then he tried to take it away. He already wasn't very nice to any of us, but how could he stab us? I'm surprised he didn't drown me when I was a baby. I was extra-tiny and had no voice box. Why didn't he kill me then? Maybe it would have been more humane.*

Jake gathered Cate up, pulling her against him before saying in his low, rumbling voice, "I love you, Cate. I can't live without you, and I mean that literally. The past two weeks have been the best of my life. You washed away years of depression the moment I laid eyes on you. From the first time we met, all I could think about was you and how beautiful and tenacious you are. I want to be with you and in you every waking moment. If you give up, then I give up. I can never go back to the freakin' emptiness I felt before you happened to me."

Cate crumpled against Jake and wept uncontrollably. She longed to verbalize what she was feeling but couldn't. Suddenly, she felt something nudge her right hand. Prying open one eye, she saw that Jake was trying to get her to take his iPhone from him. Shaking, she accepted it and shifted in his embrace.

I'm so sorry I told you to shut up.

"*That's* what your first words are after what you just went through? Christ, but I love you."

How can you love me? I'm defective, scarred by my father's attack, and a rape victim even though I don't remember it. I'm so not normal!

"Defective? What in the hell are you talking about?"

About not talking. I've never uttered a sound. Something went wrong when I was in utero. I'm so scrawny. I'm like a stick figure! Why are you so attracted to me? I'm a marked-up, messed-up, mute woman in a little body only some fourteen-

year-old girl would have! The only difference between me and a pubescent girl is that I have big breasts.

"Stop it, Cate! You're gorgeous, Baby. You're this tiny little thing who's got the perfect breasts and ass. I love your slender arms and legs and the delicate way you move. That black hair of yours is enough to drive me out of my mind, and I almost forget what I'm talking about when I look at those big, gray eyes. You know what I'd love? I'd love it if we did have a dozen kids and they were all girls who looked just like you." Pausing, he added, "Although that might be tough, seeing as I'd spend all of my time keeping the guys off them when they got older."

But my scars and the fact that I can't speak –

"The only thing that bothers me about your scars is that you were hurt in the first place and by your own father. As for not speaking, we've been through this. As a matter of fact, we've been through all of this. Why are you stewing about it now? I don't care that you can't talk. You say more with one look at me than any other woman I've ever known in my life. You gave me hope that I could finally move forward after what happened with my Dad and Mom's departure. You saved me."

Maybe if I'd been able to scream I could've saved Mom and Luca.

"Your mother didn't have a chance to scream, but your brother did. You shared that with me, remember? If his screams couldn't save the family, what makes you think yours could have?"

Maybe Daddy would've listened to me. Maybe I could have reached him if I'd been able to talk. Weary, she sighed and typed, **My father wasn't a nice man. He was distant, self-absorbed, and didn't really care about me or Luca. Why didn't he kill me when I was a baby? I didn't fit into his world. He could have easily found someone in his drug empire to suffocate me or –**

"Cate, that's enough!" Jake barked. "I'm not going to lie here and listen to you talk about your father offing you after you were born. Didn't you say your parents got you the best help available once it was discovered that you were mute?"

Because I was an embarrassment.

"Did they tell you that?"

Cate reflected on his question for several minutes before texting, **No. They never told me that I was an embarrassment. They**

didn't have to. My limitations didn't fit into their socially
conscious lifestyle. They were too fixated on appearance,
possessions, and status. Having a disabled child wasn't good for
their image.

"Did your mother show you and Luca affection?"

**Yes. She wasn't a bad mother. She just wasn't a great one.
We knew she loved us, though.**

"And him? Did he ever hug you or play with you or your
brother?"

No!

"You answered pretty quickly. Think about it for a minute,
Baby. You said you loved him. Do you think he loved you?"

Cate forced herself to truly consider his question. She recalled a
trip the family had taken to Cancun, Mexico when she'd been five.
On their first day at the beach, she and nine-year-old Luca had
played in the water and built sandcastles while their tall, curvaceous,
blonde, blue-eyed mother lounged in a chair, alternately dozing and
reading a book. Their black-haired, gray-eyed father, who was slim,
swarthy, and fit, sat in a beach chair with a drink in one hand,
working on his tan.

"I have to pee," Luca had told Cate, his shaggy, black hair
dripping from a recent splash in the Caribbean Sea. "Don't get too
close to the water while I'm gone, okay? I'll be right back."

But something caught Cate's eye not long after he'd left the
beach. It was an odd-looking, beautiful thing that resembled a
partially deflated ball that had been cut in half. Some sort of strings
hung from the flat end. Curious, Cate edged closer to the mysterious
and fascinating thing and reached out to feel the strings that floated
in the shallows.

There was instant, searing pain the moment her tiny hand made
contact with what she would later learn was called a jellyfish.
Seconds later, her father jerked her away from the thing and lifted
her into his arms, an alarmed expression on his face. She wailed
soundlessly at the excruciating pain in her hand.

"Bianca! Wake up, goddamn it!" her father shouted.

"What?!?" her mother asked, instantly awake. "What's wrong
with Cate!"

"She touched a fucking jellyfish! I'm taking her to a doctor!
Stay here and wait for Luca!"

"Where is he?"

"In the bathroom, Bitch! If you paid closer attention to our children, then you'd know that! Don't you leave this spot!"

"Giuseppe, wait!" she cried, but he was already gone.

The exclusive resort had an on-site medical clinic, and Cate was quickly examined by a doctor and given a shot. Her father never let her out of his arms, didn't chide her for crying as a result of the stings or the injection, and repeatedly demanded reassurance from the physician regarding Cate's recovery.

"She's so small," he'd said. "She was only two pounds when she was born. Nothing can happen to her."

Cate became sleepy, drowsing in her father's arms in the clinic for what seemed like a long time. The doctor came in and out to check on her. More than once, she felt her father gingerly lift her injured hand and brush his lips across the top of her head.

The swelling and pain in her hand receded, and she began to feel more alert. Finally, the doctor pronounced her well enough to leave the clinic but told her father she needed to rest for the remainder of the day and night. If she showed any signs of distress, she was to be immediately brought back for further treatment.

"You were a good girl at the doctor's," her father said. "You want ice cream?" When she nodded, he ventured, "You like chocolate? No. Vanilla? No? What do you like?"

She mouthed the word *strawberry* as clearly as she could. He strode toward one of the resort's restaurants. Cate still wore only her frilly pink bathing suit, and her father remained shirtless and shoeless.

"Table for two," he told the hostess. "Giuseppe Nasello. We're staying in the Great Tinamou Cabana for the week."

"Mr. Nasello, we require shoes and shirts in the dining room," the pretty, young hostess replied with a smile.

"I don't care," he snapped. "My little girl was hurt this morning, and I promised her strawberry ice cream. I'm paying the resort several thousand dollars this week for our stay. Make an exception this once."

"Let me just check with my manager," she said, still smiling.

Several other diners scowled at them, but her father ignored their disapproving looks as he took a seat, continuing to hold Cate against him. When a waiter approached, Giuseppe ordered a large bowl of strawberry ice cream. After it was placed before them, he fed Cate one small spoonful at a time until she indicated that she was full. He then ate what remained.

Once the bowl was empty, Giuseppe told the waiter, "Bill this to our cabana, and add a fifty percent tip." After signing the receipt, he left the restaurant and carried Cate back to her mother and Luca, who had waited on the beach as he'd ordered.

"Giuseppe, is she all right?"

"She's fine now, Bianca!" he snapped. "If you'd been watching her more carefully, she wouldn't have gotten stung by a jellyfish. But I don't know why I'd expect you to be mindful of her. If you'd taken care of yourself while you were pregnant, then she wouldn't have been premature and might have developed normally."

Her mother looked stricken. Then she straightened and said, "If I recall, *you* were supplying me with my…medication."

"I supply everything you need!" he hissed. "I always have. But you didn't take any *medication* when you were pregnant with Luca. So, don't blame me for what happened with Cate. Because of you, she almost died! Because of you, she can't ever speak! I love and protect my family!"

"You have a funny way of showing it!" her mother said angrily. Taking Cate from his arms, she cried, "Go to Hell, Giuseppe!"

"I'm sure I will someday," he said flatly. "But I won't be going there alone."

His wife looked sad for a moment before saying quietly, "I'm sure you won't." Taking Luca's hand, she directed, "Come on, Children. I think we've had enough excitement for one day. Let's go get cleaned up and have a nap before dinner. Your father will join us later."

Cate looked over her mother's shoulder as Bianca Nasello marched across the sand away from her husband. Cate bit her lower lip and stared forlornly at her father. His jaw was tight as he glared at his wife's retreating back, but his steely eyes softened when he saw his daughter looking at him. Cate watched him give her a quick smile and then he turned and waded into the water.

"Baby?" Jake's voice was soft but insistent, as he continued, "Well?"

He loved me, but that makes me even sadder and more confused. Only thinking of him as indifferent made it easier to

believe he could do what he did to us. **If he loved us, even if he only loved me and Luca, then how could he stab us then kill himself? He was a bad man but –** Swallowing hard, she went on, **How do you kill someone you love? How do you take a knife and stab them until they die?**

"I can't ever imagine doing it, so I can't answer that. All I can say is that you told me the Feds had his back against the wall. You said something about how he looked while he was stabbing you. It sounds like he just snapped."

I guess. I was so scared.

"Tell me about it."

I don't know if I can. It breaks my heart to think about it and to think about him loving us then attacking us. It hurts.

"It'll hurt you more not to talk about it."

But we're supposed to go to Everton's so I can meet his mother-in-law and daughter and –

"And we're not going anywhere. You finally remembered what it *felt* like the night your father slaughtered your mother and brother and tried to kill you. We're not leaving this room until you share it with me. Trust me, Cate."

I do but –

"But nothing. Screw everything and talk to me. Everyone else will understand, and you can send out your first blog another day."

I wrote it earlier this week and have it scheduled to automatically post today.

"You did? Are you okay with me reading it?"

Of course, but don't feel obligated.

"Obligated? You're my wife, and I love you. I don't feel obligated to do anything. I *want* to do everything when it comes to you. If I could, then I'd give you anything you wanted."

I don't want anything but you.

"That's not true, but let's not argue about it now. Just use my phone to talk to me. I think we'll be buying you another one later today. I doubt if yours survived being thrown across the room. The screen hit the edge of the dresser."

But –

"That phone is your voice, Baby." Then, "Do you really trust me?" When she nodded, he said, "Speak to me, Cate."

She began to type.

Chapter Fifteen

"Better?" Jake asked, as they left the Verizon store.

Yes. I'm glad I got the insurance on this phone, although I don't plan to throw it across a room anytime soon. Of course, I didn't plan to throw the other one either.

"You were pretty shaken, Baby. The important thing is that *you* didn't break."

I know. Not-so-smoothly changing the subject to avoid further discussion about her earlier meltdown, she offered, **I love my new iPhone case.**

Jake grinned and said, "I'm sure you do. Pink roses all over it. It's perfect for you." Opening the passenger door of the Mustang for her, he asked, "Are you ready to go to Everton's now?"

Yes, although I hate that we didn't go for lunch.

"You weren't in any shape to go for lunch. I'm glad you told me everything about how you felt after the nightmare."

And I'm glad you made love to me afterwards and helped me relax for a while.

"It was my pleasure," he smirked. "It helped me relax, too."

Everton Marshall's house was an older, two-story home in an established Sarasota neighborhood that was in transition and had been for some time. Although some homeowners had renovated their houses, other properties had deteriorated over the past few decades. Everton's place wasn't dilapidated, but it needed a facelift in the near future. As they climbed the steps to the porch, Cate wondered how long he'd owned the home.

Everton greeted them at the door and then ushered them inside, saying, "It's great to see you two! Hazel's having a beer with M'Dear while they cook dinner. Ava's working on a paper for school. She'll join us in a little while to eat."

As they followed him to the kitchen, Cate noted that Everton had good taste and nice things. His house might be older, but it held contemporary furniture and had appealing décor. When she texted this to him, he laughed.

"M'Dear did all of the decorating. She took me and Ava in after her daughter, Ava's mother, died. Once I graduated from school and had enough money, I bought this house and asked *her* to live with *us*. When I told her she could decorate the place however she wanted, she just about lost her mind. She's one of a kind. I'm real blessed. My own mother was no prize, but I found a true Mama in my mother-in-law. You'll love her, and she'll love you."

When they entered the kitchen, Hazel put down her beer, went over to hug Cate, and asked, "Are you feeling better?" When Cate nodded, Hazel hugged her younger brother and asked, "How does it feel to be a married man?" Without waiting for an answer, she continued, "*I've* had a wonderful day, so far. M'Dear is freakin' awesome."

"You're going to make me blush."

They all turned toward an older white woman who had straight, gray hair that fell past her waist. She was about Hazel's size, meaning she was of average height and approximately seventy-five pounds overweight. Unlike Hazel, who typically wore jeans and casual shirts, M'Dear wore a long cotton purple dress and soft shoes. She smiled broadly at Cate, and her blue eyes radiated warmth.

Cate didn't move. She knew she was being rude by not greeting M'Dear, but she was so shocked that the woman was white that she was having trouble processing the fact. Everton, with his brown skin and box braids, was a beautiful black man, and Cate had assumed his dead wife had also been African-American.

My mistake, she thought. *Snap out of it, and be polite.*

She smiled at M'Dear and texted, **It's so nice to meet you. I'm sorry we couldn't make it here for lunch.**

"Don't apologize," M'Dear said kindly. "Everton said you weren't feeling well. I'm just glad you're better now." Noting Cate's iPhone, she exclaimed, "I love your phone case! Where did you get it? Do they have tie-dye patterns?"

Cate grinned and admitted, **I didn't see any, but I bet you could go online and find one.**

"Good idea. Let me give you a hug. Now that you're married to Jake, you're part of the family. He's been a regular at our house since he and Everton became partners."

I'm so sorry! We should have had you and Ava as guests at the wedding!

"Don't worry yourself about that. You didn't even know Ava and me. Besides, if we'd gone to the wedding, then we wouldn't have been able to decorate your house."

Feeling as though she was acting like a complete fool, Cate texted, **I should have thanked you the moment we met! It was all magical. I can't even begin to thank you and Ava enough.** Turning to her sister-in-law, she typed, **Or you either for coming up with the idea. Everything looked amazing.**

"I'm glad," Hazel told her with a grin. "Now, give M'Dear that hug. She's like an Earth Mother and damn well knows how to give awesome hugs."

Hazel was right. The moment M'Dear took her into her arms, Cate felt as if she'd been wrapped in a maternal security blanket. It felt wonderful, but Cate started to cry.

"Baby, what's wrong?" Jake asked worriedly. "Are you okay?"

"She'll be fine," M'Dear assured him. "Why don't all of you go to the living room and leave us alone for a while?"

Jake hesitated before asking, "Is that okay with you, Cate?"

She nodded against M'Dear's ample bosom but continued to cry. The other three left the room, but M'Dear didn't move. All that she did was hold Cate, and Cate found that it was all she needed at the moment. She thought of her father holding her after she'd been stung by the jellyfish and cried harder.

"You go on and cry all you want," M'Dear said soothingly. "You cry all evening if you need to."

My father loved me, but he didn't even know what kind of ice cream I liked, Cate reflected. *What happened to him? What turned him into the head of a drug dealing empire? Was he just born like that, or did someone turn him into that man? He and my mother obviously used drugs, although Luca and I didn't understand at the time. Was it the drugs that made him like that? Was it taking drugs that drove him to stab us and shoot himself?*

Flinching involuntarily as she recalled the loud bang of the gun as her father blew out his brains, Cate wondered what his final thoughts had been. He'd believed he'd killed his wife and both of his children. Had he felt triumphant that he'd beaten the authorities? Had he been devastated and experienced remorse? Was he even consciously aware of his actions?

"How far along are you?" M'Dear asked softly when Cate quieted. When Cate pulled away and stared quizzically up at her, the older woman said, "I know you're pregnant."

I don't even know for sure, yet. How could you know?

"I can tell. Always could."

Just because I'm emotional right now –

"It's not that. Everton's told me a little about you, and it sounds like you have a lot of reasons to cry. I just get this feeling in my chest when a woman's pregnant, even if she doesn't have a clue."

If I am, then I'm only two weeks along.

"Hm. I don't know where you're going to put that Baby. You're so tiny. When are you going to see a doctor?"

Tomorrow I'll find out and see what the doctor says if I am pregnant.

M'Dear smiled and said firmly, "You are. Are you happy about it?"

If I am, then I'm happy and scared. I'm so mixed up and can't speak. I know it might be dangerous for me to be pregnant because I'm so small. I'd want the baby anyway. I want lots of babies with Jake. I want them to have the kind of childhood I didn't have.

"And what kind is that?" M'Dear asked soberly.

A happy one.

"Sit on the barstool here at the counter, and let me tell you a few things while I stir the pot of soup." Once Cate was seated with a glass of water in her hand, the woman said, "My childhood was anything but good. Not only did my father beat me and my mother, but he was also an alcoholic and rarely worked. We lived in the car or with other deadbeats like my father most of the time. As you can imagine, we didn't go to doctors when we got sick. When I was fifteen, my mother became very ill and died. My father, who by then was both a drunk and an addict, forced himself on me while he was high. Once it was over, I threw up, got dressed, and went straight to the police. I was placed in a foster home and was fortunate enough to have wonderful foster parents. They ended up adopting me. I went to school regularly for the first time in my life and graduated when I was nineteen. Then I went to college and got my degree in psychology. I went on to graduate school and became a psychologist. I met my husband, who was also a licensed mental health counselor, at a conference. We married and had our beautiful little girl, Tracy."

Cate patiently waited for the woman to continue. She was fascinated by the story and had various questions; however, she wouldn't be impolite enough to ask. She was used to listening and would take whatever information M'Dear chose to give her.

"My husband was diagnosed with brain cancer when Tracy was sixteen. The next year, the last year of her father's life, was truly awful for him and for us. After he died, she began to act out. My little honors student started staying out all night, failing tests, and smoking. I understood why, of course. I got her into counseling, but that didn't seem to help. Then along came Everton." When Cate cocked her head, M'Dear said, "Yes. Everton. He'd been raised on the streets and was one of Tracy's classmates. He started looking out for her. One night, he brought her home unconscious. He said he'd found her passed out and about to be molested by another boy. He asked if he could sleep on the couch and talk to her the next morning when she woke up. I agreed, and he had a two-hour talk with my hung-over, crying daughter. I never asked him what he told her, but she immediately cleaned up her act, actively participated in therapy, and brought up her grades. When she and Everton started to date, I was thrilled. I was less thrilled when I sensed Tracy was pregnant. I sat both of them down and asked them about it, and they admitted one of the condoms they'd used had broken. They'd been worried about telling me, but they insisted they loved one another. I never doubted that. They also insisted they wanted to get married right after graduation and continue on with their plans to go to college and raise their baby. I supported their decision."

M'Dear paused to refill Cate's glass of water and take a drink from her beer bottle. After hefting herself onto the barstool next to the one Cate was occupying, the woman remained quiet and appeared thoughtful. Cate imagined she was remembering her dead husband and child and her own terrible childhood.

"I was thinking about the day Ava was born," M'Dear confided. "Our love for her was all-encompassing. Everton and Tracy were naturals at parenting, and Ava was a wonderful baby. My daughter and son-in-law were determined to make it on their own and to finish college. None of us expected that Tracy would die of an aneurysm a year later. I'll never forget the call from Everton. He was so distraught that he was incoherent. It was the worst day of my life. Losing my husband had been heart-wrenching, but he was in such bad shape that it was almost a relief to see his suffering end. With Tracy…." She sighed and said, "Everton managed to convey to me that one minute she was talking to him and the next she was gone. She was so full of life, and then she was dead. He was inconsolable. I immediately suggested he and Ava move in with me so that I could help raise her while he finished school. He accepted instantly. It was a good solution for us since we were both devastated by Tracy's death. It was also good for Ava, of course.

"Ava had lost her mother and was confused. She was only a year old. When she was diagnosed as being deaf, I was even more relieved Everton had agreed to our living arrangement. We both threw ourselves into learning what Ava needed on top of my duties as a psychologist and his studies at college. The tragedies of the past and the difficulties of that present sealed our family bond. That's why I agreed to move in with him and Ava when he bought this house. He wanted not only to repay me but also to show me that he really did consider me to be *his* mother. So, I moved in here. Neither of us has ever regretted it."

Cate felt compelled to ask, **Has he dated at all since his wife died?**

"To my knowledge, Everton's never been with another woman since Tracy left us. Sixteen years of celibacy, but he just doesn't seem to be interested in anyone. I personally don't think it's healthy, but it's his choice. I've dated here and there over the past dozen years or so but haven't found the right man, yet. I think Everton needs a partner, but I don't know if he'll ever allow it. Maybe when Ava goes to college in a couple years." Sliding off the stool, she returned to the stock pot and said, "The soup's just about ready. Is there anything you'd like to ask me before dinner?"

Are you still a working psychologist?

"I am."

Could I talk to you about things? I had therapy only when I was a minor, and I wasn't exactly ready to deal with a lot of

what happened. Once I became an adult, I pushed it all down in order to make it from one day to the next. Jake's made me realize I can't do that anymore. I guess our wedding was the final trigger. I had the same nightmare I've had every night for eighteen years about my father stabbing us all then killing himself, but I actually felt something while I was dreaming and when I woke up. It was horrible.

"You can talk to me whenever you want about whatever you want, but not as my patient. As I said, you're part of the family now. I'm here for you, but it wouldn't be ethical for me to have you as a patient and a family member."

Thank you, and thank you for sharing your story. It makes me feel less weird and less isolated.

"We all need help at different times in our lives," M'Dear pointed out. "Some of us just need more help than others. You seem to have helped Jake quite a lot. I've been trying to convince that boy to get therapy for a long time, but he's stubborn. Everton says Jake's a lot less depressed since the two of you hooked up two weeks ago, although he should still probably get professional help. Perhaps you can push him in that direction if he backslides."

I'll do my best. He is very stubborn about certain things. I've asked him to call his mother, but he flat-out refused. I finally got him to agree not to permanently rule it out.

"That's certainly progress," the older woman declared. "He obviously adores you, Cate. He has serious trust issues when it comes to women because of his mother, but he also doesn't trust himself because of what happened with his father. He may be a big, strong man, but a part of him is still a scared boy who blames himself for the crash and his mother's abandonment. I'm betting he's asked you not to leave him more than once, even though he'd never dream of leaving you."

Cate nodded and confided, That's why I picked the inscription I did for his wedding band and had it put on the outside.

"What does it say?"

Forever, Baby.

M'Dear smiled and said, "You couldn't have chosen anything more perfect. You two certainly moved quickly when it came to meeting and marrying, but I do believe there are instances where couples know they were meant to be together from the start. I'm glad you didn't wait." Grinning, she said, "Speaking of waiting, I'm sure the others are starving. How about some dinner?"

Chapter Sixteen

After Cate and Ava were introduced, everyone took their seats at the dining room table. The hearty vegetable soup was delicious, and Cate texted this to M'Dear, who thanked her before offering her a roll. Cate ate, but her attention was focused on Ava, who was tall, shapely, and as white as her grandmother. The girl was deaf and used sign language but could also read lips and speak, which thrilled Cate, who was able to simply "talk" to Ava as much as she wanted.

She kept talking after the table had been cleared and they'd all taken their seats in the living room. Cate knew she was virtually ignoring the others but couldn't stop herself. It had been a long time since she'd had a conversation with a deaf person like Ava who could understand her and who could make herself understood to a hearing person who didn't sign. Cate longed to be able to have more conversations like the one she was having with Everton's daughter.

Ava seemed to be enjoying herself as well. At the beginning of their long exchange, she informed Cate she was sixteen and was often mistaken for a white girl instead of a biracial one. Toward the end, she confided that her shoulder-length black hair was that of an African-American. When Cate appeared confused, Ava smiled and said, "Touch it. You'll see!"

Cate did and felt the slightly different texture of the girl's hair.

"But it does feel soft," Cate mouthed. "I thought black people's hair was coarse."

"Everyone's different," Ava told her, her voice tinged with a distinct accent Cate had heard before when she'd communicated with the deaf who weren't mute. "I can change its look by changing products anytime I want. I'm half-black and half-white and love my whole self."

Cate turned toward where Everton and M'Dear were seated and texted, **You did a great job of raising Ava. She's a beautiful young woman.**

Everton grinned and thanked her before continuing by speaking and signing, "A beautiful young woman who needs to finish her research paper."

"Dad!" Ava said with feigned embarrassment. "I'll get it done."

"You bet you will because you're going to get your butt upstairs and finish it tonight," he chuckled. "You've procrastinated way too long. How are you supposed to study for your history exam when you haven't finished the biology paper? It's already 10:00 p.m. Now, go on."

Ava rolled her eyes and told them all good night before trudging dramatically up the stairs. Once she was gone, Cate apologized for keeping her away from her studies.

"Don't," Everton told her. "She obviously had a good time. She's just a sixteen-year-old junior who knows how to push the right buttons when she wants to. I'm not complaining. She's a good kid, but she is still a kid. If her old man doesn't stay on top of things, she might slip. I want my baby girl to succeed. I'm already nervous about her going off to college in a couple years."

"She'll do fine," M'Dear said confidently. "She's got a good head on her shoulders, and she won't let anyone take advantage of her."

Unless they drug her drink, Cate thought darkly, remembering the foster father who'd drugged her at dinner and then raped her while she was unconscious. *God, please keep Ava safe. Everton and M'Dear have suffered enough, and I don't want to see Ava suffer at all.*

Cate, Jake, and Hazel left not long afterwards and returned home. Hazel, who hadn't seen the decorations inside the house, was thrilled with the way they'd turned out and asked her brother and sister-in-law if they'd liked their wedding present.

"You mean baby present," Jake remarked. "What if we have ten boys?"

"Then they'll either have to be manly enough to feel comfortable wearing pink, or they'll be gay and it won't matter."

That got a full belly laugh from Jake and a grin from Cate.

117

"You *are* pregnant, and it *is* a girl," Hazel insisted looking pointedly at her sister-in-law. "I think Hazel would be a lovely name for my niece."

"We'll see," Jake said genially. Looking at Cate, he raised an eyebrow and asked, "Now?"

"Now what?" Hazel inquired.

"Cate set up this week's *Cate Speaks* blog post so that it'd upload automatically. She wouldn't let me read it before it went live, but she told me I could once we got home. Well, Baby?"

"Oh, my God!" Hazel exclaimed. "The blog! I want to read it first!"

"I'm her husband! Just because you're the eldest –"

Cate held up both hands before pointing to the two computer desks. The brother and sister made an exaggerated run for each desk, vying to see which one could read the blog first. Nervous about their reactions, Cate left the room and went to put on pajamas. She figured that they'd be talking about it by the time she changed and got ready for bed. Yet, when she emerged from the bathroom, the house was quiet. Her heart pounding with nervous anticipation, she moved hesitantly toward the living room.

Jake and Hazel remained in the desk chairs, staring at nothing in particular. Neither of them spoke.

It must suck, and they don't know how to tell me, Cate thought. *Maybe the whole blog idea was a mistake.*

"Fuck me," Jake murmured so softly that Cate almost missed it. Rising from his chair, he moved toward his wife, tenderly took her in his arms, and murmured, "That was the most beautiful, heartbreaking thing I ever read. Jesus, Baby."

"We have to really get this out there," Hazel insisted. "People need to read it. Freakin' amazing."

Certain they were simply trying to make her feel good because they loved her, Cate shook her head and shrugged. Jake suddenly looked angry, and she became confused.

"You don't believe us!" he accused. "We're telling you the truth, damn it!" Releasing her, he stalked over to where his phone lay on the desk and punched in a phone number before muttering, "And I thought *I* was stubborn."

What are you doing? Cate texted.

"Something I never thought I'd do. Something you made me realize I had to do." Pausing as someone evidently answered his call, he said, "Mom? It's Jake."

Hazel stood so quickly that the desk chair she'd been occupying tipped over. Her eyes widened, and her lips parted in astonishment. Cate held her breath and waited to see what might happen.

"Yeah, Mom. It's really me." Jake went on shakily, "I've missed you, too. I – I don't know what to say. I guess I still don't really understand, but I love you. I didn't want you to think I don't. I'm just still angry and confused."

Tightly squeezing his eyes shut as he listened to his mother speak, Jake clenched his jaw and nodded as if she could see him. Cate wondered what the woman was telling her son. Was she apologizing for her behavior, making excuses, or berating him for not contacting her? Since Cate had never met Jake and Hazel's mother, she had no idea what to expect. The only thing she did know was that Irene Genter had abandoned her children when they'd needed her most. Even though she understood how Jake's father's death had devastated his wife, Cate couldn't condone the woman's actions.

"I know, Mom," Jake said quietly. "I do forgive you, but I'm still hurt. Can you understand that? Yeah, maybe so. I'm glad I called, too. I promise. Hazel will. You, too. Bye."

He ended the call and lowered the phone but didn't open his eyes. Hazel started to move forward, but Cate shot her a warning glance and shook her head. Hazel stopped immediately and frowned at her younger brother, who left the room without a word to either of them. They listened as he went to the master bedroom, shutting the door behind him.

"Go to him," Hazel said urgently. "Please, make sure he's okay."

The way she said it made Cate look shrewdly at her and text, **Tell me why you look scared.**

"Because I am scared. Jake went through such deep depression after the accident and Mom's departure. I was worried every day that he'd kill himself. Thank God, it got better, but that uneasy feeling was always there a teensy bit until he met you. After that phone call, I have no idea what to expect. Get in there and remind him that he has you and your baby with him now."

I don't even know if I'm pregnant! Cate typed furiously. **I'll be SO happy to know one way or the other so that we can end all this speculation!**

"If it turns out you're not, then work on getting pregnant as soon as you can. Jake needs you and all those babies you're going to have in order to keep him going. Don't let him tell you otherwise."

He told me this morning that he wouldn't go on without me, thought Cate. *I figured he was being dramatic to make a point, but what if he wasn't? What if something happens to me and he kills himself? God, he can't do that!*

She went to the bedroom and quietly entered, closing the door behind her. Jake was sitting on the edge of the mattress with the phone in his hand. He didn't raise his head as she walked over to stand in front of him and took his free hand in hers, bringing it to her belly. He lifted his head but didn't smile or speak.

Releasing his hand, Cate texted, **I want to name her Rosa. It means "pink" in Italian.**

Jake smiled and nodded before wrapping his big arms around her tiny body and burying his face against her chest. She didn't ask him what his mother had said. She knew that he'd tell her when he was ready.

"Mom was so happy I called," Jake began. "She started crying when I told her I loved her, but she doesn't understand how I can continue to be hurt, angry, and confused by her remarrying and leaving me and Hazel after Dad died. She said we were adults, and we should have been able to handle things." He barked a mirthless laugh and muttered, "*She* couldn't handle things, but *we* were supposed to? She was the parent, and we were her children. I was barely eighteen when she left. She just doesn't get it. Maybe she never will. At least I told her I loved her and forgave her. At least if I die tonight, I know I said it. It does make me feel better, and it made me feel better to hear her say it to me, no matter what."

I'm glad, even though you're not going to die anytime in the near future. I need you, and Rosa needs her daddy.

"What if there is no Rosa?"

Then we'll continue working on creating one.

"Maybe we shouldn't. As much as I want us to have kids, I can't risk your life."

The doctor will tell me if there are risks, and we'll be careful.

"Something could go wrong."

That's true. Something could go wrong with anyone at any time. If anything does go wrong with me, then promise me you won't give up. It would kill me if you hurt yourself.

"If you died, I'd want to join you."

And abandon Rosa in an even worse way than your mother abandoned you?

"No. If we had kids and I lost you, I'd stick around for our children like Everton did after Tracy died. He told me once that if it hadn't been for Ava, then he would've killed himself. I believe him. I didn't know him then and never knew Tracy, but they were obviously soul mates. The way he lost her...."

M'Dear said he told her they were talking one minute and then Tracy died the next.

"That's not quite true, but don't ever tell M'Dear. I think it's the one thing he's never shared with her. They were talking all right, but it was while they were having sex. They were in the middle of making love, and Tracy had just told him how much she loved him when she cried out and collapsed. She died in Everton's arms with him inside her. Jesus, it's no wonder he's never been with anyone else since. To lose the woman he loved and in that way...."

Oh...my...God.

"Don't leave me," he rasped. "Swear you won't leave me."

Pulling him closer to her, she kissed his brown hair then drew away and texted, **I'll never willingly leave you, Jake. I swear it. Now, swear to me that you'll never do anything like kill yourself, whether I'm with you or not. You're so precious to me. Don't ever even consider robbing the world of all that you are.**

"Cate –"

If you love me, then you'll promise.

"I – I promise."

Good. Now, make love to me. I want to not think about anything bad for a while and feel you come with me.

He sighed but smiled tiredly up at her and said, "It's always my pleasure to pleasure you, Baby. I can't ever get enough of you...."

As he held her afterwards, Cate texted, **You really thought the blog was that good?**

"It made me call my mother after ten years, and I thought Hazel was going to dissolve into a puddle of tears while she was reading it. She's right. We have to get it out to people. You're so damned talented, and you have so much to say. You *should* be heard by as many people as possible. We'll figure it out. Somehow, you'll speak to everyone."

"I've got it!" Hazel announced the following morning as they sat in the living room. "Jake can tell everyone at work about the blog. I think I can reach more people by talking to all the truckers while I'm driving, and they'll spread the word. My friends on the highways will make it their mission once they get hooked. But I think your best bet is Dana Montgomery from the TV station. If she makes this awesome video like she says she will, then she can mention the blog at the end. Maybe there could be a link. Ask about it when she calls."

Wouldn't that be shameless self-promotion?

"Hell, yes! There's nothing wrong with that. Use whatever's at your disposal to reach more people. You have a lot to say, and that's not going to stop after one blog. Trust me. People are going to be hooked. They just don't know about you, yet. All that is going to change soon. You have a real gift, Cate."

Jake's phone rang. As he glanced at the display, he said, "Speak of the devil. It's Montgomery." After a brief conversation with the woman, Jake stood and said, "She wants us to come down to the station. She and the videographer have been working on the video since the wedding. It didn't sound like she'd had any sleep. I told her we'd be there as soon as we could. She sounded exhausted but exhilarated. I'm damned curious."

Me, too.

"Me three," Hazel added. "I hope it's not schmaltzy."

The video was not "schmaltzy" as Hazel had feared. When they had finished watching the piece, Cate and Hazel were in tears and Jake looked deeply affected. Montgomery and the videographer waited anxiously to hear the threesome's thoughts.

It's beautiful, Cate typed. **It's unbelievable.**

"No, you're unbelievable. I remember your blog being mentioned during the reception at The Peking Palace. We read the first post today. It was amazing!" Taking a seat beside Cate, the woman said, "I want to air this as a story and put it out on YouTube.

I can guarantee you, it's going to go crazy viral with the right promotion. I'd like to add a line near the end about your blog and include a link. I also want to send the piece to our parent corporation to see if they'll highlight it on the national morning show or on the evening news. My bosses think they will. Would you be all right with that? People might come out of the woodwork, but you could reach so many who need to hear your message if we do this. Who knows? Someone might offer you a deal on the rights to work with you on a book about your life story. If they do, then hire an entertainment lawyer. Be careful you don't get screwed. We can help you with that."

Why? Why are you doing this? To advance your own career?

"It certainly won't hurt our careers," the woman said with a glance at the videographer. "But that's not why we're doing it."

"Why then?" Jake prodded.

The woman looked away before admitting, "My first real news story was a report on a family who'd been murdered by the father. He'd shot his wife and six kids before turning the gun on himself. That story's haunted me ever since. I always wished I could have done something to make their story more meaningful, to make it really reach people. I just wasn't sure how. Perhaps this is my way."

"What do you think, Baby?" asked Jake, as he slipped an arm around Cate's shoulders. "I can tell you now that we'll have to move."

I think we'll have to move anyway. We'll have to have a bigger place for our family, right? If this will help us and others, then I think we have to do it. Maybe it's why I survived.

"You survived to save me," Jake reminded her. "But maybe you also survived to save others. Most of all, you survived to save yourself."

Chapter Seventeen

You're sure? Cate texted. **There's no doubt?**

"No doubt," the thirty-something female OB/GYN confirmed. "You are pregnant, and we do need to consider this a high-risk pregnancy because of your small frame. We're going to do some tests to check the size of your pelvis and other things, but I can already tell you that you're way too small for your body to allow for a natural delivery."

How many C-sections can one person have?

The woman chuckled and asked, "Anticipating a large family already?" When Cate grinned and nodded, the doctor said, "We'll take it one baby at a time. If I feel as though your body can't handle another pregnancy no matter whether it's after this baby or several, then I'll let you know. Will your husband be understanding if you can't have more children?"

His main fear is losing me. If you say my life is in danger, I'm thinking he'd be at a surgeon's office getting a vasectomy the same day.

"I'm glad to know you're his main concern."

The way she said it made Cate uneasy, and she asked, **Why?**

"Because if something does go wrong and a choice has to be made between terminating the pregnancy or compromising your welfare, then I want to have some sort of idea regarding where he stands."

Feeling unnerved by this line of conversation, Cate texted, **If he comes with me for a regular appointment and there are no problems, then please don't say anything like that. I think losing me is the only thing that really scares him. I want him to feel reassured unless there is some serious issue.**

"Of course. One major bonus is that you said you're married to a paramedic. The fact that he has a medical background is a huge plus if there are any issues with the pregnancy."

What types of problems should I be looking for?

"None at this time. You're in the beginning stages of pregnancy. My hope is that all goes well until we get to a scheduled C-section date and welcome a healthy baby into the world. However, I will have you come in more frequently than the average expectant mother and send you to a specialist if I think it's warranted. Just as each pregnant woman should, listen to what your body tells you. If something feels wrong or if you begin spotting, then contact my office or go to the hospital right away." Scanning her computer screen, she noted, "I recall you telling me you were a preemie. How early were you, and do you know what led to the premature birth?"

I have no idea how early I was. When I was five, I heard my father tell my mother that she should have taken better care of herself when she was pregnant and not used drugs. He said I weighed two pounds at birth and that it was her fault I almost died and couldn't speak. The ironic thing is that he was the head of a powerful drug cartel and was certainly her supplier. I guess he didn't see his culpability in my premature birth or internal deformity.

The OB/GYN nodded somberly and then said, "Cate Speaks."

Cate jerked back as if she'd run headlong into a brick wall. The first blog post had only gone live two days before. How had this doctor she'd never met until that morning already heard about it?

As if reading her thoughts, the woman said, "I saw the story about your wedding on the Sunday evening news and immediately went to look up the blog. It made me cry. I called my sister and told her to check it out, but she said she'd already seen the video on YouTube and had just finished reading the blog. They replayed the story on the news this morning, and all of the staff has been talking about it. When you checked in, you caused quite a stir back here. The receptionist practically flew around the place, telling everyone on the staff that you were our new patient."

Why didn't you say anything when you met me?

"Because you're a new patient, a newlywed, and a newly expectant mother. I'm here to be your doctor, not ask for your autograph." Smiling, she added, "Although I still might do that."

I signed in. You all have it. You'll get another signature each time I have an appointment. I guess you could sell them on the Internet.

"Ha! Good one. I wonder if someone's already snagged the sign-in sheet?" Sobering, she said, "Your blog was amazing. I can't wait to read the next one. I don't think you realize how much you touched everyone with your honest words. You have a beautiful voice."

Cate's nose stung as her eyes filled with tears. She thanked the doctor and bid her farewell until the next visit, paid for the appointment, and left the clinic. Then she walked home, entered, went to her computer, and pulled up her first *Cate Speaks* post.

Cate Speaks

I've always had something to say, but I was never allowed to speak. Born prematurely and without a voice box, I couldn't make a sound. I learned to communicate, but my brother was the only person who truly paid attention to what I thought or felt. I had that beauty until I was eight. That was when our father killed my mother and brother and tried to kill me. That was when he killed himself. That was when my isolation became complete.

My father was the head of a drug cartel, and he was about to be brought down by the authorities when he decided not to let them best him. I woke one night to my brother's screams, his cries for our father to stop, and his pleas for me to lock the door to my room and not to let our father in. I didn't know at the time that our mother was already dead.

After he killed my brother, our father came for me. I tried to stop him, but there was no hope of that. He repeatedly stabbed me until he thought I was dead. Then, he went out to the garage, sat in one of his fancy cars, and shot himself in the

head. I heard the shot before I lost consciousness. That night, I died inside.

Abandoned by my remaining relatives, I spent the next ten years in foster homes, graduated from high school and college, and found a job. I lived my life trying not to feel, remember, or love. I kept myself apart and never, ever turned out a light. After all, bad things happen when no lights are on in a house, right?

Two weeks ago, I opened my heart to a beautiful man who listened to me speak without a voice, just as my brother had listened before his life was taken. This man managed to reach me in a way no one else had for eighteen years. I came alive and realized that life was too short not to truly live. I *needed* to make myself heard.

There are others out there who can't speak, see, hear, or walk. Some people suffer from mental illness, chronic health conditions, and despair. Some of us have been the victims of violent attacks, emotional abuse, and sexual abuse. All of us want to be heard, and some have the courage to enlighten others by example. It's time I did the same. Maybe if I do, then others will be less afraid.

I know what I've lost and what I never had. What I don't know is what I *might* have – now that I've found the strength within myself, thanks to the love of a wonderful man. If I can reach people and show them how they can face whatever fears they have in order to lead happy lives, then this blog will be a success. I'll talk openly about my past, my present, and my dreams for the future. I'm Cate, and it's about time I stopped hiding and had my say.

Cate stared at the screen long after she'd finished reading the post. So much had happened since she'd written it the previous week. Since then, she'd become a wife, a sister-in-law, and a confirmed mother-to-be. That didn't take away her fears, new concerns, or questions about what lay ahead.

That's part of the journey I'll blog about, she told herself. *I can decide each week whether to review current events in my life and how I deal with them or past events I'm working through. If people are interested –*

She started, remembering there was a feature on the blog page that would allow her to see how many hits she'd had per week and in total. She glanced at it, glanced away, and then glanced back in disbelief. She'd already had almost fifty thousand hits.

Quickly going to YouTube, she searched for and found the newscaster's story on the wedding. She gaped at the screen. Over seventy-five thousand people had *Liked* it. She looked at the clock. It was noon.

Oh...my...God.

Her phone chimed, notifying her of a new text. She wondered if Jake had taken a break to text her in order to find out the results of the pregnancy test. He couldn't keep his phone turned on all the time when he was working for obvious reasons. However, the text wasn't from Jake. It was from Beth Kirkland.

Congratulations on your wedding! We watched the story on the news last night, and it was fabulous! Then, I read the blog, and it made me cry. Logan listened to it with his screen reader and wants to have a long talk with you. He came from a pretty bad childhood himself and is always trying to help others with special challenges. He wondered if maybe there was a way you could combine your efforts to reach even more people. He'll be texting you later today. Congratulations again! We can't wait to see you and Jake soon!

Cate texted back, **Thank you so much for all the kind words. I'd love to work with Logan on reaching more people. How are you doing? How are Deacon and Mary Margaret? I need to talk to you soon since I just found out I'm pregnant and am thrilled and panicked.**

She sent the text and waited nervously for a response. It wasn't long in coming.

OMG!!!!! Congratulations! OMG!!!!! What are you doing right now? I'm not working in the store today, and Deacon and Mary Margaret will be taking naps in about an hour. Come over, and we can talk. OMG!!!!!

Smiling, Cate remembered Logan telling her and Jake that Beth was rather ADHD. When they'd seen one another face-to-face, Beth had seemed energetic but not abnormally so. However, her texts were obviously indicative of what she experienced inside. Before Beth could text again, Cate quickly texted back that she'd be at the apartment in an hour but would knock softly.

After eating some of the leftovers from her wedding reception, she set out for Beth and Logan's condo. She was riding up the elevator when she got a text from Jake.

Well? was all it said.

Yes, everything went well, she typed, grinning.

You're killing me, Baby. You know what I mean. Well?

You'll have to wait until you get home and we take our drive into the country.

Cate, don't torture me like this.

Don't be so impatient. You've waited two weeks. What's a few more hours? I have to go. See you tonight. I love you.

I love you, too. You know there's going to be payback for your making me wait, don't you?

You can torture me with pleasure all you want as payback. ☺ <3

Cate pocketed the phone as she stepped off the elevator and went to the Kirklands' door. She knocked softly and was soon ushered inside by Beth, who greeted her and then said, "I'm so glad you're here! I've been hyper as all get-out after getting your awesome news!" Gesturing toward the couch, she said, "Have a seat. You want something to drink? No? Okay."

Once they'd settled onto the sofa, Cate typed, **Do you mind if I ask you some questions? I'm kind of freaking out, even though I'm happy. Jake doesn't know, yet. I'm going to tell him tonight. We'd both discussed talking with you and Logan about how to raise a child when one parent has physical limitations. You two have obviously done a great job with Mary Margaret and Deacon.**

"Thanks. We made some mistakes, but we learned from them. We were kind of scared about having kids ourselves and not only because Logan was blind. He had wonderful caregivers who were like mothers to him, but he and his brother grew up in an orphanage. He was concerned about not knowing what to do in a normal family situation. Luckily, Logan's biological father found him before I got pregnant with Mary Margaret. His dad is a wonderful man, and my mother is a wonderful woman. They actually fell in love and got married, which was amazing for them and us. They've been so supportive."

Cate was dying to ask where Beth's father and Logan's mother were but didn't want to be rude. Instead, she texted, **As you know from my blog, my own childhood was pretty awful, and I can't speak. How can I raise a child? Jake had a wonderful childhood but lost his father about ten years ago. His mother remarried and moved away. I think he's worried about how we'll manage as parents, even though he wants as many kids as we can have.**

"Logan and I can be there for you, but we're far from perfect. You and Jake will do great! You'll figure it out. I still can't believe you're pregnant!"

It happened the first time…our first time.

"Have you seen a doctor? Is everything okay?"

This morning. She says all's fine for now, but it's a high-risk pregnancy because I'm so small and was a preemie myself. It sounds like I'll be having a C-section for sure. I don't have a choice there but –

Her phone chimed. After apologizing to Beth for the interruption, she read the message and almost dropped the phone. Beth asked in a concerned tone of voice whether or not Cate was all right. Lifting her gaze to meet Beth's, she held up the phone so that her friend could read the message.

"Oh, my God! Cate, you have *got* to do it! Text Jake right now!"

They can't keep their phones on at work. If I tell him it's an emergency, he'll lose it when he gets the message and think something's wrong with me. I can't just share this with him in a text.

"Of course you can! He'll have to ask off work, but I can't imagine they wouldn't give him the day or two, especially if he does a little promotion for them at the same time. Go on!"

Knowing this moment was an enormous turning point in her life, Cate texted Jake, informing him that Dana Montgomery had just texted saying her station had been contacted by its parent company.

They wanted to fly Cate and Jake to New York to appear live on their national morning show on Friday. To her surprise, Jake immediately texted back, **Hell, yeah. It's your moment, Baby. I wouldn't miss it for anything.**

What are you still doing on your phone?

I thought you might change your mind and text me about your visit to the doctor. I guess you're going to make me squirm until tonight. I'm damned glad I left the phone on, though.

But Jake –

I'll work it out with my job. Trust me. They'll understand, especially if I tell them I'll plug our team on national news.

Beth already suggested that.

You're with Beth?

The kids are taking a nap, and she asked me to come for a visit. She and Logan saw the news story and read the blog. He wants to work with me on a project to help others like us who've had bad childhoods and are physically challenged.

Sounds good. Did you tell her about Rosa, yet?

Cate's heart swelled with love, but she wasn't about to take the bait.

Rosa who?

Killing me, Baby. Text the news lady back. Get details, and then text them to me so I can let my bosses know. Love you.

Love you, too.

After an exchange with the newscaster, Cate allowed Beth to read the chain of messages. Mary Margaret toddled in while her mother was reading the texts, and the child climbed up onto her mother's lap while rubbing sleepily at her eyes. She yawned and smiled at Cate. When Cate smiled back, Mary Margaret moved over to lean against her. Cate put her slender arms around the child and enjoyed the feel of the little girl's body snuggled against hers.

"Mary Margaret likes you a lot," noted Beth. "I hear Deacon stirring. Will you sit with her while I go get him? We can talk while I nurse him and give Mary Margaret some apple juice."

Cate spent another two hours at the Kirklands and listened to Beth share information about pregnancy, babies, and children. By the time she left, she felt totally comfortable with Beth and more comfortable with the idea of having a baby and being able to care for it. Cate hoped that Jake would be as comfortable with the reality of fatherhood as he purported to be.

I'll find out tonight, she thought. *I'm sure it'll all be fine.*

Chapter Eighteen

"Fuck me, Baby," Jake said huskily, once he was capable of speaking again. "That was some freakin' intense sex."

Just the way you like it, Cate thought, as she nuzzled her face against his neck. *Just the way I like it with you.*

After they'd eaten a hasty dinner, Jake had driven them to a deserted area outside of Sarasota. Cate had insisted he give her a driving lesson before the sun went down, and he'd grudgingly agreed. She promised she'd tell him about the visit to the OB/GYN as soon as it was dark and the lesson was over. She'd kept her promise by texting him "Rosa" once she'd put the car in Park. Then, *she'd* proceeded to make love to *him* in the front seat until they both came hard. Since Jake was usually the dominant partner when they made love, Cate was pleased that she'd gotten good results after taking charge for the first time.

"So, your doctor says you're okay?" Jake asked, once he'd come down. "When's your next appointment?"

Cate held up two fingers.

"Two months? No? Two weeks? What's wrong? That seems awfully soon for someone who's in her first trimester."

Cate disengaged herself from Jake, picked up her phone, and typed, **I'm small and was born early myself. She says I need more careful monitoring and that I'll probably need a C-section. She doesn't foresee any major problems, but she wants to be thorough.**

"I'm going with you to your next appointment."

You don't have to.

"I'm going."

But Jake –

"It's my baby, too," he said petulantly, making Cate laugh noiselessly.

You sound like a little boy who has to have his way.

"You're my woman. As your husband and the kid's father, I want to take care of both of you. I have a right to go with you and ask questions and hear what your doctor has to say."

Of course you do. I just don't want you to obsess about me and the baby.

"Too late. I won't lose you, Cate. I'm telling you right now that if anything goes wrong and it's a choice between saving your life or the baby's, I *will* choose to save you. You've got to understand that and don't blame me if it happens." Tightening his bulky arms around her, he said, "You're so damn small. I love you exactly as you are, but you think I don't know how risky pregnancy can be for you? I'm a paramedic, for Christ's sake. I know you can't deliver naturally. There's no way your body would allow it, and that scares the hell out of me."

C-section, remember? I'll be fine.

"I'm counting on it. I guess our family will have to be a little smaller than you want."

What? What do you mean? The doctor said we'd take it one baby at a time, and she'd let me know if we shouldn't have more. We could still have ten kids.

"No, we can't. Generally, it's not recommended that women have more than three C-sections. Each one brings with it more risks of complications for the mother. I'm setting our limit at three."

You can't do that! Cate texted angrily. **It's my body, and they're my babies, too! It's not your decision to make alone!**

"Now who sounds like a little kid wanting her way?" he teased. Sobering, he said firmly, "Three babies at most. Your doctor's right about taking it one baby at a time. Pregnancy could be very dangerous for you. One baby at a time up to three. Then, I'll have a vasectomy, and we'll be done."

You don't have to do that.

"I'm not taking any chances. Jesus, you have no idea how happy and uneasy all this makes me."

Yes, I do, she thought. *You are so overreacting, but that probably wouldn't be good to text. If only you weren't so scared of losing me....*

"Have you told anyone else, yet?"

Beth. I wanted to tell you first, but I couldn't help but tell her when she texted me."

"Are you going to announce it on your next blog post?"

I was thinking you could call Hazel, Everton, and your mom. We can let everyone else know when we're on the national morning show this Friday. The news people would love it, and it would be a spectacular way to share the surprise.

"I'll call Hazel right now, but she'll be the one calling Mom. Then, I'll call Everton, but I'll tell him to share the news with only M'Dear and Ava until we tell the world on Friday." Putting his arms around her, he said, "I have the most amazing, weird feeling right now. I'm worried, excited, and so turned on that I can barely think straight."

You better think straight if you're going to teach me how to drive.

"You did great tonight, Baby. You're a natural. You'll have your license in no time."

We'll need another car. How are we going to afford it?

"We'll figure it out. You have to get your license before we need to purchase another vehicle. By then, maybe we'll have worked out a way to afford it."

Are you excited about being on TV?

"Yeah, but it's strange. I never imagined being on the national news."

Me neither. I'm excited but scared.

"You have nothing to be scared about. Did you see how many hits you had on your blog today and how many people dug the YouTube video? I checked at lunch and when I got off work. Fate's been on our side since the moment we connected that second time we saw one another. It's all good."

What if it doesn't stay good?

"Then we work through it. I may have only *really* known you for two weeks, but you're my Cate. I *know* you, and you *know* me. Forever, Baby."

Forever, she agreed.

When they arrived home, Cate went to the basket of baby things Hazel had given them and removed all of the tags from the pink clothing, booties, and blanket before going to the washer and starting a load of clothing that included the items. While she did this, Jake called his sister and Everton, and she half-listened to his animated voice as she took the pink toys to the second bedroom and placed them on the nightstand. As she surveyed the room, she imagined a crib, dresser, and changing table. Reminding herself it was way too early to purchase such things, she returned to the living room and went to sit by Jake on the couch. He put his left arm around her shoulders and told Everton he had to hang up and would see him in the morning.

"Hazel and Everton are over-the-moon happy for us. Hazel's already talking about only doing hauls in Florida or limiting her region to the Southeastern U.S. She says she doesn't want to miss Rosa growing up. She's going to call Mom right away and tell her."

I'd love to have your sister around more often. Hazel's a fabulous person, Jake.

"Yeah. I got lucky, having her for a big sister. Maybe she'll decide to settle down and stop hooking up with other drivers she doesn't really know. Hell, she could get remarried and have kids of her own. She's only thirty-five. This could make her rethink things."

Or not. She seems comfortable with her life.

"She is," he admitted. "I'm not. She lives life her way and enjoys it, but it worries me."

Maybe she and Everton should get together.

Jake laughed loudly at this suggestion and said, "Everton and Hazel like each other, but they wouldn't make a good couple. After losing Tracy, Everton's main focus is on his daughter and mother-in-law. He wants predictability. Hazel is anything but predictable."

Still, it'd be nice for each of them to find a special someone.

Jake looked contemplative but said nothing. She didn't ask him what he was thinking and was satisfied, savoring the feel of simply being with her husband. She had thirty-eight weeks to truly get to know him before Rosa would enter the world and change the dynamics of their relationship.

The buzzer on the house sounded, and Cate jumped involuntarily. Her thoughts instantly returned to the man who'd attacked her six months earlier, and she stiffened, looking wide-eyed at Jake. After telling her to stay in the house, he went out of the door, leaving it partially open. Once he was on the side porch, he exclaimed, "What the hell do you think you're doing here?!?"

Cate tensed and moved toward the open door, her phone in her hand. She was ready to text 911 if need be. She waited, one finger poised over the number 9.

"I have lost my job because of you!" Cate heard her ex-friend, Yana, cry. "They have fired me! It is your fault!"

"It's your own damned fault," Jake snapped. "Get off the property, and don't come back or we'll call the police."

"I will not! You have turned Cate against me! You are using her!"

"Get off the steps," Jake rumbled in a low voice. "Then, get some psychiatric help."

Cate heard Yana let out a cry of indignation and then say something in Ukrainian. Although the woman kept speaking, alternating between her native tongue and English, her voice became fainter. Cate strained to hear more of what she was saying but couldn't. Jake returned to the house and pulled his phone from his pocket before hitting one of his contact numbers.

"I need the police," he said grimly. "No, it's not an emergency at this moment, but my wife and I were just threatened." After rattling off their address, he said, "Thanks. We'll be waiting."

What did you do that for? Cate asked, shaking slightly as a result of Yana's appearance and the exchange she'd overheard. **She's gone. She won't be back.**

"Maybe she won't. Maybe she will. Maybe someone else will."

I don't understand. You said she threatened us. She didn't.
"She did."
What? When?
While she was leaving."
You speak Ukrainian?

"No, Baby. She was going back and forth between that and English. One of the things I heard before she got out of earshot was that she was going to contact someone to teach us a lesson. I'm guessing that means the Ukrainian mafia. The Ukrainians I've come across in North Port have all been great people, but it's no secret that there's a mafia presence in that area. Everyone's scared of them. If Yana approaches them, that could put you, our baby, me, and Yana in danger. I can't do anything to protect her, but I sure as hell can do something to try to protect our family."

It had to be an empty threat. Yana's family is terrified of the Ukrainian Mob.

Jake rested his hands on her shoulders and bent to kiss her before saying, "Baby, something is definitely wrong with her. I get that she wasn't like this at all before, because I know you wouldn't have been friends if she had been. I guess my appearance made her feel threatened or something, but this is way beyond being upset. She's not rational. She *does* need professional help. I'm sorry for her and you that she's lost it emotionally. Obviously, the people at Combine saw it after her tirade. Perhaps she kept on about it. We need to tell the cops. That way, it'll be on record in case she tries anything. The cops may go to Combine and have a chat with your former boss. Were there ever any indications she was unstable?"

After her husband left her for another woman, she kind of had a breakdown. It was a rough few months. Then, he was killed in a home invasion, and she was a mess again. One day, she came in and said she was fine. She was her old self again, and life returned to normal.

"You repeat that to the cops when they come. Something tells me there was more to her return to normal than was normal."

They heard a car pull into the driveway. Knowing it was the police, Jake kissed her again and said, "I'm going to keep you safe, Baby. You and Rosa stay here."

She couldn't help but smile, as Jake went out onto the side porch and unlocked the gate for the policemen who'd responded to his call. For the next hour, they explained to the two men about Cate, Yana, Jake, and the events of the past couple weeks. Cate had expected the officers to dismiss Jake's concerns, but they didn't. This both frightened and comforted her.

Before they left, one of the policemen said to her, "My wife and I read your blog." When Cate blinked in surprise, he continued, "It really hit home for us. Our youngest kid's autistic, and a lot of folks say there's nothing going on in his head. We've always felt like he's got a lot going on up there, but he just can't get it across to us. After we read your post, we decided to bring him to some new doctors. We can't give up on him. We think he has something to say, too. Thanks for giving us the boost we needed to do that."

Cate smiled and nodded before texting, **Everyone has something to say that's important to them. I'm glad your son has parents who want to listen.**

Once the cops had left, Jake said, "You're an awesome example, Cate. Are you going to keep blogging once a week or start doing it every day?"

I don't know if I have enough material to blog every day.

"Are you kidding me? After twenty-six years, I'd think you'd have more stored up inside than I can begin to fathom. Try it, and see what happens."

Cate tried it for the next three days and loved it. Jake was right; she had plenty to say. As she gained more followers, she gained more confidence. She and Logan Kirkland met for lunch and began to "talk" about their pasts and their mutual dream of reaching those like them who had physical limitations. Before she and Jake left for New York City Thursday afternoon, she typed a post that would automatically go live during the airing of the morning show.

This could be truly great, she thought, once she'd set up the automatic posting. *We could make such a huge difference in the world if it works.*

Friday morning, Cate sat nervously beside Jake on the set of the national morning show. Her stomach was in knots because of her nerves. Jake was wearing khaki pants and a green fisherman's sweater that brought out the green in his eyes, highlighted his sandy brown hair, and accentuated his ruggedly handsome features. Cate wore a pink, sleeveless knit dress with a coordinating crocheted pink sweater. Jake told her the outfit flattered her small, sexy body and made her long, black hair and gray eyes even more pronounced and beautiful. His comments and the way his hands roamed over her before they left for the studio made her breasts tingle and her body ache for his touch.

I know he'll give me what I want anytime I want it, she reminded herself. *Later. We have all the time in the world. Right now, we have something very important to do. Actually, we have quite a few important things to do. Life is calling.*

Chapter Nineteen

"You have such a touching, unique tale to tell," Janie Halbreck, the popular, African-American morning show host commented before tucking some of her long hair behind one ear, which was her signature gesture during interviews. "As you know, we've been highlighting your story, the news report, your wedding video, and the *Cate Speaks* blog throughout our broadcast this morning. Viewers are emailing, posting to our Facebook Page, and Tweeting us about the two of you and about how inspiring you are. Your honesty is refreshing. What do you hope to achieve by being so open?"

Cate smiled and typed on the laptop Logan had given her that had speech reader software installed on it. It was meant for the visually impaired but worked very well for her, despite the fact that the laptop was too unwieldy to carry around to use in casual conversations. She'd been surprised by how realistic the female voice sounded as it read what she typed, although the program did have a few quirks like not stressing italics. The national morning show's crew had plugged the laptop into something that allowed those at home to also read what Cate was typing on the screen.

"We want to show people they don't need to be afraid of life, their pasts, or any physical challenges they might face," the synthesized voice said. "It took me a long time to realize I didn't have to live in fear and isolation. I was already very independent, but I was scared and ashamed of my past and my inability to speak. Jake taught me I didn't have to live like that."

"What about you, Jake?" the woman prompted. "What did Cate teach you?"

"That I can be loved for who I am and not what I look like or for what people expect from me. Without being able to speak, she told me how worthwhile I was."

"That's beautiful," the host said with sincerity. "How far are both of you willing to go in order to be examples to others?"

"We're simply living our lives," the computer voice said as Cate typed. "We're not trying to impress anyone. We're real people with real hopes, dreams, and problems."

Nodding, Halbreck said, "Your childhood was definitely atypical, Cate. You've been very open about your father's position as the head of a drug empire and what he did to you, the rest of your family, and himself. Have you come to terms with what happened?"

"What happened was horrible. I don't know if anyone who survives such things ever truly comes to terms with them."

"I see at least one scar on your hand. Is it difficult for you to show your scars to others or to look at them yourself?"

"It used to be. Not anymore." Steeling herself, Cate typed, "Everyone can see."

She passed the laptop to Jake, who nodded but said nothing. Then, she unbuttoned her crocheted sweater and slipped it off, revealing all of the scars on her arms and chest that weren't covered by the material of her dress. Turning to Jake, she mouthed, "Eighteen."

"Eighteen," he repeated. "She was stabbed eighteen times by her father eighteen years ago."

Halbreck, obviously startled by Cate's actions, quickly recovered herself and said, "That took a lot of courage."

Motioning for Jake to return the laptop to her, she typed, "Before I met Jake, I was strong, but I also lived in fear. I won't do that anymore. I'm going to live my life with my husband, blog, and work with Logan Kirkland, the owner of Sight Unseen, to help others with physical or emotional challenges."

"What is Sight Unseen?"

"It's a store that carries products that the visually impaired can use in order to function more easily in the sighted world. Sight Unseen has a physical location in Sarasota, but there's an online store as well. Logan himself is blind. He and I want to start a nonprofit organization that will help those with physical limitations learn more about empowerment. That's what my blog post today is all about."

"We'll be closely following your story. It seems like you have quite a few projects in the works."

141

Jake grinned and said, "Our most important project in the works is a small one."

"Oh?" Halbreck asked with interest. "And what is that?"

Using the letters she'd learned from Everton, Cate signed *R-O-S-A*. Once Jake translated, he explained, "That's what we're going to call her. She should be here in less than nine months."

"You're pregnant?" the host asked, sounding both shocked and delighted. "Congratulations!" As the others on the set clapped and cheered, Halbreck added with a chuckle, "Where *are* you going to *put* that baby?"

When they were no longer live on the show, Cate and Jake were escorted out of the studio to a lounge. Cate shivered in the chill of the room, and Jake held up her sweater so that she could slip into it and button the front. She smiled and signed "thank you" to him.

A blonde man wearing gray slacks and a black sweater entered and then introduced himself as Albert Fuentes, the producer of the morning show. He thanked them for coming, asked them to have a seat, and then proceeded to discuss the possibility of doing a one-hour special on Cate's life.

I don't know, Cate texted on her phone. **What would be involved?**

"Our people would put together a piece and then interview you about different aspects of your life. We'd hit the high points. I don't want to take away interest from your blog. I'd actually like to draw more interest to it and this nonprofit organization formation you're working on. I also know someone else who'd like to talk with you." Once Cate and Jake had exchanged confused looks, he said, "My partner, Einar Nielsen, is here in the studio."

The producer mentioned the man's name, and Cate immediately recognized it. He was a Pulitzer Prize-winning journalist who'd written several bestselling biographies of famous people, including former Presidents, heads of industry, musicians, and actors.

But he writes about important people. I'm not a celebrity.

"I think you're wrong about that," the man countered. "He really wants to talk with you. He'd like to do a book about your life. He's very thorough, and he likes to work with the subjects of his books."

"Look, we don't know anything about Cate's rights," Jake told him. "I don't want to see my wife used in any way for other people's gains."

We were told to get a lawyer who specialized in entertainment law if we were approached with a book deal or anything like that. I don't want anyone to take advantage of me or my family.

"That's a very wise move. You don't have to do anything today, but will you at least meet Einar and see what his thoughts are regarding a book? Will you consider our idea for a special on your life?"

Cate nodded, and Fuentes thanked her again then excused himself in order to summon Nielsen. While he was gone, Cate texted, **My head is spinning. What do you think about all of this?**

"I think it'd be freakin' awesome if we make sure you're protected."

I agree. I'd like to know everything about my family but don't even know where to start. I'm too close to the situation. Plus, I'm thinking a big-name writer will have more success with investigative journalism than I would. He could tell me about my parents, their families, the drug cartel, and all of that.

"True, but what if he finds out something really terrible about your father and what he had done to people?"

Do you think it would bother me if that came out? He stabbed us and shot himself! I'm sure he did lots of bad things before that night.

"I'm sure he did, too. If it doesn't bother you that everyone knows about those things, then that'll work out fine. But what about you?"

What about me?

"Are you going to talk about the rape? If you don't, someone else might come forward and talk about it to gain notoriety. Hell, the rapist himself might come forward."

Cate pondered his question for a few minutes before typing, **I'll tell everyone about my rape. Do you know how many other foster kids are sexually abused while they're in the system? Maybe my telling about that would help others who've had similar things done to them. Would you be okay with me telling people I was sexually assaulted?**

"It's your choice. All I'm saying is that it's good to be an example of a real survivor, but we're not only talking about being an example in our community. Everyone in the world will know. You've got to be ready to deal with that. I don't want you to lose yourself in your newfound freedom and in your desire to help everyone else. Rosa and I need you."

You wouldn't lose me. Sighing, she continued, **We will definitely have to move soon, though. We'll probably go home to tons of mail, reporters, and whack jobs waiting on our steps. If I do sign a book deal or something like that, then we'd have enough money to move and get another car. I could stay home with Rosa, blog, and work with Logan on the nonprofit.**

"Don't do any of it for money," advised Jake. "We can make it on our own."

I know we can, but I don't see a conflict if I sell my story to people and use the money to help make our lives easier. What I went through was hell. I might as well reap some reward from all those years of suffering.

"No hasty decisions, okay?"

Promise. Whatever we do, we'll do it together. It's not only my life we're talking about here. It's yours, Rosa's, Hazel's, and everyone else we care about. We have a lot to consider.

They returned to Sarasota, pleased with the outcome of their appearance on the show but exhausted. When Jake pulled into their driveway, several reporters approached them. Curious loiterers gawked. They politely declined interviews, accepted business cards from the reporters, and managed to get inside their gate and wish everyone a good night before going into the house.

Once inside, Jake blew out a breath and muttered, "Maybe we should stay with Everton, M'Dear, and Ava for a while until we figure out what we're going to do."

I want to sleep in my own bed. This weekend, we'll review what we want and then contact a realtor if we go forward with the news show and book deal. If not, all of this will eventually blow over.

Her phone chimed, and she glanced at the new text. It was from Logan Kirkland.

You guys rocked on national news. And the blog post you did about the nonprofit that uploaded while you were on TV was

great. **How about coming over to have lunch with Beth, the kids, and me on Sunday? We can hang out, relax, and then talk about the nonprofit for a while. BTW, I'm glad the laptop and speech reader seemed to work for you. Beth said it looked like you didn't have any problems with it. It sounded fine, but I am totally blind and wanted to be sure. We should install the program on your home computer. You could really use it there and on a laptop. Since you don't have your own laptop, keep the one I lent you for now.**

She texted back, **That all sounds great. Thanks. See you guys Sunday.**

"I have to work Sunday, remember?" Jake told her once she'd shown him the chain of messages. "You go ahead, but make Beth drive over here and pick you up. Until things are settled, you're vulnerable."

I'll be fine.

"Do it for me, Baby."

For you.

The next week was frenetic. With the exception of her trip to Logan and Beth's condo, Cate stayed in the house while Jake was at work. She continued to blog each day and to text or email the entertainment lawyer she'd retained, the TV producer, and the award-winning writer. She also received various offers from filmmakers who wanted to buy the rights to her life story and was communicating with the lawyer about their offers.

When Jake wasn't working, they went together to The Peking Palace, which was now filled with even more customers thanks to the wedding video and news coverage of the place. Jake gave Cate more driving lessons. The two of them went to Everton's house to hang out and learn more sign language. They also made love as often as possible.

"You're going to kill me, Baby," Jake murmured one night after a particularly lengthy and intense lovemaking session. "I'm not complaining or anything, but it seems like you're becoming insatiable when it comes to sex."

It must be the hormones. I want you more and more each day, and I wanted you so much from the beginning.

"I'm happy to make love to you anytime you want. Just text the word, and I'm there."

How about if I sign it? I think we're getting better at sign language, don't you?

"Yeah, but I'm kind of used to the texting. With signing, I don't get all the words like when you text. It's a different kind of language."

True. Maybe we can alternate.

"We should try. After all, you'll be signing to Rosa, and I'll sign and speak at the same time so that she can learn to talk from me and other speaking people."

I wish I could speak to her. I want to sing my baby to sleep.

Jake sighed and admitted, "It breaks my heart when you say things like that. I wish I could make it happen. Maybe someday."

She kissed his jaw, wrapped her arms around him, and didn't text a response.

Chapter Twenty

"Is that what I think it is?" Jake asked hoarsely, as they stared at the monitor in the OB/GYN's office. "Tell me I'm seeing things."

"You're seeing things all right," confirmed the doctor. "It looks like I'll be referring you to that specialist, Cate."

Why? What's wrong with my baby? I've never seen an ultrasound before. Is it okay?

"You're only a month along, and everything looks fine. That's not the problem."

What is?

The OB/GYN pointed to a dot on the screen and said, "There's your baby." Moving her finger to another dot, she added, "And there's your baby. You're carrying twins."

Twins? she texted in disbelief.

"Yes, twins. I already had you on the high-risk pregnancy list. Now, you've moved up a lot closer to the top. Carrying one baby would have been enough for you. With two, you could have double trouble. You and your babies might be fine, but you'll all need even closer monitoring until your C-section. I'll work with the specialist to ensure we do that at the appropriate time. The twins may have to be delivered early in order to prevent serious complications for you or them. Your risk of miscarriage is also greater with more than one."

"Any restrictions at this point?" Jake asked intently.

"Not from me. If you can wait, then I'll call the specialist's office and see if they can work you in this morning so that you can meet him together."

"We can wait," Jake said after taking another glance at the monitor.

Once the doctor had left the room, Cate texted, **Relax. I'm fine. The baby…I mean…the babies are fine. We'll all be okay.**

"Maybe. Maybe not. Because you're so tiny, carrying two babies could put a real strain on your body. You might have to go on bed rest early on. You could have other issues. You could lose them. I could lose you."

You won't. If they come early, then maybe I wouldn't need a C-section. I could deliver them naturally.

"Not a chance," he said quickly. "You'd be risking your life and theirs if you tried that. No way in hell I'm letting that happen."

It's my body, and they're inside me. They'll stay in there until I tell them it's time to come out and play.

"Stop screwing around with me. I'm freakin' scared, Cate. This is serious."

She squeezed his hand and smiled gently up at him. He was a big, strong man who was frightened only by the thought of losing her. She loved that he cared so deeply but hated that he was so consumed by his fear of loss. She wondered if he'd ever be able to let it go.

Two hours later, they were at the specialist's office. The man examined Cate, reviewed her file, and informed her that she would alternate between seeing her regular OB/GYN and him for the remainder of her pregnancy. By the time they left the man's office, Jake was so tightly wound that Cate worried he might explode.

Let's go home, Cate suggested once they were in the Mustang. **You need to call Hazel and Everton, and I need to text Beth and Logan. I also feel the need to blog about this. The thought of one baby was exciting but daunting. Now that we know there are two, I don't know what I'm going to do. How am I going to manage with two babies while you're at work? What if I can't do it?**

"You're only four weeks pregnant," Jake said reassuringly. Sounding in control again, he went on, "We have time to figure it all out. If they survive –"

Cate glared at him and texted, **IF they survive? You're counting on me losing them? If I miscarried, then you wouldn't have to worry about me dying, would you?**

"I am *not* counting on you miscarrying," he ground out. "They're my kids, too! Would I be relieved if your life weren't in danger? Hell, yeah! Would I be sad about the loss of the babies? Of course. I'm not hoping they die. I'm only being realistic."

Realistic. Realistic is that we're having twins and need to pick another name for the second baby.

"Cate, you have to face the fact that –"

Don't, Jake. Don't you dare go there again!

"Okay, okay," he said soothingly. "How about Mitzi?"

Are you serious?

"Why wouldn't I be? You don't like it?"

Not really. Well, not at all. Any other suggestions?

"Francesca? That would go along well with Rosa."

Francesca and Rosa. I love it. What if we have boys?

"We're only having girls, remember? Girls who are as beautiful as their mom."

If we did have boys, then what would you name them?

"Bubba and Abner."

No way!

"Gotcha! I *was* teasing there," he snickered. "What would you name them?"

Jake and…I don't know.

"Now we have to have girls. I don't want to have any son of mine named I-Don't-Know."

She swatted him playfully on the arm and shook her head. Both of them relaxed and enjoyed the ride home. Once there, Jake made his calls, while Cate texted Beth and Logan. Then she settled into her desk chair in order to write her next blog post. When she finished, she realized she was ravenous.

Let's go to The Peking Palace, she told Jake. **I'm starving.**

"At least you're putting on a little weight."

Since I'm having twins, I'm thinking I'll be putting on a lot more weight than I thought.

"As worried as I am about you and the pregnancy, I can't wait to see you big with my babies."

Cate was shocked by how his words turned her on and typed, **If I wasn't so hungry, I'd take you in me right now. When we get home, I want you to make love to me all night.**

"That's my insatiable little woman."

Are you calling me your little woman in the literal sense or being sexist?

"Literal, of course," he answered with amusement. "I may be a man's man, but I'm no sexist pig. God, you've got me wrapped around your little finger."

Ha, ha, she texted, but she was grinning at the joke. **Forever, Baby.**

"That's my plan."

Once they were seated at "their" table near the kitchen in The Peking Palace and had ordered dinner, Cate typed, **Everton's mother-in-law is going with me to look at houses tomorrow. I wish Beth could join us, but she said Mary Margaret's coming down with a cold. I hope Deacon doesn't get it.**

"I hope you don't get it. I'd hate to see you sick, period. Being pregnant limits a lot of the medications you might need if you got a sinus infection or the flu."

I can't hide from the world the whole time I'm pregnant. If I get sick, then I'll deal with it. I hope I don't catch anything because I want to spend our first Thanksgiving dinner together healthy and happy. I'm so excited Hazel will be coming.

"Me, too. It'll be great to spend Thanksgiving with my four best girls."

Four?

"You, Hazel, Rosa, and Francesca."

Giggling noiselessly, Cate texted, **You are TOO much, Mr. Genter!**

"I know," he said with mock arrogance. Sobering, he continued, "I think I might have an idea about how you can manage the twins while I'm at work. Tell me if you think it's nuts or if you want to take longer to consider it."

Cate waited patiently and chewed nervously on her lower lip. Whenever Jake wore a distracted expression on his face, she knew he was worrying over something and trying to find a way to control whatever situation was making him anxious. She wished he'd talk to a therapist but had temporarily suspended her efforts to get him to do so. Every time she brought up the subject, Jake became angry and an argument followed.

"Your blog's doing great, and things are really looking up with all the TV, book, and movie deal talk. I don't want to count our chickens before they're hatched, but it seems like your crappy start in life is going to leave you in a very comfortable financial position for the rest of it. We should know just how comfortable in the near future. The entertainment lawyer has told you what he thinks you can end up with monetarily by going through with all these deals and future ones. What if we buy a nice house in a secure neighborhood that has a smaller guest house on the property? Hazel could quit trucking and live in the smaller house to have privacy for her and us, but she could come when I'm at work to help you out."

You want to stop her from doing what she loves.

"I want to protect her like I want to protect you and our kids. I want her close. I need her close."

You want to save her. You want to save everyone. You can't, Jake. Sometimes people can't be saved. Her fingers hovered over the keypad on her iPhone for a few moments before she texted, **You couldn't have saved your father. You need to stop blaming yourself.**

"Hazel's been telling me that since I was seventeen. She'll never understand, and neither will you."

Make me understand. Talk to me about it.

"I can't. Ever."

That makes me very sad for you.

"It's not what you think."

Then what is it?

"Never mind. What about you? Do you still feel like you might have stopped your father or saved anyone else if you could have cried out for help?"

No. I've come to accept that nothing would have stopped him, except another adult who was stronger or armed. Our mother, Luca, and I didn't stand a chance.

A thought struck her, and she frowned as she mulled it over in her head. Their food was placed in front of them, but Cate didn't move to take a bite. Jake asked her what was wrong.

I was just thinking that maybe my father didn't stab us and kill himself to stop the Federal government from besting him. What if he did it to stop the heads of other drug rings from taking us or him? Maybe they'd threatened to torture or kill us if he talked to the authorities. We would have given them leverage. She looked away then back before typing, **He probably thought it was better for him to do it himself. That would give**

him the satisfaction of knowing no one had beaten him and eliminate the risk of anyone controlling him in any way.

"Any of those scenarios is awful. What he did is unforgivable." Reaching across the table, Jake cupped her left cheek in his large, right palm and suggested, "Maybe the author of the book about your life will unearth the truth. It won't make any explanation better."

No, but it would be nice to know the truth in the end. I can't change the what, but I'd like to know the real reason why.

The following morning, Cate and M'Dear set out with the realtor Cate and Jake had chosen in order to find them a house that met all of the "must haves" on their list. This had proven challenging to the woman, since the list included a neighborhood that was gated but had no deed restrictions and a house that had four bedrooms, three bathrooms, and a large, fenced yard.

Cate had admitted to Jake that, although she would be happy to have Hazel live nearby, she didn't want her living in a guest house on their property. She knew her sister-in-law would want to be an integral part of their lives, but she'd feel trapped by such a living arrangement. Plus, Cate knew the realtor would have been seriously challenged by having to add a guest house to the "must have" list. In the price range they'd given her and with the other requirements they'd included, the woman would have probably suggested building in a new development. Neither Cate nor Jake wanted a cookie-cutter house, which was another challenge for the realtor because of their other requests.

The first two properties they looked at didn't interest Cate at all. Although she liked the layout of the third, it lacked a feeling of warmth, and she texted that it wasn't the home for her and her family. They'd just entered the fourth house when M'Dear's phone rang.

"It's Everton," she said with a frown. "It isn't time for his lunch. I wonder why he's calling. I'll step outside to take it. You go ahead. I'll catch up."

By the time Cate finished her tour of the house, M'Dear still hadn't returned. Concerned, she was about to text the realtor a message stating that she was going to find the older woman when M'Dear entered. Her face was ashen, and she appeared grim.

Jake, Cate thought, her knees almost buckling. *Something must have happened to Jake.*

As if reading her thoughts, M'Dear hurried over to her and said reassuringly, "Jake's not hurt or anything, Honey." Putting her large arms around Cate's small shoulders, she went on, "But he's not okay. We need to go back to your house."

Pulling away, Cate texted, **What happened?**

M'Dear turned to the realtor and asked her to leave them alone for a few minutes. The woman quickly stepped outside to make some phone calls of her own. Once she was gone, M'Dear suggested to Cate that the two of them sit on the couch in the living room.

No. Just tell me. What's wrong with Jake? And why didn't Everton text me?

"Because it was news one shouldn't receive in a text, but he knew he couldn't call you because you couldn't speak in response."

Cate nodded and waited, her stomach muscles clenched in anticipation and fear.

M'Dear combed her long, gray hair with her fingers before saying quietly, "Hazel lost control of her rig on an icy road, and it went over the side of a mountain. She's dead."

Oh...my...God.

Her eyes burning with unshed tears, Cate texted, **Did her cab explode?**

"Yes, Honey. It did."

Oh, God. Why? Jake's father didn't listen to his son's warnings and burned to death during that race. Hazel wouldn't quit trucking when Jake asked her to, although he was more worried about her being attacked by some guy during a one-night stand rather than thinking about her dying in a wreck. Now, she's been killed in a fiery crash. Jake is going to...to...I don't know what he'll do.

Will you explain to the realtor that there's been a family tragedy and tell her we'll contact her when we're ready to resume looking for a house? She texted M'Dear. **Then, I need to get home to Jake as quickly as possible.**

"Of course. It's going to be very rough on Jake, but he'll make it through because of you and the baby...babies. Just be patient but persistent and follow your instincts. You know I'm always available if you need guidance or want a referral to a psychologist or

153

psychiatrist for either of you. Keep in mind that we're family. I'm your friend, not your therapist."

A friend with benefits, just different kinds of benefits. Thank you so much.

"Everton and Jake are best friends as well as coworkers. They're like brothers, Cate. I'm hoping that Everton will be able to help Jake through this but in a fraternal way. You're Jake's lover, wife, and the mother of his children, and you've been through your own trips to Hell and back. Everton's had some trips there as well. I'm sorry for the two of you, but your individual experiences will help you to help Jake."

What if I can't? Cate worried. *We've only truly known each other for one month. I know we both feel like we're meant to be together, but what if love and desire aren't enough? What if I can't reach him like he reached me?*

Thinking about the two tiny "dots" she was carrying inside of her that were their children, Cate's resolve grew stronger. She *would* reach Jake. She *would* see him through this. The alternative was unthinkable.

Chapter Twenty-one

How is he? Cate texted Everton, who was sitting on the porch swing when she and M'Dear arrived home.

"I was trying to comfort him, but he told me to get the fuck out. You know how he gets when he's upset? This is, like, a hundred times worse. I told him the only way I was leaving was if he promised not to hurt himself. He said he'd already made that promise to you and to get the fuck out of the house. I thought he was going to punch me. If I hadn't known you were heading here, I would've let him and insisted on staying. Instead, I came out and sat on the swing. He locked the door behind me. Of course, I have the extra key, but I wasn't about to use it unless I thought he'd –"

Cate held up a hand and emphatically shook her head. She remembered the sound her father's gun had made when he'd shot himself. She wondered if Jake knew how to use a gun.

"Would you like for us to come in with you or wait here?" M'Dear asked.

Wait here. Once I understand what's going on with Jake and see if I can do anything for him, then I'll come back out and talk with you. I may be a while.

"I'm not going anywhere until I know he's somewhat settled," Everton muttered. "I thought he was losing his mind when he got the call."

Who called him with the news?

"Someone from the trucking company Hazel works…worked for. Jake was her emergency contact. I think they only intended to tell him she'd been in an accident and send a representative to meet with him to disclose the truth, but it didn't work out that way. We had our phones off because we were working. So, they called the second number Hazel had listed for Jake, which was Dispatch. They had to tell them it was an emergency, and Dispatch radioed us and

155

told us to contact them once we'd finished at the hospital with our current case. They knew we were wrapping things up. When Jake radioed back, they gave him the number to call. I swear he knew Hazel was dead right at that moment. When he called and they started talking to him about a meeting, he lost it and said something like he knew his sister was gone and to just tell him the goddamned truth. So, they did.

"I watched him fall apart while he listened. Once he disconnected the call, I drove him back to work, parked the ambulance, told him to stay put, and went to let everyone know what'd happened and called M'Dear. Then, I came out, took him to my ride, and drove straight here. His car's still at work."

Good. I don't want him driving right now anyway. Cate hugged Everton then signed, "Thank you."

"I lost my best girl fifteen years ago," he said quietly. "I don't want to lose my best friend. You go make it better. He damn sure won't let anyone else in when it comes to this."

Cate nodded, turned away, then turned back to Everton and texted, **Has Jake told his mother, yet?**

"He said there was no way he was calling her. None of us has her phone number. He's never even told us her married name. I just know her first name's Irene, and she lives in Indiana."

Jake has the number. If he won't call, then I'm afraid I'll have to ask one of you to do it. If I could speak, I'd call myself.

"You know we'll help in any way possible," M'Dear assured her. "Now, go to Jake."

Cate unlocked the door and stepped into the living room, which was deserted. The house was eerily quiet, and her pulse quickened. She began to panic, imagining that Jake had hung himself or cut his wrists. Then, she heard the noises.

At first, Cate didn't know what to make of the sounds. They were foreign and frightening. After several seconds, she understood and walked to the master bedroom where she found Jake sitting on the edge of the mattress with his back to the door. His shoulders shook as he sobbed.

"Why?" he asked hoarsely without turning around. "Why, Baby?"

Cate went around the bed, sat beside her husband, and put one small arm around his waist. Placing the palm of her free hand on his chest, she lifted her chin high and kissed his wet jaw. He didn't move, open his eyes, or stop sobbing. It broke her heart. Sliding her palm up until her fingers were in his hair, she sighed. She wanted to talk to him without breaking their contact but knew it was impossible. So, she stood, withdrew her phone from one pocket of her jeans, and sat in his lap. His arms automatically went around her, and he rested one cheek on the crown of her head.

I'm so, so sorry, Jake. I don't know why Hazel died any more than I understand how my father could have attacked me, Luca, and our mother.

She held up the phone, and Jake raised his head from hers in order to read the message. Still crying, he said bitterly, "I *told* her not to drive anymore. I *told* her life on the road would kill her. She ignored me, and now she's gone."

It's terrible, but it's not your fault. She died because it was her time to go.

"Bullshit!" Jake growled. "Her death was senseless and could have been avoided if she'd listened to me!"

You are NOT God. You can't control anyone but yourself.

"And don't I know it? My big sister and our father are dead; my mother couldn't care less about anyone but herself; and you're risking your life for nothing!"

Cate scrambled up, her temper igniting, and typed, **NOTHING? Our babies are NOTHING?**

Jake ceased crying, shot to his feet, and boomed, "You'd risk death for them! You'd risk leaving me alone because of them!"

You're right! If I have to, then I'll risk my life to make sure they have a chance to live! You want to lose me, Jake? Just TRY to tell me to have an abortion! I'll walk out on you in a minute! Your mother might not have done right by you, but I'll be damned if I don't do right by my children! They're innocents created out of pure love, and I WILL NOT end their lives in order to make you feel better! Do you even really love our babies? Do you really love me, or are you just afraid of being alone? Plus, I'm pregnant, not dying. Yes, it's a high-risk pregnancy, but I'm fine and might stay fine for the next eight months. What is WRONG with you?

Jake stiffened, his hands clenched into fists and his breathing rapid. All of the anger left his face, and tears began to seep from his eyes once more. Muttering a curse, he reached forward as if to pull Cate to him. Still furious, she stepped back.

"Christ, Baby! I'm sorry. I love you *and* our girls. Don't leave. I – I want to explain."

Start explaining then! Our daughters and I are waiting.

He winced. Cate was ashamed to admit that it gave her satisfaction. However, as she watched big, strong, angry Jake deflate in front of her, returning to his seat on the bed with his head down, her heart ached. Thinking about her babies, she made herself remain where she was. If she capitulated, she feared he wouldn't explain and she'd be forced to leave him. If that happened, she suspected she knew what he might do to himself. Cate shivered with dread.

"My father was my hero when I was little," he began. "He was everyone's best friend, a loving husband, and an attentive father. He loved Hazel, but I was his favorite."

Why does the way he said that last part make my skin crawl? wondered Cate.

"Once it was determined I was dyslexic, Dad insisted on being the one to help me learn how to read properly. He spent time every night in my room working with me. At least that's what he said to others. No one suspected a thing. No one knew what he was really doing with me in my room."

Suddenly feeling ill, Cate reminded herself to breathe. She prayed that Jake wouldn't look up and see her expression. She was certain he'd misinterpret it and think she was disgusted with *him*, which wasn't true at all.

"I was so confused. After all, I was only a kid who looked up to his father. But I knew it was wrong and pretended it didn't happen. I knew he wouldn't stop until I learned how to read, so I did everything I could to learn quickly. Once I was doing fine, he had no reason to be alone with me every night. I was relieved that he stopped, but he told me if I ever said a word then I'd lose everyone I cared about. I was...six? Seven? I don't even remember. All I remember was that I couldn't tell. If I told, then I'd be alone forever." Resting his palms on his thighs, Jake continued, "He didn't try anything with me again for years. I was afraid he was hurting Hazel, but I couldn't ask her. I couldn't tell. I'd been programmed to keep silent and pretend Dad was as great as I'd thought before he'd hurt me. It got easier as time passed, and I kind of shoved what he'd done to the back of my mind.

"When I was seventeen, he came after me again. I wasn't some scrawny little kid; I was bigger than he was. So, I told him to go fuck himself and leave me alone. I told him I was going to tell Mom and Hazel what he'd done when I was little. He was livid, and we argued. I think that was when he started having the stroke. I warned him not to race. I told him he'd put other people's lives in danger…." His voice trailed off, but Jake resumed momentarily by saying, "He died in that crash. Watching it was horrible, but the whole time I was screaming that he deserved to burn in Hell. Everyone thought I'd lost my mind because of my grief. They had no idea I was freakin' serious." Sighing heavily, he went on, "After the funeral, I told my mother about what he'd done. Hazel was out of the house, and I felt like I had to tell Mom. I was scared to death that she'd leave once I shared my story with her. And she did."

Cate moved forward and rested her small hands on his broad shoulders, but Jake didn't look up at her. A part of her mind was blank with shock, but another part was already trying to formulate some response to his admission. One thing of which she was certain: Jake was going to start therapy immediately. So was she. They'd both waited too long to begin real healing when it came to their pasts.

"When I told Mom what Dad had done, she…she didn't act stunned or anything. She seemed sad and wouldn't look me in the eye. That was when I knew she'd known or at least suspected what Dad had done to me. Within a month of my telling her, she married that guy and left for Indiana. I reasoned Dad was right. I'd told him I'd tell, and he'd left me. I'd told Mom, and she'd left me. I vowed never to tell Hazel. I couldn't lose her. So, I stayed quiet but got really depressed. Then I focused on my desire to become a paramedic and help people, and I moved forward. I pushed everything down. It stayed down, although I never did quite lose the depression. I'd loved my parents; I'd hated my parents; and I'd lost my parents. When I wasn't working, hanging out with friends, working out, or hitting bars in an attempt to find some woman who might actually care about me, it was like I was wandering around in a fog. Then, I met you.

"I loved you from the moment I saw you. You're so freakin' beautiful and fragile-looking, but you're also so damned brave. When I first saw your scars and found out how you'd gotten them, I was in awe of your willpower. When you shared your rape story with me, I was even more amazed. The fact that you'd survived all that trauma in addition to never being able to utter a single word was inspiring and made me want you even more. I wanted to share what had happened to me with you, but I couldn't. I was so conditioned that I was continually fighting my urge to be honest with you about my abuse. I couldn't lose you. I love you so much, and I couldn't chance your leaving me. Never. I knew if you did, that'd be it for me. But I felt torn.

"I finally broke down and told Hazel this morning. I went to work early and called her from the car and talked and cried. She *was* shocked and angry at our parents and apologized again and again for not realizing what Dad had done to me. She told me she'd never leave me, and neither would you. She urged me to tell you. Now, she's left me, too. Now, I wonder if you'll leave or if God will take you like He took Hazel today."

Kissing the top of his head, Cate moved her hands from his shoulders and typed, **I would never, ever leave you because of what your father did. God didn't take anyone away from you. Your father was a very sick man, and I'm not sorry he's dead, although I'd never wish that kind of death on anyone. Your mother should have apologized and gotten help for you and her instead of running away. And Hazel's death was a senseless accident.**

"What if I caused it? What if she was so upset by what I told her that she lost control of her rig and died?"

You've told me that she was an excellent driver. Did she ever drive before when she was really sick?

"No. When she was really sick, she stayed off the roads."

If she hadn't been able to handle her truck because of what you said, then I'm sure she would've done the same. I'm sure she was devastated, but she obviously thought she could handle her rig.

"She always said driving was her way of relaxing and thinking things through. That's why she loved it so much. She had fun, freedom, and the soothing rhythm of the road."

Her death was an accident.

"I wish I could believe it. I feel responsible."

You're not. You can't control life, Jake. What your father did was heinous on so many levels, and I want you to swear to me here and now that you're going to start talking to a professional about everything you shared with me today. I'm going to see one, too. I wasn't really committed to therapy when I was a child, but I certainly see the value in it now that I'm an adult who's going to have children of her own. We both had such dysfunctional childhoods, although they were dysfunctional in completely different ways. If we're going to be good parents, then we have to be emotionally healthy ourselves. We want our girls to grow up happy and secure, which is something neither of us had.

"At least people knew your father was a bad guy. Everyone thought mine walked on water. They loved him. I loved him. The bastard."

Chapter Twenty-two

"It's perfect. Let's do it."

Heartened, Cate texted, **You're not just saying that because you know I love it?**

Shaking his head, Jake smiled tenderly down at her and placed his palms on each side of her belly, which was now the size of a basketball. Bending low, he kissed her long and hard before straightening and adjusting the front of his pants. Cate grinned, pleased that they continued to enjoy intense and frequent sex despite Jake's heightened battle with depression, their hectic schedules, and her growing midsection.

"This house fits all of our needs, and it has character," Jake remarked. "Plus, you're five months pregnant, and the girls are getting bigger every day. I know everything's been fine, so far. I also know that if they keep growing at this rate, your C-section will be sooner rather than later. We both want everything to be ready when they arrive." Glancing around, he went on, "If we put in an offer on this house and they accept right away, we'll still have to have an inspection. Assuming all's good, we'll work with the realtors and title company in order to close on the place. It could be another month before we move in. This feels like home. Let's make it our home."

She nodded and opted to stay in the kitchen while Jake went to inform the realtor that they wanted to put in an offer on the house. The past four months had been filled with emotional highs and lows, and Cate was ready for relative stability. Her life had been so dramatically altered from the moment she'd encountered Jake Genter on the street five months earlier, and she was thankful but also tired.

Since Hazel's death and Jake's revelation about his childhood sexual abuse, he'd been meeting with a psychiatrist once a week. Cate had been seeing a psychologist every other week, and the two of them met with the same therapist once a week for couples counseling. Jake had been slowly but steadily improving, and they'd both worked diligently to make their marriage stronger after their whirlwind courtship.

Cate Speaks had also grown stronger and was reaching millions of people daily. That, in combination with the development of Limitless, the nonprofit organization she and Logan Kirkland were creating, made her feel as though she was having a truly positive impact in the world. Her collaboration with Einar Nielsen, the author who was writing her biography, provided her with an even greater impetus to work through her issues with her therapist. The entertainment lawyer was finalizing a deal with a major motion picture studio that wanted to create a film about her life's tragedies and her efforts to surmount them. She'd become the poster child for victims who persevered with quiet determination.

She and Jake enjoyed weekly visits with Logan, Beth, Mary Margaret, and Deacon. They also found themselves at Everton's visiting with him, M'Dear, and Ava, and always ate Sunday dinner with the family. Their Monday-through-Friday evening meals at The Peking Palace had been altered to Saturday nights only. Jake had discovered he liked to cook more than simply chicken and fish and prepared the rest of their nightly meals at home. Cate, who had no interest in cooking, happily ate whatever he prepared and was now within her normal weight range and not only because of her pregnancy.

There continued to be several major obstacles in their attempts to achieve balance in their lives and recovery. Following Hazel's death, Jake had unleashed his suppressed rage regarding his abuse and his mother's complicity and had vowed never to speak to her again. Cate didn't blame him at all and felt it was his right not to talk to his mother after what she *hadn't* done in order to protect him. However, the woman had begun to call Jake daily on his iPhone to make excuses. It made him furious each time he saw her number appear on the screen. Finally, Cate had suggested he change his number, and there had been no more calls. Both of them were relieved, but Cate worried that the woman might simply appear on their doorstep one day.

At least once we move in here, she can't just show up, Cate thought. *There's a guard house at the front of the development, and*

*we definitely won't put her on the list of people who can come in.
We can also keep out stray reporters, curious strangers, and those
who want my direct help.*

With the notoriety that had followed the wedding video gone
viral and their appearance on national television, the couple never
knew when one of them might be approached by someone wanting
money, an autograph, advice, or inside information. Jake, already
protective of his wife, had announced that there was no way he was
going to spend every moment apart from Cate worrying about her
and the babies. He knew that she wasn't going to remain a prisoner
in her own home, but he wanted her and their daughters to be more
secure. When he'd suggested hiring a bodyguard, Cate had put her
foot down and refused. He'd sulked for days after they'd argued
about it, but she didn't back down, despite the fact that she was
touched by the depth of his love and protectiveness.

"The realtor's making the call now," Jake announced, as he
returned to the room. "She says she thinks everything will be easy
and that we might be able to close in two weeks. That would be
great. At least we don't have to do anything to the house, except
decorate. Do you want to take one more walk-through before we
leave today?"

In response, she held out her hand and nodded. The house had
four bedrooms, three bathrooms, a large eat-in kitchen, a dining
room, a family room, a laundry room, and a home office. It was all
on one level and had been completely gutted and renovated by the
previous owner, who'd put in hardwood floors, updated appliances
and fixtures, and new cabinets. Each room had been painted a
different color, but the chosen shades were muted and tasteful. A
wooden playscape had been built in the expansive, fenced backyard.
The outside of the home was almost the same shade of pink as their
current house, and they'd taken that as a sign that it was, indeed,
meant for them.

When they stepped out onto the front porch, the realtor beamed
at them and said, "They accepted your offer. The seller was thrilled
to find out who was buying her house. She's a follower of your blog
and declared it would make the sale of the property much more
meaningful to her. That's good for us, since you went in with an
offer that was $25,000 below her asking price. Congratulations!"

"Now we just have to put the other house on the market," Jake said, squeezing Cate's hand.

"It'll sell in no time," the woman remarked. "I have no doubt you'll get what you want for that house because of who you are. People who are enamored of the two of you will be clamoring to buy your old home. It should be a breeze."

Once they'd thanked the realtor for her help and discussed what lay ahead, Jake and Cate went to Jake's new dark brown Honda SUV and agreed they were both hungry. As they drove home, Cate thought about how much happier she was now that Jake had sold his father's Mustang GT. As much as he'd loved that car and the good times he'd had working on cars with his father, his willingness to allow himself to acknowledge what the man had done to him had granted him license to release years of pent-up fury and frustration. Selling the car had been easy because of its make, model, age, and condition, and Jake seemed relieved to be rid of the reminder of the elder Jake Genter.

As for Cate, she'd gotten her driver's license and bought a white Volvo SUV. She loved driving and wished she'd learned a decade earlier. The freedom that came with it was liberating. Simply driving aimlessly around town excited her. She was constantly discovering new places to shop, eat, and explore. She couldn't wait to take her daughters on excursions, although she continued to worry about how she would cope with raising children as a mute parent. She and the psychologist were working on her self-confidence issues regarding that as part of her therapy.

"Fuck me," Jake hissed, as they pulled into their driveway. "Shit! Freakin' unbelievable!"

Cate tensed, and her heart began to race. She didn't have to ask the identity of the woman seated on the steps. She knew it had to be Jake's mother. Touching him on the arm, she shook her head.

"Don't worry, Baby," he said in a low voice. "I won't make a scene outside the house. No promises about inside, though. Take your car, and go to Beth and Logan's or Everton's. I'll come and get you once I'm done here."

I won't leave you alone with your mother.

"She's not going to shoot me, Baby."

That doesn't mean she can't hurt you. You can hurt her, too.

"We've already hurt each other, and I don't plan to make amends with Mom. Ever. I forgave her for leaving, but I can't forget, especially now that I'm being open about what happened with Dad."

I don't think you should forget. I think you should tell her what you told me and ask her to leave. Don't invite her inside. It would be a mistake.

"There are people hanging around on the street. I can guarantee you she'll cause a scene and draw unwanted attention. If we're going to hash it out, then it needs to be done in private."

Before she could stop him, Jake unbuckled his seatbelt and pushed open his door. She hastened to do the same and hurried around the SUV to stand beside him as he approached his mother. The woman stood slowly, and tension radiated from her. Cate wondered if Irene would begin to cry.

Jake's mother was tall like her son, but she had red hair and was heavyset. Hazel had definitely resembled her. Cate could tell that the woman had once been pretty, but her face was lined with years of what her daughter-in-law suspected was hard living and hard drinking. Her skin had a yellowish hue to it, and her red hair looked dry and damaged even from several yards away.

"Not out here," Jake said in a menacing tone when he and Cate got close to the steps. "We'll talk inside." Taking his wife's right hand in his left, he quietly ordered, "Move over so I can unlock the gate. Now."

Irene stepped aside and looked between her son and daughter-in-law while she waited. Cate did her best to appear impassive, but the truth was that she was slightly afraid. She didn't believe her husband or mother-in-law would inflict violence upon each other, but she did believe a vicious argument was about to ensue. She wished she could excuse herself long enough to text Everton and get him to come to the house, but she dared not leave Jake. Only she understood how emotionally fragile he still was.

Once the three of them stood in the living room, Jake ordered, "Say what you came to say then get out! I never want to talk to you again, and I sure as hell never want to see you again!"

"I came here because I love you and wanted to meet your wife," Irene answered in the graveled tones only a lifelong chain smoker could have. "She's carrying my grandchildren. I want to be a part of their lives."

"You think I'm going to let you be around our children?" Jake asked in disbelief. "No freakin' way! You wouldn't stop Dad from hurting me, but you want me to trust you with *my* kids? Are you crazy?"

"I made mistakes," she countered with obvious shame. "I didn't know for certain what your father was doing. I couldn't just go to him and ask him if he was…hurting you!"

"You expect me to believe you didn't notice anything out of the ordinary during that time when Dad was helping me in my room? You didn't think it was odd that he'd lock the door every night when we'd start the tutoring? Maybe you were just plain stupid!"

"Jake, please!" Irene pleaded. "I might have…noticed some things, but I couldn't talk to your father about them. Everyone thought he was so wonderful, but he could be a mean son-of-a-bitch! If I'd told him what I suspected, he would've hurt me!"

"You goddamned bitch!" Jake shouted hoarsely. "You stayed with the bastard because you were afraid he'd hurt *you*, even though you knew he was hurting *me*? I was a little boy, Mom! You did the laundry! You had to know! How in God's name could you stay with such a man?"

"I stayed because I *loved* him! He was my husband, Jake! He was my world, no matter what he did!" Breathing heavily, she added, "We never wanted children to begin with! We wanted it to just be the two of us forever, but accidents happen! You and Hazel are proof of that!"

Cate was aghast. Irene might not have repeatedly stabbed her son with a knife like Cate's father had stabbed his daughter, but she was certain that the woman's words were slicing through her son just the same. He was shaking with rage, and his expression vacillated between shock and revulsion. For a few seconds, Cate battled the urge to throw up. The feeling of nausea passed. Unfortunately, a feeling of pressure began in her lower belly.

Her eyes widening with fear, Cate grabbed Jake's wrist and tugged as hard as she could. He glanced back at her, looking dazed. Then *his* eyes widened.

"Baby? Baby, what's wrong?"

I don't know. There's pressure inside. I'm scared.

He nodded, drew himself up to his full height, turned toward his mother, and said, "Get out now before I call 911. If you don't, then the police will be coming as well as an ambulance."

"An ambulance? Something's wrong with –?"

"Get…the…fuck…out!"

"And if I don't? You'd have me arrested?"

"Gladly!" he snarled, lifting his wife and carrying her to the couch.

"But wouldn't that cause a scandal? You wouldn't want people knowing what happened to you, would you?"

Jake froze in mid-stride. Still holding his pregnant wife in his arms, he asked, "Are you trying to threaten me?"

"Of course not. It's just that you have a comfortable life now, and my husband and I are going through a divorce. I could use some money. If you'd just give me some to tide me over, then I promise I won't tell anyone. I know how mortified you'd be if people found out about what Dad did to you."

Cate was heartbroken for Jake, who squeezed his eyes shut for a moment before opening them again. He walked to the couch and then took a seat. Continuing to hold Cate, he slipped one arm from under her knees and placed his palm on her belly. In the same calming tone he'd used when he'd been the paramedic tending to her injuries almost a year earlier, he reassured Cate that he was going to take care of her and help to make it better. Then, he kissed her forehead, withdrew his iPhone from his pocket, and dialed Dispatch. Irene didn't move, seemingly encouraged by Jake's silence.

"Yeah, it's Jake Genter. I need an ambulance at my house. Cate's having abdominal pressure, and my mother is trying to extort money from me. Thanks. We'll wait here for the paramedics and the cops. I appreciate it. Great."

Disconnecting the call, he told Cate, "Two minutes tops, Baby. It'll be okay. I'm going to move and lay you back, all right? Try not to worry. Everything will be fine."

Jake's mother launched into an angry tirade while Jake did as he'd said. They heard sirens in the distance, and Irene began to back away. She looked as if she was ready to run, and Jake grabbed her by one arm and offered her a humorless smile.

"You didn't think I'd call your bluff, did you? Jesus, Mom. I always thought you loved me."

"I *do*! What I said before wasn't true! I was just upset!"

"Fuck that! It was obviously the truth! As if every mother who loves her kids lets their father violate them. As if every mother who loves her kids tries to blackmail them. You think there's a Mother's Day card for that? Christ! I told you I forgave you, but I take it back. You're not worth forgiving. You're not even worth thinking about. I'm pressing charges against you for what you did tonight. You can sell your story to the highest bidder and tell them everything for all I care. Tell them how you let your husband rape your child for months on end while you did nothing. *I* have nothing to be ashamed of. I wonder what people will think of you?"

Cate rubbed her belly, worried about her babies but also so proud of her husband. She hoped his brave decree hadn't been one last burst of strength before a surrender to despair. As the sirens got closer and the pressure inside her increased, she tried to calm herself. If Jake was going to fall, then there was no way she could catch him in her present state. She had to stay strong.

Chapter Twenty-three

Cate felt Jake's lips brush across hers before he asked softly, "You need anything, Baby?"

A little normalcy would be nice, she thought.

"Cate? Are you still hurting?"

Opening her eyes, she shook her head and held out a hand for her phone. Once Jake had placed it in her palm, she texted, **I still feel pressure, but there's never been any pain. I could use some water, though.**

Jake helped her to sit up slightly so that she could drink. Once he laid her back onto the bed, he put the glass on the nightstand and stretched out beside her on the mattress. Caressing her belly, he kissed her again before saying, "Mom won't be bothering us anymore. Evidently, she didn't care about exposing my secret if it tarnished my image, but she didn't want to tarnish her own. I spoke with the cops, and she wants to cut a deal. She'll never tell anyone what happened and never come near us again as long as I don't tell others what *she* didn't do when I was little and what she tried to do last night. I'm not sure what I want to do, though. I kind of want to come clean about what happened. I need to consider telling others, giving them courage like you did when you started sharing your story."

That exchange between you and your mom was awful. I feel so bad for you. How are you handling it?

"I'm not. I've been too insane with worry about you and the girls to dwell on it. It'll hit me soon, I'm sure. I'll talk to the psychiatrist about it during my session tomorrow."

Our couples counseling is tonight.

"Not this week. You heard the doctors at the hospital. Everything's okay right now, but you have to stay in bed for the next

170

week then be reevaluated, assuming you don't go into labor before that."

I can't go into labor now, she insisted. **The babies would never survive.**

"Rest and try to relax. M'Dear's coming to take care of you while I'm at work. If you feel the slightest pain or have any problem, then she'll contact your doctor and me or call 911 if it's necessary."

I'm still scared.

"I know, but I think you'll be fine. That was a pretty terrible argument, and I can understand why you got so stressed. I should've insisted you leave like I suggested before we got out of the SUV."

You can't order me around.

"Tell me about it," he said with a wry smile. "You'll be the death of me, Baby."

I'd rather kill you with pleasure than by scaring you about the babies and me.

"Great minds think alike, but I'm thinking sex is over for us until the girls are here. Hell, you might be on bed rest until they come because of this. I'm sorry."

She drew her fingers along his collarbone before typing, **It's not your fault. It's hers.**

"I know. I'd give anything to have Hazel back, but I'm glad she never had to find out how Mom really was and that our parents never really wanted us. Jesus! My father raped me, and my mother knew and kept quiet about it. That makes them both monsters in my eyes."

Mine, too. My poor Jake.

Sighing, he said, "My poor Cate. We're a pretty screwed-up pair, aren't we? Maybe somehow we innately knew and that's why we were instantly drawn to one another. I'm really glad you pushed us both into going to counseling. God knows we need it. Besides, I want our girls to have the kinds of lives we never did. I wish I could protect them from the world."

The world didn't do as much to hurt us as our own parents did. It makes me sad. Rosa and Francesca are going to be so blessed because we're not going to perpetuate the badness of our fathers and mothers. We're going to love and care for them. We're going to give them nice, wholesome childhoods.

"Damn straight."

Jake?

"Hm?"

Do you regret marrying me?

"Regret it? Why would I ever do that? I love you, Baby. You're the best thing that ever happened to me."

With the blog, the book, the TV documentary, and this movie deal we're working on, we'll never be anonymous. What if you decide you don't want to share what your father did, and someone finds out because of all the attention focused on us? What would you do then?

"What you've done for as long as I've known you. I'd tell the truth about it and hope it helps someone else who's been through the same thing. I meant what I told Mom. I'm not afraid of people knowing what Dad did to me. My only real fear is that I'll lose you and our daughters."

Her eyelids growing heavy once more, Cate nodded and texted, **I love you so much, Jake.**

"Yeah, Baby. I love you so much, too. You rest. I'm counting on everything being okay."

For the following seven days, Cate stayed in bed and was pampered by Jake and M'Dear. Although she insisted on blogging every day, she spent the rest of her time sleeping, reading, getting up to shower and eat, and then going back to bed to sleep and read more. With each day that passed, the feeling of pressure inside her belly receded. By the time she went to the specialist for her follow-up exam, she felt fine.

"You're doing very well," the man told Cate and Jake after he'd examined her and performed an ultrasound. "The girls are looking good and continuing to grow. However, I do want you to take it easy. You can resume most normal activities, but avoid lifting, exercise, and sexual intercourse. I may lift those restrictions as the weeks pass, but I'd rather err on the side of caution for now."

"Any idea about when Cate might need the C-section?" asked Jake.

"If she and the babies continue to do well, she may actually get close to full-term."

But?

"But your body may not be able to handle the strain. I'd be happy if we could get the fetuses past twenty-eight weeks."

Twenty-eight weeks! That's still way too early! Isn't a normal, full-term pregnancy between thirty-nine and forty weeks?

"I have to think about the welfare of the mother as well as the babies. If your body can't support you and them without compromising your kidneys or heart, then you'd be putting yourself at risk and your babies could die in utero. Better to take them early and treat them outside the womb and save your life in the process." Waving one hand dismissively, he said, "One day at a time. One week at a time. Follow my orders, and call me if there are any new problems or you have a recurrence of the feeling of pressure. Put your feet up as often as possible, and try to stay calm. I'll see you next week."

As Jake drove them home, Cate stared out of the window and thought, *Seven more weeks at the least. Nineteen more weeks at most. I can do this. I'll do whatever it takes to give the girls more time. But what about Jake? He's already worried about losing me. What is he thinking after what the doctor said about the babies putting a strain on my body and possibly killing me? And what about the fact that we can't have sex?*

"Stop worrying about me needing sex," Jake said suddenly. "You need it, too. But we both know we're not going to do anything that will put the girls' lives in danger. We can make it for a few months without it."

How did you know what I was thinking?

"Because I'm your husband, and we both like intense sex. Once the babies are born and you're fully recovered, then the sex will be explosive again. Until then, we can wait."

Are you scared about what the doctor said?

"Which part?"

You know which part.

"Of course, but I can't do a damn thing about it. Just promise me you'll do what he said and not fight him if he tells you it's time for a C-section, no matter when that is. We can always have more babies, but I can never have another you."

173

You and I both know we won't be having any more babies. I know how you think. I'm sure you've already researched vasectomies.

"I'm a paramedic. I didn't have to do much research."

I wanted us to have more children, she texted disconsolately.

"I know, but we shouldn't."

If…if the girls don't make it, then I plan to try again, though.

"The girls *will* make it, but you're never getting pregnant again," he declared with certainty. "That's all there is to it."

But Jake –

"But Jake nothing! I will *not* lose you, Cate! I don't' care how much freakin' therapy I have, that'll always be my greatest fear. Accept it and deal with it."

Accept and deal with what you WON'T accept and deal with?

"Yeah. They always say women are stronger than men. I say bullshit, that men and women have different strengths and weaknesses but that they all even out in the final analysis. I'm a strong man who lives to love and protect you, but that also makes my fear of losing you my greatest weakness."

All right, Mr. Know-It-All. What's my greatest strength and my greatest weakness?

"Your tenacity is your greatest strength, and your concern about returning to your former isolation is your greatest weakness. That makes losing me *your* greatest weakness since I'm the one who brought you out of your self-imposed exile. I remind you to stay connected. You need me to complete you as much as I need you to complete me. The only difference is that you'd go on if I died. I'm not sure I could go on if I lost you and the girls. I wouldn't see the point. My love for you *is* my sole reason for being."

You have so many reasons for being! she texted, both pained and frustrated by his words. **Please, don't ever make me think about you killing yourself. It's enough that I heard my entire family die. If I die, then I can't imagine you taking your own life. It would kill me!**

"You'd already be dead, Baby. I'd just be joining you."

Becoming more and more tense as they spoke, Cate rested her hands on the swell of her stomach and tried not to panic. Then, she lifted her phone and typed, **We can't talk about this anymore. It's stressing me out, and I'm scared it'll cause more problems for the babies. Promise me you'll talk to the psychiatrist about this again. Please.**

"I promise, Baby. I was trying to be honest, but I don't want to dump on you and make you worry. I won't talk about it anymore unless it's with the therapist. I promise."

Thank you. Attempting to relax, she texted, **Depending on when the babies come, M'Dear says she'll help me once you're not on paternity leave anymore. Ava's going to help, too. She can't wait to take care of the babies. She says she wants a lot of children herself one day when she gets married.**

"Really? Jesus, she's seventeen now. Just think, Everton could be a grandfather in the next few years, depending on what happens. If Ava meets and marries a man at college, she might start having babies. Grandpa Everton. I'll start calling him Gramps."

Don't tell him what I said. I don't know if Ava's told him. I know he worries about HER having kids and doesn't want her to be sexually active, yet. She's still so young. It may be a long time before she marries and has children.

"Okay. I won't say a word. Will you be able to keep quiet?"

Ha, ha.

Jake laughed, and Cate grinned. Relieved that he wasn't focusing on the negative possibilities for the time being, she rested her left hand on his right thigh and gave it a squeeze. When he reminded her that they couldn't have sex, she bit her lip and fought the urge to giggle.

"What?" he prompted.

I can't have sex. You can.

"What are you –?"

I can't take you in me in the traditional sense and can't do anything strenuous, but I can take you in my hands and my mouth.

"I'm not going to let you get me off when I can't reciprocate."

We'll see about that….

During the night, Cate woke, visited the bathroom, got herself a glass of water, and then returned to the master bedroom. She was extremely pleased that she'd done it all without turning on a single light. For someone who had spent years living in fear of the dark, she was no longer afraid. True, she still kept a nightlight on in every room, but it was more for convenience sake rather than as a result of anxiety.

Cate climbed back into bed and didn't hesitate to reach for the front of Jake's pajama bottoms. He was hard and murmured her name in his sleep as she lightly ran her hand over his concealed erection. Smiling, she undid the string on his waistband.

"Baby, what –" he began then jerked and groaned, "Christ, Cate!" when she took him in her mouth. Putting his hands on her shoulders, he eased her gently but firmly back until she was forced to separate from him. She sighed with disappointment, as Jake switched on the light.

Cate grinned at Jake. His brown hair was mussed from sleep, and his cock stood at attention when he knelt in front of her. She playfully reached for it, but he grabbed her wrist. His grip wasn't tight, but it did halt her efforts. She pouted.

"Don't give me that look," he said with a hint of exasperation in his voice. "Baby, I meant what I said earlier. No sex means no sex for either of us. You're supposed to be taking it easy. The position you were in and what you were about to do counts as exercise in my book, and you're not supposed to exercise, remember? Plus, I refuse to let you pleasure me when I can't pleasure you at the same time." When Cate tried to pull her wrist from his grasp, he wouldn't let go and continued, "I want you more than anything, but I'm not going to chance causing harm to you or the girls. Got it?"

He allowed Cate to disengage from him so that she could text a response. When she did, he burst out laughing and put his muscular arms around her, pulling her into his lap. When she squirmed provocatively, he cried, "You are so not playing fair."

All's fair in love and war. This is both.

"You're right, so I'm ignoring your text. I know you want me in you *now*, but it's not going to happen."

But –

"If we have sex, you could go into labor tonight," he said seriously. "It could happen. I know that's not what you want. Maybe we can use this time to practice those intimacy skills the psychologist suggested."

We've done them before, she pointed out.

"And we always end up having sex, which we're *not* supposed to do during those exercises."

You just reminded me that I'm not supposed to exercise.

Jake chuckled and said, "We'll be exercising restraint while staying connected."

But we can't stay connected. We can't even GET connected!

"Ha, ha. When the doctor okays you for sex again, then we can make love every spare moment we have."

Promise?

"I'll pinky swear you."

Pinky swear? My big, hunky, hard husband is going to pinky swear?

"Hey, real men aren't afraid to pinky swear!"

Prove it, Tough Guy!

Jake extended his right pinky finger, and Cate linked hers with it. As they slowly moved their linked fingers back and forth, Cate ached to take Jake between her legs. He was still rock hard, and she knew there was no place he'd rather be. Their fingers still entwined, Cate snuggled against Jake and worked on practicing her non-sexual intimacy skills. Jake shifted and settled them both back onto the mattress but never let her go. She drifted to sleep in his arms and wondered how they were going to survive being celibate together.

Chapter Twenty-four

"I think that's the last form for this round," Logan said before sitting back in his office chair. "At least our application for the nonprofit organization status is moving forward without many issues."

I'm relieved that it hasn't been as challenging as I'd anticipated, Cate texted. **Everything has fallen into place, lately.**

After Logan listened to the text using Siri, he agreed and asked, "Are we still on for the big barbecue at your house this weekend?" After she'd confirmed that they were, he added, "Thanks for inviting our parents, too. They both love spending time with you and Jake, and they enjoyed it when we all went over to Everton's house for dinner last month. They're looking forward to seeing Everton, M'Dear, and Ava again."

Beth's mother is such a nice woman, and your father is a sweetheart.

He paused, listened, and then thanked her before asking, "Did Beth text you that Deacon started walking last night?"

No, but she told me this morning when I arrived at the store before you and I started working on this. I can't wait to see him. I bet he looks so cute when he walks!

"I bet he does," Logan responded, and Cate was surprised by how sad he sounded.

You want to see him walk.

"Of course, but that will never happen. I've been blind since birth and have no idea what it's *like* to see. I can't miss what I never had, but I can wish I'd had it. Once in a while, I let myself imagine what it would be like to see for a day. People tell me how beautiful my wife is and how adorable my children look. They talk about colors, the beauty of plants and animals, and things like the way the sun looks when it hits the waves as it sets when we're at the beach.

They tell me I bear a striking resemblance to my father. A part of me would like to experience all of that in a visual way. Having sight would make my life easier. Since I've never known any different, I just live my life the way I always have – independent, determined, and thankful for the great things I've been given and earned."

I totally understand.

"I know you do. Only someone else with significant challenges could truly get it."

You're such a wonderful father, despite your physical challenges. What if I suck at being a mother because of mine?

"Impossible. You're going to be an amazing mom. Actually, you already are."

Cate smiled and typed her thanks and then her apologies. She needed to go home and read more of the final draft of her biography. What she had read was alternately intriguing and horrifying. She'd joked with Jake that she wondered how the book would end.

Rising awkwardly from her chair, Cate texted Logan a parting wish that he enjoy the rest of his Friday and declared it was time for her to waddle to her car, which was parked down the street. He laughed and said, "Waddle all you want. You've earned it. Beth told me your specialist is amazed that you've made it to thirty-five weeks."

Me, too. My belly's as big as a beach ball, but I'm fine with that. The girls are doing great. The doctor thinks I might be able to go another two weeks before we do the C-section. I see him again on Monday. He may change his mind.

"At least Rosa and Francesca should be well-developed and a good size at this point. That'll be a huge plus. Who's going to help you with them until you recover from surgery?"

Jake will be taking paternity leave for twelve weeks. M'Dear will help after that if need be. She swears she wants to take the time off from her practice and play grandma to the babies. I'm relieved and pleased for me and the girls. Ava's going to help out since it's summer and she's not in school.

"Sounds like a great plan. Of course, we'll be there for you guys, too. You know if you need help you can always call me and Beth."

We know, but you have your business to run and two small children of your own. We will call if we need you, though.

Thanks for being such a good friend, Logan. I'm so glad I literally ran into you over a year ago.

"Me, too. See you Sunday."

Very funny.

Cate waved goodbye to Beth, who was helping a customer, as she waddled out of Sight Unseen and into the June heat. She hadn't been kidding about her "beach ball" belly. She'd retained her sparrow-like frame, so the twins had nowhere to go but forward. She was amazed she continued to be able to get up on her own with the added weight in the front and the way it altered her balance. By the end of each day, her back hurt terribly. She suspected her C-section would be the following week. Although the prospect made her nervous, she sensed that her body wouldn't be able to withstand the strain of pregnancy much longer.

Cate walked two blocks down the street toward where she'd parked. She glanced at her watch. It was 9:14 a.m. Foot traffic on the sidewalks was light in downtown Sarasota at this time of day, and she paused to look up at the clear blue sky while waiting for the light to change so that she could cross the street. For once, there weren't many cars on the road, and she could hear birds chirping. She smiled as two of them hopped around on a tree branch above her Volvo.

"Hello, Cate."

Confused, Cate turned and looked up into the face of a dark-haired, muscular, middle-aged man she didn't recognize. She moved to withdraw one of the cards she carried that stated she was mute. The stranger casually reached for her wrist, took it in his hand, and squeezed hard. She winced.

"You are Yana Tarasenko's former friend," he said menacingly, his English heavily laced with a Ukrainian accent. "We have come for you."

Cate experienced instant panic. She would have to be dense not to realize the stranger was part of the Ukrainian Mob. She also knew that she couldn't speak or scream for help. She was thirty-five weeks pregnant with twins and had no chance of fighting the man or running away.

"Time for us to go," the man announced.

Her heart pounding with dread, she expected him to drag her toward him. Instead, a vehicle pulled up to the curb behind her, a door opened, and strong arms hauled her inside. The stranger smiled wickedly as he slammed the door. Then, he jogged around and took the front passenger seat. Knowing she had to get out as quickly as she could, Cate reached for the door handle closest to her fingers, but the man who had pulled her in quickly stopped her by hitting her on the side of the head with the butt of a gun. She heard a *crack!* and saw stars before losing consciousness.

She woke feeling disoriented and sick. As she gradually returned to full awareness, Cate realized she was lying on her back on the ground in the country somewhere. The stranger who had spoken to her and was obviously the leader of this operation stood over her with a gun aimed at her belly.

"I know you cannot speak," he said coldly. "Still, I am sure you wish to ask me why we are doing this. You are wondering if Yana has become deranged and done something to lead us to you. The answer is yes and no. The bitch is dead herself. Her death had nothing to do with you. She had become a liability over the years." When Cate's eyes widened, he said, "Yes, she was working for us. I made an…arrangement with her after she approached me about killing her ex-husband. I took care of that in exchange for her loyalty. She did feed us much information on you before your friendship ended."

Swallowing the bile rising in her throat and blinking back tears at Yana's betrayal, Cate mouthed the words "Then, why?" and prayed for a miracle. If no one came to rescue her, she and the girls were going to die. She couldn't let that happen. She knew that it would bring about Jake's death, too.

"Your father was a calculating son-of-a-bitch," the man told her. "His operation was vast, and he made quite a lot of money trafficking drugs. But then you know that by now, I am sure. What you do not know is that he had many of our people killed during his rise to power. We swore to avenge them by having him and his family murdered, but then he decided to take care of that himself. You survived and were only a child. You posed no real threat to us, so we decided to allow you to live. We cannot do that any longer. All of the publicity surrounding your life has led to much investigation and speculation by too many outside eyes. We must stop this before it goes any further. If we kill you and those who would expose us, then all will return to normal eventually."

Frowning, he said, "I have never killed a pregnant woman before and have no wish to do so now. But I have no choice. I will make it quick."

Tears streamed down Cate's face, but she glared at the man and mouthed the word *no* with conviction. He glared back at her then shouted something in Ukrainian to the two other men who stood behind him. They immediately turned, hurried back to their vehicle, and then drove away. The stranger approached Cate and crouched beside her, allowing the muzzle of his gun to point toward the ground as he did so.

Glancing at her belly, he said, "I am truly sorry. You do not deserve this, but it must be done. I promise you will not suffer. I swear it in my heart."

The man placed the gun across his chest as if to emphasize his words. Then, he bent forward and kissed Cate on the forehead as if she were a child he was tucking into bed for the night. Repulsed by his actions but seizing the opportunity, Cate raised her hands and shoved the stranger away with as much strength as she could muster. He simultaneously yelped, stumbled back, and reflexively pulled the trigger of his gun. Cate watched in horror as he literally – albeit accidentally – blew his brains out.

Don't think about it, she told herself. *Don't think about him or how what I just saw is what Daddy did after he stabbed us. Surely, this man is supposed to rendezvous with those other goons or someone else soon. If he doesn't show, they'll come back here and finish what he didn't. I have to find a way out. I can fall apart later.*

Scanning the scrub surrounding her, Cate was startled to see her purse several yards away. She supposed she shouldn't have been surprised. The murderers would have wanted her found as a statement to other mobsters and to the world. Once people had figured out she was missing, her phone would have been tracked and her body located. She shivered, even though she was unbearably hot after lying in the midday sun for an indeterminate amount of time.

Rolling onto her left side, Cate struggled to rise. She hoped her would-be killers hadn't taken her too far out of town and that help could come soon. Her head hurt, and she suspected she was slightly dehydrated. She made it to her feet but battled dizziness as she staggered toward her purse. Once she reached it, she managed to pick it up and stumble to one of the few trees in the area. She'd just reached the trunk when pain shot through her lower belly. Her purse slipped from her hand, and she fell to her knees, placing one palm against the tree trunk and putting the other on the underside of her midsection.

Something is wrong, she thought. *Something is wrong with the girls. I don't think that was a contraction. What if the men threw me to the ground before I woke up? God, if I am in labor and no one finds me, then the girls and I will die for sure. I'm not big enough to deliver them. Even if I were able to have them naturally, I can't imagine giving birth out here in the middle of nowhere by myself. Oh, God. God, please let my phone get a signal wherever I am. Please, don't let me and my girls die. I've suffered enough, haven't I?*

Repositioning herself so that she sat with her back against the tree trunk, Cate dug out her phone and looked at the battery level. She was grateful it was at eighty-five percent, but she knew it might drain quickly, depending on the remoteness of her location. She wanted to use the app that would tell her where she was but didn't want to drain the battery any more than necessary.

She checked the time on the phone. There was a chance that Jake might be on his lunch break, so she decided to text him first before texting 911. If he didn't text back right away, then she'd immediately contact the authorities.

Help me, Baby. Help us.

Almost instantly, she received a text from Jake that read, **Baby, what's wrong? Where are you?**

I'm in the middle of nowhere somewhere. I was taken and got knocked out. I woke up here, but I don't know where here is. There's nothing around. Two of the men are gone but might come back anytime, and the one who was going to kill me is dead. I –

The intense pain ripped through her again, and she screamed silently and wondered what was happening inside her belly. The babies seemed to shift in position, and Cate experienced enormous pressure deep within. There were still no contractions, and her water didn't break. There was no bleeding. She tried to push past the pain in order to text, but it was too great. She was faintly aware that her phone was receiving one text after another.

Knowing that she had no choice, Cate forced herself to look at the phone. Jake had texted questions asking about her physical condition and pleading for her to respond to his texts so that he'd know she was okay.

Not okay, she typed, finding it almost impossible in her present state. **Pain. Lots of pressure. No bleeding or contractions. Concussion? Find me, Baby. Help me. Please. Scared. Need you. Love you. Think the girls are dying. Save them. Love you. Not going to text anymore unless something changes to save battery. Love you, Jake.**

I'm coming, Cate. Forever, Baby. Hold on.

She placed the phone beside her and "talked" to her daughters, telling them to hold on, that their father was coming to save them, and that she loved them. She refused to look at the time and see how long it had been since she and Jake had last communicated. She hoped it hadn't been as long as it felt. Eventually, she heard sirens in the distance.

What if they're not for me? What if they're on their way to another emergency and pass me by? I should get up and go toward the road. I should...I should....

The sirens got closer. They were obviously coming for her. She closed her eyes and prayed that the girls were still alive and would stay that way until they could be delivered at a hospital via C-section.

"Cate!" Jake screamed, but his voice echoed from somewhere far away. "Baby, we're here!"

"Cate, throw a rock or something so we can find you!" cried Everton. "Come on, Girl! Help us out so we can help you!"

She glanced around but saw nothing she was currently strong enough to throw so that they could see it. Instead, she lifted her phone in trembling hands and texted, **Under a tree. Hear you.**

Jake, Everton, policemen, and paramedics came into view. Naturally, Jake and Everton wore their paramedic uniforms but were unencumbered by medical paraphernalia and ran toward her at top speed. They skidded to a halt and dropped to their knees, one on either side of her.

"Cate, look at me! *Cate!* Jesus, Baby! I love you. Don't leave me, Baby! I –"

And that was when Cate lost consciousness.

Chapter Twenty-five

Cate woke in a hospital with one hand resting on her belly and instantly knew that she was no longer pregnant. Her stomach was only slightly rounded, and she hurt inside and out. She was certainly medicated, but the narcotics didn't eliminate all of the pain. The pain didn't matter to her at that moment.

The girls, she thought desperately. *They took the girls, but were my babies still alive when they were delivered? Are they okay?* Beginning to cry, she silently yelled, *Somebody help me! Jake! Jake!*

"Baby, no!" Jake said from beside her, as he took her hand. "You need to stay still. Please, Cate. Listen to me. Everything will be all right. Trust me."

She looked up at her husband, who stood next to her bed still wearing his paramedic uniform. He radiated anxiety, exhaustion, and sadness. There was stubble on his face, and she wondered how long she'd been unconscious. She looked pleadingly at him. He would know what she wanted to ask.

"The girls are fine," he said quickly. "Promise me you'll lie still, and I'll explain." When she stilled and nodded, he leaned forward, kissed her, and murmured, "That's good, Baby. It's all going to be good."

She frowned at his words. She could sense his underlying uneasiness and wondered whether or not she was actually going to die. Perhaps he didn't want to admit that to her or to himself. She reached up to touch his jaw with her free hand, and he turned and kissed her fingers before beginning his explanation.

"After you lost consciousness, we evaluated you and then got you to the ambulance. Those bastards had taken you to a remote location about thirty minutes south of Sarasota. The cops were escorting us, but we could only go so fast. A couple minutes away from Sarasota Memorial, you suffered placental abruption and started to bleed heavily. We were so goddamned close to the hospital, but I was worried you'd bleed to death before we got there and that the girls wouldn't make it even if you lived." He swallowed hard and cleared his throat before continuing, "Of course, we were in constant contact with the hospital throughout the ride. Your specialist was waiting in the O.R. by the time we got you there. I kind of lost it when they told me I couldn't go in with you, and Everton and the other paramedics had to restrain me. God knows what I said to them. I was scared and pissed, but I'm glad they did hold me back. I shouldn't have been in the operating room seeing you like that, especially not as emotional as I was. The girls were out within a few minutes, but the doctor kept you in there for a long time. He was finally able to get the bleeding under control."

"Rosa and Francesca?" Cate mouthed distinctly.

"Weren't breathing when they were delivered but were resuscitated almost immediately. It doesn't look like they went without oxygen for long, and the neonatologists say that newborns brains can repair themselves a lot better than any others that have been similarly affected. We'll have to wait and see, but everyone thinks they'll be perfectly normal."

Cate held out her free hand in the familiar gesture that meant, "Please give me my phone so that I can talk."

Sighing, Jake dug in his pocket and pulled out his own phone. After releasing the hand he'd been holding, he waited patiently while she typed.

If I'm alive and the girls should be fine, then why do you look so sad? What aren't you telling me?

Rubbing his face with one hand, Jake admitted, "I named the first baby who was delivered Rosa, since that was the name you picked when we thought we were just having one baby. I named the second twin Francesca."

That's perfect, Jake. I'm fine with that. But it's not what you're worried about. What's wrong?

"I told you I wanted our daughters to be just like you, and they are. They're gorgeous identical twins and are delicate just like their mother. I couldn't be more thrilled, especially since they're both healthy."

Jake –

"They can't cry, Baby," he said quietly. "Just like you."

What on earth are you talking about? She texted in confusion. **Of course they can cry.**

"You couldn't when you were born."

But I was born without a voice box and – Realization dawning, Cate began to shake and typed, **Both of them? Both of the girls have no voice box?** Reflecting on how hard it had been to live her life without the ability to speak, she allowed the tears to fall as she texted, **But I didn't want them to have to live like me! I didn't want them to have the burden of existing in silence!**

"I know. I'm sorry, Baby. The specialists they called in are doing tests, but they said it looks like a genetic mutation. They say they've never seen this before and really don't have a clue as to what allowed for the girls to develop without voice boxes like their mother. Like I said, the babies are identical twins. One of them might not have inherited the condition if they'd been fraternal twins. Hell, I don't know. I also don't care. I love you and them and don't give a rat's ass whether any of you can speak. We'll use sign language with them from the beginning, get them occupational therapy like you had when you were little, and use the technology you use today that wasn't available when you were a kid to help them communicate. It'll be easier for them to grow up mute than it was for you."

Cate knew that what he was saying was true, but she also knew her girls would carry an unwanted challenge with them for as long as they lived. Also, if the condition she'd unwittingly passed along to them had some genetic link, they might choose never to have children in case the result was the same. She wondered whether they would resent her and blame her for their inability to speak.

They'll hate me for making them mute, she typed.

Jake offered her reassuring words and wiped at her cheeks with one tissue after another. Finally, between the exhaustion, medication, and her weakened physical state, Cate was pulled back into unconsciousness. When she woke, Jake was not in the room. Instead, Logan sat beside the bed listening to a book using his iPhone. When she shifted slightly, he stopped reading and pulled her phone from one pocket of his jeans.

"Hey, Cate. Jake charged your iPhone. Here you go." When she didn't take the phone from his hand, he moved it closer to her and said, "Please, take it. We need to talk, and this is the only way you and I can do that."

Reluctantly, she accepted the phone and forced herself to type, **Thank you for being here. It's comforting to have one of my best friends with me right now.**

Cate meant every word, but she didn't feel like communicating with anyone just then. She waited while Logan listened to her text then texted, **Where is Jake?**

"With your girls. They're really cute. You know Beth and I had decided two kids were enough for us, but she's trying to get me to reconsider now that she's seen your girls. I'm not sure if I'll change my mind, but I certainly won't protest if she wants to try to get me to reconsider by seducing me later."

Thanks for trying to make me feel better, but it's not working. I haven't even seen my girls, but I'm already afraid they're going to hate me.

"Hate you for what?"

Causing them to be mute like me.

He paused after listening to the text then asked, "If you'd known early on, would you have aborted them?"

What? No. It's irrelevant now. It's my fault.

"It's your fault you inherited a genetic defect that caused you to be mute and unintentionally passed it on to your daughters? I don't think so. Neither will they. They're going to love you."

How would you know?

"Because I don't hate my mother or my father, and they certainly caused the problems that led to my blindness."

Cate inhaled sharply and licked her dry lips. She had never asked Logan or Beth what had led to Logan's lack of vision and had assumed it was due to a birth injury or a genetic defect. She knew nothing of his mother other than the fact that the woman was dead. His father was kind, highly intelligent, charismatic, and loving.

"My parents had two things in common when they met: drugs and sex. I'll spare you the details for now. Let's just say they were mixed up and knew when they found out she was pregnant that they should get clean. They tried and failed miserably. When she started having issues with the pregnancy early on, she was told not to have sex. They couldn't seem to stop doing that either. I was born way too early and was given too much oxygen in the incubator at the rural hospital where I was delivered. I was lucky that blindness was my only long-term physical challenge. As small as I was, I should have died or had severe developmental delays, cerebral palsy, and the like. I'll tell you everything another time, but I'll give you the abbreviated version of how things went down. I was raised in a wonderful orphanage by loving nuns. Even once I found out the truth about my parents and my birth, I didn't hate them or blame them. I pitied my mother and felt bad for both her and my father because they were severely screwed up at the time they created me. They didn't mean to harm me. They were just in a very bad way at that point in their lives. What happened drove my mother deeper into drugs and prostitution, and she had my brother way too early a year after I was born. She overdosed the day after, and he joined me at the orphanage. He's blind for the same reason I am but also has developmental and emotional issues." Removing his black glasses and rubbing at his eyes, Logan muttered, "At least my father got clean, primarily because he thought I'd died and felt such overwhelming guilt. He found me a few years ago, and I'm so grateful for that. We have a great relationship, as you can surely tell. I guess we'll never know which of my mother's Johns was my brother's father. It's really tragic. The whole story is really tragic." Shaking his head, Logan said, "So, if I don't blame my mother and father for *their* complicity in causing me to end up blind, then how could your girls hate you for conceiving them out of love and putting your own health at risk in order to make sure they survived?" When she didn't text a response, Logan went on, "Let's say I go home with Beth and tonight we start another baby. What if, by some freak chance, that baby is born...I don't know....um...severely ADHD." Shrugging, he admitted, "I'm kind of winging it here. Anyway, what if our baby is ADHD to the extreme? Do you think he would hate Beth for giving him life but with an added challenge that she struggled with, especially during her childhood? I'm sure Beth would probably feel some guilt, just like you are. But she'd know, just like you do, that she certainly didn't intentionally pass on that challenge. We'd love that child with all our hearts, just like we love Mary Margaret and Deacon. He'd have extra struggles, but we'd all love one another." Returning his glasses to his face, Logan said, "Rosa and Francesca are alive because of you and Jake. They'll be loved completely by you and Jake. It's not going to be like what you went through when you were growing up. You'll have a happy home, just like I have a happy one with my wife and children. Everything will be okay."

I'm still unsure.

"Time will prove me right," he said firmly. "No doubt everyone in the world will agree."

Everyone in the world?

"Your story is all over TV, newspapers, and the Internet. As if it wasn't affecting enough before yesterday, it's everywhere now that you were kidnapped, somehow shot your Mob attacker, and barely survived the emergency delivery of your twins. No one even knows about their muteness, yet. It'll be up to you to address that in your blog or in an interview. As for the rest, it's garnered international attention. The Feds have rounded up a bunch of mobsters, and a lot of arrests have been made. They're working on eliminating any threats to you, your family, the author writing your life story, your friends, and business associates. The publicity surrounding all of it should actually help to keep all of us safe. What a twist of fate."

Cate supposed she should have considered how newsworthy her kidnapping and survival would be, but she'd had more important things to consider. The author would most definitely be adding to the end of the biography he'd written, and it and the movie about her life would certainly be even more dramatic than anticipated. She prayed that recent events would end the unwanted drama for her and Jake.

I need to see my girls, she texted. **I know they won't let me up. Do you think they'd bring them to me?**

"I'll go and tell Jake. Rosa and Francesca both weigh over five pounds and aren't on oxygen, so I think the staff will probably be all right with rolling them in for a while. You need to see your daughters. Once you do, all of this worrying will stop. I guarantee it."

Cate remained unconvinced, as Logan left the room in order to tell Jake that she was awake and wanted to see her babies. When Jake entered, grinning, Cate couldn't help but grin back. When she raised an eyebrow at him, he explained that he'd gotten to hold their daughters for the first time while Logan had been sitting with her.

"They're so amazingly beautiful," he said. "Just like you."

Cate was about to text that she was certain she looked anything but beautiful in her current state when they heard people approaching her door. Her heart rate increased, as two bassinets were wheeled into the room. Soon, Cate was cradling Rosa in her arms, as tears of joy slid down her cheeks. The tears continued when Jake lifted Rosa and Francesca took her place. Cate longed to tell everyone in the room how much she loved her babies and how perfect they were.

I'll tell everyone soon enough, she thought. *I don't have to be able to talk in order to be heard. I have to be an example for my daughters in a very practical way. They're going to look to me in order to gauge how they should deal with their muteness. They need to know that they, too, can always be heard. They need to know their lack of speech doesn't mean they lack worth.*

Epilogue

"Cate Genter? Oh, my God! I'm Brooklyn Quinn. I'm a senior at Manatee High and want to go on to college so that I can work to help people who have disabilities. You gave me the courage to believe in myself."

Cate, who'd been about to take another bite of her stir-fry vegetables with rice, lowered her fork and lifted her iPhone to text a "thank-you" to the brown-haired, brown-eyed teenager. From beside Cate, three-year-old Rosa signed her name and told the girl that her Mommy was the best in the world, which Jake, who was holding Francesca in his lap, translated.

"She's amazing," Brooklyn agreed. "You and your sister look just like her! I wish my mom was like her." Looking at Jake, she added, "You're really lucky."

"Tell me about it," Jake said with a wide grin. Sobering, he went on, "Sorry your mom's not great. Mine isn't either, but I found a wonderful partner in Cate and held on for dear life. If you find someone great when you get older, don't let him go."

"I won't," Brooklyn said seriously. "I read about you, too." Glancing at the twins, she paused, choosing her next words carefully. "What happened to you was awful, and it took a lot of guts for you to be open about it. You're an inspiration yourself."

It seems like a lot of good has come out of our bad, Cate typed. **Do good things, okay?**

"You two have kept me going through some rough times. I've been a follower of *Cate Speaks* for two years, and I went back and read all the previous blogs. I've set Google alerts for *Cate Speaks* and your names. When I feel like giving up, I watch the movie about your life or read *Better Left Unsaid*. What a great biography, Mrs. Genter! It makes me believe I can overcome my own problems. I want to help people, just like the two of you do."

Francesca signed that she was hungry, and Jake snickered and said, "This little princess doesn't like to feed herself." He laughed when she signed again and explained to the girl, "She says princesses always get their way."

"Not if they're going to grow up to be queens," Brooklyn remarked.

Cate and Jake exchanged glances at the young woman's wise words, and Francesca picked up a spoon and ate a mouthful of rice.

"I have to go," the teenager said. "Sorry to interrupt your dinner. It was great to meet you. Thanks again!"

When she turned to leave, Cate rose and touched her on one arm. Brooklyn turned and cocked her head. Cate looked back to Jake, who nodded his agreement. She withdrew one of her cards and handed it to the girl. It was not one of the cards that declared that she was mute. It was a business card.

If you're interested in volunteering at Limitless, then email me, she texted. **We can always use dedicated volunteers.**

Brooklyn's eyes widened, and she asked, "Are you kidding me? Really? I could work at the nonprofit you and Mr. Kirkland formed? For real?"

As a volunteer for now. If you finish school and things work out well with the volunteering, then who knows? You might end up with a job when you get out of college.

The young woman beamed at her, but Cate could tell she was tearing up. She wondered what the girl's story was and knew she'd probably find out soon. Cate smiled at Brooklyn, who wiped at the corners of her eyes.

"Thank you," she said softly. "You can't imagine how much this means to me."

You're very welcome.

Cate watched young Brooklyn leave The Peking Palace. She hoped the teenager would email her and that she, Jake, Logan, and the others involved in Limitless could continue to make a difference in the girl's life. She wished someone could have made a difference in hers when she'd been younger.

"She'll email," Jake said from behind her. "Come on, Baby. Your food's getting cold."

They finished their meal and offered their goodbyes to the Asian family as they left the restaurant. Then, they walked through the

September evening heat to Logan and Beth's condo and spent two hours visiting with the couple while six-year-old Mary Margaret, four-year-old Deacon, and Rosa and Francesca played. When the Genter girls began to rub tiredly at their eyes, Jake and Cate announced that it was time to go home. Each of the children protested, but their parents reminded them that they'd all be gathering the following day at Jake and Cate's for a backyard picnic and playtime. Once they were reminded that Everton, M'Dear, and Ava would also be present, they ceased their protests and asked if they could go to bed right away so that tomorrow could come sooner.

Later, when Rosa and Francesca were asleep, Cate headed for the tub while Jake worked on Limitless business. After the twins' births, Jake had volunteered to take a variety of business courses and offered to run the nonprofit that Cate and Logan had formed. He'd quit his job as a paramedic two years earlier and was relieved to find that he loved the career change. Thankfully, he was extremely good at his "new" job, and this had allowed Logan and Cate to continue with their own careers as well. It also helped Cate and Jake to equally share parental responsibilities for the girls.

Cate sank into the tub and sighed. After everything that had happened in her life, she could finally say that she was completely happy. Nothing could erase all of the trouble in her past or Jake's, but they had a fulfilling marriage, healthy, loving daughters, financial security, and purpose. Cate was no longer plagued by self-doubt because of her inability to speak, and Jake had been liberated from his long battle with depression. Life was good.

Jake came into the bathroom and began to strip off his clothing. Cate smiled up at him. She knew her husband and knew that he'd decided he could work on Limitless business after spending quality time with her. They were still passionately in love.

Jake stepped into the hot water, settled back against the opposite end of the tub, and opened his arms to her. By the time Cate made it across to him, he was already hard. His mouth slammed down on hers, and she gasped as he lifted her up, repositioned them both, then thrust upwards while pulling her down.

"Fuck me, Baby," he murmured, as they increased their rhythm and water sloshed over the side of the tub and onto the tiled floor. "Speak to me, Cate. Tell me how much you love me."

As usual, the sex was intense. Jake growled out Cate's name as he came. Cate gave in to her own release and knew she'd spoken volumes without uttering a sound.

Other Books in The Limitless Series

Sight Unseen
Unheard Of
Under Her Skin
Brain Storm
Out On A Limb

ABOUT THE AUTHOR

Lauren Cutrera, who also writes under the name Barbara Cutrera, has published over 20 contemporary romance, romantic suspense, paranormal romance, mystery, and fiction novels. Diverse people and plots highlight her works, drawing readers into the characters' unique journeys as they navigate their way through their struggles and triumphs. Lauren and her husband, Budge, are the proud parents of a grown son. They live in southwest Florida and have a cute and naughty Yorkie, Hadrian, who sleeps next to Lauren as she writes each day.

Explore other published works by the author at amazon.com and goodreads.com

Check out all things Lauren (and Barbara) at www.laurencutrera.com

And connect with her there or on

Facebook: https://www.facebook.com/profile.php?id=100063631654302

Instagram: https://www.instagram.com/laurencutrera/

Pinterest: https://www.pinterest.com/laurencutrera/_saved/

OTHER BOOKS BY THE AUTHOR:

The Essential Elements Series

Kindred Spirits
Scorched Creek
Spirits Corner
Memory Lane
Homeward Bound

The Limitless Series

Sight Unseen
Better Left Unsaid
Unheard Of
Under Her Skin
Brain Storm
Out On A Limb

The Seneca & Michael Duet

A Lovely Dream
A Lovely Reality

The Gift Series

The Healer's Gift
Jordan's Way
Bound by Grace
The Nameless

The Real World Series

Over, Under, Across & Through
A Good Man's Life
Mercy
Unfinished Business (Final Chapter)

<u>Standalone Novels/Short Stories</u>

In A Manner of Speaking
Prim & Proper
Lucky
Compromising Positions
True: 3 Short Stories